SUCCESS

— IS THE —

BEST
REVENGE

KATHY SECHRIST

ARCHWAY
PUBLISHING

Archway Publishing books may be ordered through booksellers or by contacting:

Archway Publishing
1663 Liberty Drive
Bloomington, IN 47403
www.archwaypublishing.com
844-669-3957

Because of the dynamic nature of the Internet, any web addresses or links contained in
this book may have changed since publication and may no longer be valid. The views
expressed in this work are solely those of the author and do not necessarily reflect the
views of the publisher, and the publisher hereby disclaims any responsibility for them.

Any people depicted in stock imagery provided by Getty Images are models,
and such images are being used for illustrative purposes only.
Certain stock imagery © Getty Images.

ISBN: 978-1-4808-9839-4 (sc)
ISBN: 978-1-4808-9840-0 (e)

Library of Congress Control Number: 2020921293

Print information available on the last page.

Archway Publishing rev. date: 01/11/2021

Dedicated to my patient husband for being my cheerleader throughout the four years it took to write this book, and to my son for always being the anchor in my life.

Contents

PART 3: WHIDBEY ISLAND

PART 4: LONDON

PART 5: WHIDBEY ISLAND

PART 6: HEALING, HOMELESS, AND HOPEFUL

ONE

Whidbey Island

Chapter 1

Either give me more wine or leave me alone.
—Rumi

My apartment had been decorated 1970s style with gold shag carpet. The passage of time had added a yellowish tinge to the once white walls, and the bathroom permeated the air with the funky odor of the sewer. My new home was like me: empty of life and energy.

The day before, I'd had a husband, a family, and a beautiful waterfront home on Whidbey Island. We'd had twenty years together and built a supportive and loving life, nurturing each other's dreams. Before, we'd had everything. Now Ray had everything, and I had nothing. Nothing but that run-down apartment; my son, Jackson; and my cat, Kitty.

My mind was dead; my heart was numb. I sat in the pit that had become my world and watched rats scamper across the patio. Six months ago, I wouldn't have been able to predict that new low in my life. Six months ago, I'd been happy, doing well in my business, and working toward new dreams with my husband. Six months ago, I hadn't known what I knew now.

Wiping salty tears away with an angry swipe, I walked with determination into the kitchen and opened the refrigerator, which was stocked with enough pinot grigio to help me through this rough patch. I'd faced many potholes in my life's path, potholes I'd dug myself out of. But this time was different. The only thing that would get me through this was wine—lots of it.

I poured the refreshing white wine into a Russian crystal wineglass, a treasure salvaged from my past life with Ray. With my first sip, the wine tickled my palate, cascaded down my throat, and settled in my stomach, spreading its warmth throughout my body.

Grabbing the glass and the bottle, I muttered, "Come on, old friend; let's keep each other company," and made my way to the tattered upholstery of the love seat. And there she was.

Again.

Whenever I failed in my life or made the wrong decision, her ghost came to visit me. But instead of looking like the old lady she'd been when she died, her ghost appeared with beautiful, thick, curly brown hair, wearing the negligee she always had loved to wear.

"Drinking will not make this go away, young lady." Her voice was full of recrimination and loathing.

I drained the glass and poured another before I responded. I lifted my glass toward her voice. "Cheers, Mom. Happy to see you won't be missing this opportunity to remind me of what a loser I am."

"What number is this, Sara?"

"This is my second divorce, Mom, as if you weren't counting."

"Don't get testy with me. What is it with you and men? Have you been lying again?"

"You never believed me, did you?" I looked at her apparition through squinting eyes.

"Sara, how is drinking helping?" Again, she spoke with a soft, passive-aggressive voice, as if she really cared.

"Didn't answer my question, Mom. Getting forgetful, are ya?" I sat back with the full wineglass in hand and waited for what I expected her to say.

"You were a liar then, and you're a liar now. Your stepdad didn't molest you. You were an eleven-year-old liar, and I made sure everyone in the family understood to never believe my little girl. Dammit, Sara, you will never amount to anything." Her words, as cold as ice, wheezed through my lungs, freeze-drying my heart, as if it were the first time I had heard her say those things.

"Did you ever love me?" I asked. But she was gone.

The wind that blew rain against the windows brought me back to reality. The early summer storm outside didn't even begin to match the storm that raged inside—divorce number two. A divorce I hadn't wanted.

How can two people who started out as friends and fell in love end up hating each other? Do we really hate each other? Could it be we just hurt each other so horribly that the only emotion that made us feel anything toward each other again was hate? I wondered.

Taking another sip of wine, I revisited Ray's suspicion that I'd cheated on him. I knew my weird behavior had given him cause to suspect me. I never had stepped outside the marriage, but what had Jimmy Carter said that got him in so much trouble? He had lusted in his heart. Well, I'd lusted in my heart, which had caused my behavior to turn from that of an overweight, menopausal, mature woman with frizzy, naturally curly dyed-brown hair into that of a giddy, flirty teenager. Burning heat crept up my neck as I remembered how my flirting had become unleashed after I lost a few pounds.

Ray had not taken kindly to the new me.

Did I think he was grieving for losing me? Hell no, he wasn't! Anger built and ignited inside faster than the wine soothed it away. I didn't know if the wine quenched or fed the rage, but soon my glass and the bottle were empty. I stomped into the kitchen and grabbed another bottle. This would be more than a two-bottle night, so I grabbed a third bottle and stumbled back to the love seat.

I heard my phone ring through the alcohol fog wrapped around my brain. It was Ray. What the hell did he want now? I poured a fresh glass of wine and placed a crooked smile on my lips. I'd always heard that one sounded happier when smiling.

"Hello?" Honey dripped from my voice.

"Hey," Ray responded in his usual greeting.

"What do you want?" The honey turned to sharpness.

"When are you coming to pick up the rest of your stuff out of the house?"

Yep, I had put him on the defensive. I took a large gulp of wine. "When you tell me why you got a court order giving me just thirty minutes to pack up twenty years of my stuff out of my house." I'd been the one to run away from the family home, but he'd stepped out of our marriage. So why had I been the one given the court order? I took another gulp of wine.

"Listen, bitch, you are the one who left, so just come get your shit."

"I left because I share no one with his girlfriends!"

The conversation escalated into a shouting match in which neither of us listened to the other. Our words were sprinkled with vulgar name-calling and accusations that maybe were true but more than likely were not. Every word Ray spoke was like gasoline feeding my anger. The more my anger grew, the faster the wine went down, until I finally hung up on Ray. Or maybe he hung up on me. I didn't remember.

Just like I didn't remember drinking that third bottle of wine.

Chapter 2

Ever has it been that love knows not its own
depth until the hour of separation.
—Kahlil Gibran

The next morning, the phone jarred me awake. I swam through a
fuzzy cloud and tried to wake from my drunken stupor. I clamped
my eyes shut against the morning sun and willed the ringing to stop.
After four rings, the call went to voice mail.

An ax had been planted in my head, and sandpaper scraped my
throat. Last night, the wine's fragrance had been intoxicating, but now
the stench made my stomach roil. Snippets of the argument with Ray
flooded into my consciousness. Each angry word and accusation pierced
my heart that much more. My rage from last night had evaporated. It
probably was in hiding until the next time he called.

That year, we would have celebrated twenty years of marriage, yet he looked at me like a stranger or, worse, an enemy. It was as if all the love we'd shared had become pain, the pain had become fear, and the fear had sown hatred strong enough to break us. We both had become self-righteous in the belief the other was the cause of our pain.

"What number is this, Sara—number two? You are useless," Mom scoffed in my ear like an old tape.

She was right, of course. Marriage number one had dissolved after the birth of a beautiful baby boy. Jackson had been the child we'd wanted so badly after three miscarriages. Then my first husband had come home from the bar to announce he no longer loved me.

"Oh, shut up, Mom," I snapped, and I rose from the sofa and headed to the kitchen to flip on the coffeepot.

While I watched the black liquid fill the pot, tears slid down my cheeks as I tried to remember the last time I had felt loved by my mom. At the tender age of eleven, the year I'd become a woman, my stepfather had begun to molest me. I'd believed Mom would protect me from him and make my world right again. That was the year I'd learned life was not all princesses and unicorns, and moms didn't always love and protect their children. I also had learned what the word *betrayal* meant and, worse, what it felt like. From the moment I'd told her, I'd become the outcast of the family and been branded a liar. My life had been one of struggling to earn her love back and to stay out of my stepfather's way to prevent him from touching me. I had not been successful at either.

Sadness hung over me like a gray cloud waiting for the rain to fall. I thought maybe a shower would make me feel better, but when I turned to leave the kitchen, I yelped as I caught the scurrying of rats on the patio. I made a mental note to call the property manager after my shower.

Wearing my favorite oversized sweater and sweats, I walked into the living room just as my phone rang again. I flopped onto the couch and noticed the caller ID: Thomas Hunter, my business partner from London. We'd been partners for five years; he was the database whiz, and I was the design and client satisfaction whiz. Most of our clients were in the United Kingdom, which meant I had made several trips to London. No doubt my visits had fed Ray's suspicion we were having an affair. That accusation couldn't have been further from the truth.

"Good morning, Thomas."

"How ya doin', Sara?" His respectful British accent enamored me.

"Oh, ya know. Emotions are flip-flopping all over the place. I can't seem to focus on work." I glanced guiltily toward the three empty bottles of wine on the coffee table. *Really, Sara? Three bottles?*

"Yeah, well, I figured. Phillip called me today for an update on his project. Said he couldn't reach you."

I grimaced at the news. It must have been Phillip who had called earlier. He was one of our most important—and most lucrative—clients in London. Through all my misery, I had missed the deadline to present our proposal for work. When had it been anyway? Hadn't it been weeks ago?

"What did you tell him?" I asked.

"Told him I would check with you, and we would have the proposal delivered to him by the end of the week. Sara, we cannot put him off any longer, or we'll lose him." Then, in a softer, nurturing tone, he said, "Love, how can I help you? I can be in Seattle tomorrow and work with you on the proposal if it would help."

Maybe what I needed was Thomas to come jolt me back into reality. My days had been spent on the sofa, mindlessly watching television and napping until five o'clock in the afternoon. That was my designated time to open a bottle of wine and start my evening drinking and feeling sorry for myself.

"Sure. I suppose I do need someone to put me back on track with work. Are you going to try to catch a plane out tonight?"

"Yep. I'll text you when I know what time I land in Seattle. See you soon, sweetie."

The nurturing warmth in his voice, along with the endearments, reached me in the place in my heart that long had been void of the feeling someone cared about me. I clicked the off button on my cell and decided a nap was in order.

In the few weeks since Ray and I had separated, inertia had taken hold. I couldn't focus my thoughts on working on the project. I had no desire to go anywhere, except to Walmart for my supply of wine. I'd go early in the mornings, hoping to avoid running into anyone I knew. I only answered calls from my son, Jackson; Thomas; and Ray, of course.

Jackson had trouble accepting the separation. Even so, he understood my sorrow and grief over the ending of the marriage between Ray and me. We had always had a close relationship. Because he was an only child, he related well with adults, and I was fortunate to be one he told his secrets, fears, and dreams to. I cherished our mother-son relationship; he was the anchor in my life.

Sleep had become my coping mechanism—well, sleep and wine. Television too. Maybe *coping* wasn't the right word. *Escape* probably was a better one. I wanted to escape from all the failures my mom had self-righteously pointed out to me and others—so many in my forty-five years on earth that I couldn't remember them all. But she remembered them. She had memorized every single one.

Each new memory of my life with Ray brought a fresh cut on my heart that bled tears. I still loved him as deeply as I had the day we married. I had been the one who pulled us apart when I followed through with those silly dreams of mine. Dreams of owning my own business. Dreams of traveling the world.

All those thoughts exhausted me. I laid my head on the couch pillow and closed my eyes but not before the rats ran across the patio. Damn, I hadn't called property management. The thought arrived too late; I escaped into a better world.

Chapter 3

A friendship founded on business is better than a business founded on friendship.
—John D. Rockefeller

Thomas landed at SeaTac around six o'clock the next evening. It had been a half-day journey to arrive at the airport. I couldn't help but smile when I spotted him at the designated pickup outside the baggage claim. He stood leaning his tall, lanky body against a pillar. Damn, why had my heart just skipped a beat?

We had met five years ago in an online tech chat, shortly after his cost-saving invention had allowed him to retire early from British Tel. Though I knew nothing about database-driven websites, I knew website development, and I eventually had accepted the business deal he proposed. I'd become the people person, working directly with our clients, and he'd become the brains on the back end.

The two-hour car ride home flew by. Thomas had much to fill me in on, particularly with potential clients. I loved listening to his charming English accent; he sounded almost lyrical to me.

"I've only got one bedroom, and it's yours; I'll sleep on the love seat," I told him after we got back to my apartment.

"No, Sara, I'll sleep on the love seat. I wouldn't dream of taking your bed. Besides, I sometimes get up in the middle of the night, and I don't want to disturb you."

With our sleeping arrangements settled, I suddenly became shy toward him. My tongue got all twisted up, but it didn't matter, because my brain forgot how to structure a sentence. Good Lord, why was I acting like a silly teenager with her first crush? I saw his lips moving as if talking, but my ears buzzed from the hornet's nest that had taken up occupancy in the last few minutes.

"Huh?" was all I could utter in response to whatever he had said.

"You look like a deer in the headlights. You okay?" he asked with concern.

Struggling to shake out the hornets and regain my composure, I responded, "Yeah, sure, just tired." I glanced at my watch and added, "It's my bedtime. Mind if I hit the sack? You are welcome to stay up if you'd like. You can watch television; it won't bother me."

"No problem, love; I'm a bit tired after that never-ending flight here."

I got out extra blankets and a pillow, placed them on the love seat, said good night, and closed the bedroom door.

I leaned against the closed bedroom door, surprised by my reaction to being alone in the apartment with Thomas. I'd never had any attraction to him—well, perhaps his brilliant mind had been exceptionally attractive to me but not in a romantic sense. Was I feeling romantic? Or was I just horny and feeling unwanted? I shook my head and changed into my pajamas.

After I pulled the blankets up to my chin and snuggled into them, I decided what I felt was lust and not a romantic thread needled through my heart. I still loved Ray.

⊶⧓⊷

The aroma of freshly brewed coffee teased me awake. Vowing to keep my newly discovered lust under control, I wrapped my flannel bathrobe around myself and toddled out to the kitchen.

"Mornin'. You're up bright and early," I said, taking the cup of hot, steaming coffee Thomas offered.

"Mornin', love. How'd you sleep?"

"Fast." It had been late when we finally got to my apartment. How could he be so frigging cheerful that early? "How'd you sleep?" I knew his six-foot frame would never have been able to stretch out on the love seat that had been his bed.

"Like a baby." He grinned. "Let's have our coffee on the patio and discuss this proposal we need to have to Phillip in two days. Bring the drafts with you," he said as he started to open the slider to the patio.

"No! Shit, we can't go on the patio!" I yelled in panic.

"Why?" He looked charming with one eyebrow raised.

"Because rats are out there, and I keep forgetting to call the property management company to get pest control here."

"Gawd, Sara, call them now!" Thomas looked a little pale at the thought of sharing his coffee with local rats.

"Look, let me jump in the shower and dress while you look over the drafts. I'll call after my shower, and then we can go over your edits and finalize it."

Thomas flashed bedroom eyes at me, which brought a flirty smile to my lips. "Go on with ya then," he said, reaching for the papers lying on the dinette. The dining room and living room shared the same space, and I felt his eyes on my rear as I walked to the bathroom.

I did my best thinking in the shower, and while I lathered up, my thoughts went to my relationship with Thomas. We had gotten close, like friends. I could tell him things I couldn't have told Ray. Well, to be fair, those things were mainly about Ray. Thomas had always listened, not judged, and offered advice only when asked. *He'd make someone a fabulous husband*, I thought. I dressed in jeans and a crisp green blouse that made my eyes pop and joined Thomas at the dinette.

We spent the rest of the day working through the proposal, fine-tuning it until we were satisfied Phillip would find it acceptable. Finally, after a long day of paying attention to tedious details, I sent an email to Phillip with the proposal attached. Thomas asked if I had some wine to celebrate our achievement.

I blushed as I remembered the three bottles of wine I'd finished the night before last. "Nope, but we can run down to the store and get some."

"Is your license store open still?" he asked.

I looked at him blankly. "What is a license store?"

"It's where we get liquor," he responded.

"Oh, the *liquor* store," I quipped with a grin. "It's open, but we'd better go now if we want to make it before they close at eight tonight."

Off we went. We got wine for me and Pernod for Thomas. I'd never heard of Pernod before—it looked a little sickly with its yellow hue. Thomas explained Pernod was an anise-flavored liqueur imported from France. For more than two hundred years, it had been a favorite of chefs worldwide for its ability to flavor a meal without overpowering its natural taste.

"Sounds good to me. Should we stop at the grocery store to get what you need to cook with it?" I asked with a teasing smile.

"Don't be daft," Thomas said. "You drink the wine; I'll drink the Pernod! By the way, love, I left London so quickly I didn't have time to get American dollars or notify my credit card company I would be in the States. Can you pay for these? I'll call my bank in the morning."

With reluctance, I handed my card to the cashier. What would I need to cut out of my budget to pay for this?

I checked my email as soon as we got home and was delighted to see a message from Phillip. I turned to Thomas with a massive grin on my face. "He accepted the proposal."

The rest of the evening was spent drinking and munching on pizza in celebration of Phillip's acceptance of our proposal.

"Why don't you come to London to work on the project? The work would be much easier if you're with me."

Thomas's suggestion threw me off balance. I wasn't prepared financially or, especially, emotionally to leave the island just now. "I'll have to think about it. Okay if I let you know tomorrow?"

"Sure. Just as long as you say yes."

I had a lot to think over, but thoughts of my impending divorce were pushed to the back of my mind as I toasted in glee to the last words Ray had spat at me: "You'll never make it without me."

Well, watch me make it without you now, Ray.

Chapter 4

Anger, resentment and jealousy don't change
the heart of others—it only changes yours.
—Shannon L. Alder

The next morning, I was awakened by the sounds of Thomas in the kitchen, supposedly making coffee. I snuggled back down into the covers to await the freshly brewed coffee's aroma before getting out of bed. As I lay in bed, my mind wandered to Thomas's suggestion that I go to London. If I went, we could finalize the contract with Phillip and start the work. I was torn. I knew I should stay in Washington until the separation agreement with Ray was completed. However, most of the work could be accomplished electronically.

I had been nervous when Thomas and I talked it through last night, and I was apprehensive about bringing it up that morning.

Would he insist I go back to London before the separation agreement was finalized? *Wait a minute, Sara. He's not the boss of you. Grow up, and just tell him no.*

"Coffee, love?"

Startled, I popped my head out from underneath the covers and grinned. He leaned against the doorjamb, tall and lanky in faded blue jeans and a denim shirt. His sandy hair skirted his earthy brown eyes. If it hadn't been for his British accent, no one would have guessed he was not a true-blue American. He held a cup of coffee in one hand and a single red rose in another. "I thought you could use a strong cuppa after we stayed up so late."

"You are a godsend! Where did you get the rose?" I asked as I got out of bed and threw my robe on.

"You were out of milk for the coffee, so I grabbed your car keys and popped down to the store to buy some. This rose begged me to bring it home to you. It's my way of saying thank you for all the hard work you put into Phillip's proposal and a down payment on all the work that is still to be done."

"You are so nice to me. Thank you," I said as I took the rose and coffee from him and walked into the kitchen.

"Hey, Sara, did you forget about my flight this morning?" he asked while I found a vase for the rose.

"Nope. Let me put this rose in a vase, I'll take a quick shower, and we'll be on the road."

"Need some help?" he asked with a mischievous look on his face.

"Heck no, I've put roses in vases before," I quipped. I placed the vase with the rose on the tiny dinette and then scurried past him, heading for the bathroom.

"Just trying to be helpful."

His innuendo made me feel uncomfortable. Ray and I had bantered like that. It was a part of us I missed. I wasn't ready to banter with another.

We got in the car and headed for the ferry that would take us to the mainland. I struggled to find the courage to bring up the timeline of when I would come to London. It had never been like me to go against another's wishes, but that day, I had to fight the lack of confidence that threatened to keep the words from spilling out.

"I'm not coming to London until the separation agreement with Ray is finalized. I can work from here, gathering requirements over Skype, which will keep us on track with the project." I didn't realize how tightly I gripped the steering wheel until my knuckles were white.

"When is it scheduled to be finalized?"

"In a couple of months. Around August or September. After we agree and sign, I'll come to London, and as long as we have no hiccups, I'll stay for as long as my visa allows. That's three months, right?"

"Right. Look, you couldn't stay focused on the project until I came here and lit a fire under you. What makes you think you will be motivated and focused when I'm not here? I'm worried about you as it is. If you stay here, I fear we will lose the contract and any that may follow."

I let go of a heavy sigh, more to calm my racing heart than to breathe. "Your visit has motivated me. That, and I need the money. I can't allow the project to slip anymore." I managed a smile in the hope of reassuring him.

"Sounds like you have all this pretty well planned out. I suppose it wouldn't hurt if you stayed here until August and worked on the requirements. But, Sara, one little slip in time, and I will be coming over to kick your butt."

I almost laughed, more out of relief than because of his saying, "Kick your butt." *You have a win, Sara—the first one in a long time.*

We filled the rest of the drive to the airport with talking over our plans and dreams for future business and mapping out our next steps. Both of us were excited at the prospect of our business future together.

At the airport, we got out of the car, and I opened the trunk for him to get his luggage. I was awkward as we stood facing each other. *Do we hug? Do we kiss? No, no kisses. Not even close to kissing him yet, if ever. Should I just say goodbye and get in the car?* I stood like a frozen statue.

He reached for me and gave me a light hug. I headed back to my car and turned around to wave just as he yelled, "See you in August!"

I was happy to return to my tiny apartment after dropping Thomas off at the airport. *Kinda weird, isn't it, Sara? This crummy, run-down apartment is starting to become my sanctuary, where I can shut out everyone and everything and feel nothing.*

My phone rang before I could even put my car keys on the holder in the hall.

"Hi, Ray," I said in a tired voice.

"Lover boy gone?" he asked.

"Good God, he's not my lover boy; he's my business partner, and he left this morning! How in the hell did you know he was here?"

"I have my spies." He laughed.

Ray had long ago earned a reputation as the island gossip. After retiring from the navy, he'd found his niche in painting, renovating decks, and mowing lawns, but mainly, he gossiped with the people he did odd jobs for. He probably knew when I had gone to the bathroom last.

"What do you want?" I asked.

"Look, I talked to my attorney, and we want to set the separation date soon and settle the money and property. Then we can move forward with the divorce."

His voice held a touch of anger, and I was too exhausted emotionally to fuel his rage. I grimaced, remembering he had drained our joint bank account before I left him. I almost said, "What money?" but stayed away from the potential of another argument.

"Fine. I'll let my attorney know to move forward with the separation agreement as soon as possible. Anything else?" I just wanted to get off the phone with him.

"Nope. Have a good day," he responded sarcastically.

At forty-five years old, my life is falling apart, and he says to have a good day?

I headed for the couch and the television remote. My so-called good day resulted in a long nap, after which I stared mindlessly at the television until wine time arrived.

Chapter 5

Shame plays a huge part in why you hate who you are.
—Angel Ploetner, *Who Am I? Dissociative Identity Disorder Survivor*

It was another day of typical Whidbey weather: rain. I thought the island should have been named Soggy Island for all the rain we ended up getting. Still, we didn't get as much as Seattle or Everett. The island, situated between the Olympic and Cascade Mountains, was protected from much of the rain that blew over. I didn't mind the weather as much lately; the gloomy and wet days matched my mood and energy level. The locals said the island summer did not start until July 5, and I'd sat through many a soggy firework display to prove it.

I sat at the dinette and held my now cooling mug of coffee, hoping to direct its warmth into my soul. A hint of clearing weather teased over the marina and harbor. *Hopefully we'll have beautiful weather for tomorrow's Fourth of July parade*, I thought. I could sit on my patio and watch the parade participants go right past my apartment. I cringed, remembering the rats.

I reached for my phone and called the rental agency, but they were closed. *Crap, they won't be open until July 5, so the heck with the stupid rats. It will be them and me on the patio tomorrow to watch the parade. If I'm brave enough, that is. I could go get some rat traps, but what would I do if I caught one?* The thought sent shivers all the way down my spine, and goose bumps erupted on my skin. *Nope, I will wait for pest control.*

I pushed my now cold coffee cup away while the emptiness in my heart, the nothingness that had taken hold of my soul, once again threatened to engulf me. The lump in my throat made it almost impossible to breathe, yet the tears would not come.

July 4 had been a special holiday for my family, one we always spent together, just the three of us. Jackson had marched in the parade as a Webelo, then a Boy Scout, and later an Eagle Scout. Ray and I had been proud of him—nothing else in the parade mattered until Jackson marched by, straight and tall, his eyes straight ahead. Later, we'd made our annual trip to the carnival. It had been a hokey one meant for a small town such as ours. I remembered how the rides and games had mesmerized Jackson. The aroma of *lumpia*, pansit, cotton candy, and grilled burgers with grilled onions had wafted over to us, tempting us to each vendor. We'd sat on the park's grounds, next to the harbor, enjoying our meals, savoring every last bite. After finishing our food and tossing our paper plates and napkins into the trash, we'd strolled through the carnival and watched Jackson ride the rides. They'd been simple times—the best memories ever.

Although it was just noon, I replaced my coffee with a glass of wine. I enjoyed the refreshing golden deliciousness while my thoughts shifted to my mom and stepfather. I held up my glass in a toast to their thirty-something-year anniversary, which would have been that day. I had remembered it days ago. I didn't have the energy or desire to battle the *should*s and the ever-present shame and swallow the guilt of not calling to wish my stepfather well. I shook my head and ran my hands through my uncombed, wild dyed-brunette hair. *Divorce must be a genetic thing with my family. Mom divorced my biological father, my brother divorced after a thirty-year marriage, and here I am, on my second divorce.* I wondered if my mom and brother still had been in love with their spouses when they divorced. I shrugged and finished my wine. *I guess it's too late to ask them now.* Both were dead.

Memories of what my stepfather had done to me visited more often since I'd left Ray. Could my unresolved issues with my mom and stepfather have been an invisible barrier to my giving my heart entirely to Ray? Maybe he'd felt my not giving all of myself to him while I safeguarded my heart and put distance between us with my work.

After unwrapping myself off the couch, I poured the last of the wine into my empty glass. The flashbacks always emotionally drained me and threw me into a deeper depression. After drinking the full glass of wine in one long gulp, I lay down on the sofa and fell asleep to a movie I would never remember in the morning.

Chapter 6

The people you love become ghosts inside of you, and like this you keep them alive.
—Rob Montgomery

I woke to the sounds of people gathering for the parade outside. *I should get up to watch*, I thought, but apathy encircled me like a spiderweb and trapped me in a warm, cozy state of nothingness. There was nothing wrong with me—no cold, no flu, no headache, no hangover. I could get up, I thought, and work until it was time to go to the carnival. There wasn't much left to do, and the data and spreadsheets were due tomorrow. But I felt like staying right there on the sofa and staring blankly at the TV, shutting out the laughter and happiness outside. *I'll finish it up tomorrow.* In apathy, there was time to think and to wallow in self-pity and self-loathing.

Later, I made myself get up off the couch, dress, and walk down to the carnival. I wouldn't waste this holiday; I needed some sense of normalcy.

The fresh air felt good and woke up my feelings, and I started to feel alive again—until I saw Ray and his new girlfriend together at the carnival. The scene before me was a sweet one: his arm encircled her waist, and she looked up into his eyes with a smile while they waited in line to order their food. He leaned down and gave her a light kiss, holding her closer to him.

At that moment, I realized I had clung to the hope we would get back together as if it meant life or death. It was also the moment I realized we would never renew our relationship.

People milled through the carnival, with ice cream toppling precariously on cones and kids energized by the cotton candy they had filled their tummies with. Screeches came from the rides, and barkers called out for people to come play their games. It was all surreal, as if I floated above and watched it all unfold before me. *This isn't real. It can't be.*

What the hell is reality anyway? I've lived forty-five years of my life for others and tried my hardest to make them proud of me, to make them love me. And I failed at every attempt. Who the hell was I anyway? What had happened to the little girl who'd been full of hopes and dreams and excited about the adventure of life before her stepfather molested her? Why hadn't her mother believed her? Why had her mother let him continue to molest her for seven more years? And why had her mother painted her own little girl as a liar who would never amount to anything?

The questions came too late. Mom was dead. I remembered the day she'd passed. I had been too scared to confront her with my questions. In her last moments, I'd looked deeply into her dark brown eyes and hoped to see some sign of repentance or even acknowledgment of the pain her actions had given me. I'd seen nothing but dark brown pools with the lights inside dimming.

My feelings were mixed between the profound loss of my mom and intense disappointment in myself. Why had I been so afraid to confront her? Her actions toward me had screwed me up worse than the molestation. *Oh, Sara, you missed your chance, and now it is forever gone.*

In my effort to win my mother's love and respect and feel her nurturing and not her anger, I'd perfected a mask of calm and competence that projected a mature and capable professional. It had been a charade. On the inside, I'd been terrified the facade would crumble down around me to reveal the abandoned child within, the child who still mourned for the person I'd been before my world turned unrecognizable.

Back in my youth, I had floundered for someone—anyone—to fill the void. Was it wrong to have been so needy and vulnerable that I screwed anyone who wanted me, all because I felt so unlovable? My heart clenched, and my cheeks flamed at the memories of giving so much of myself away. All I wanted to do right then was to run from the reality of my life. Instead, I left the carnival and went back to the security of my apartment. I'd be away from the laughter and joyfulness of others but not safe from the thoughts that invaded my mind.

Back in my apartment, I decided it was wine time. I threw my keys and purse onto the table in the dark and narrow hall and walked into the kitchen. A comforting feeling settled in when I opened the refrigerator door and spied my bottles of pinot grigio, which had waited for me like a trusted friend. I took a half-empty bottle out and poured the crisp golden liquid into the crystal wineglass, lifting it to catch the sunset's rays. "Tonight you are my lover," I whispered to my friend the wine. My spirits were lifted as the wine passed through my lips and warmed my stomach. Until tomorrow.

Tomorrow I would go back to the home I loved to clear my things out—all in thirty minutes or less. Worst of all, I would see the man I still loved, who would never love me again.

Chapter 7

To say goodbye is to die a little.
—Raymond Chandler, *The Long Goodbye*

It seemed unreal, packing as much as I could in thirty minutes. When I left, I would never enter that home, my dream home, ever again. My heart was broken on many levels; seeing Ray was painful and twisted my heart in a tight band. Our future together, the one we had mapped out for ourselves, was nothing now but a chapter in a book of fiction.

As I rummaged through old cards and letters, a birthday card I had given Ray one year surfaced and begged me to pick it up. On the front cover was a picture of a man in a boat on a mountain lake, fishing. Ray's passion in life was fishing. On the inside cover was a sentiment that, even though not written by me, expressed how I felt toward him exactly. Tears ran down my cheeks when I remembered that was why I'd kept it. The front cover was him, and the verse inside was my love expressed for him.

I left for the kitchen and carried the card with me. Ray was still on the deck, so I laid the card on the counter and went back to my packing. Why I left it there was clear to me: I wanted Ray to see it. Did I secretly hope he'd read it and have a change of heart?

Come on, Sara. Of course you do.

With my court-imposed thirty minutes about up, I took one more sweep through the house to make sure I had grabbed the most important things. Satisfied most were packed up, I went back to the kitchen, where the back door was, prepared to leave. Ray leaned against the counter, holding the card I had left behind. I searched his face to see if there was any softening of his heart. His blue eyes turned to ice, and he ripped the card into little pieces. Tears fell onto my cheeks as quickly as the pieces of paper fell to the floor. I turned away from him so he wouldn't see me cry and promptly left to join Jackson in the truck. No goodbyes were said as we left for the storage units that would be a new home to my things.

Twenty years of marriage filled the truck, including my grandma's dining room set, which had hosted many happy family dinners; my great-grandpa's rocking chair; my grandma's double bed; and my clothes and books. It didn't seem like much to have acquired in twenty years. But marriage wasn't material things at all, I realized. It was two souls bonding, working together to make a life, and making promises to each other and to their children. Promises that were easily broken.

"How about I buy ya some dinner for helping me?" I asked Jackson after we had unloaded the truck and locked the storage unit.

"Yeah, sure. But I have to get back to Seattle right after to study for a heavy-duty exam tomorrow."

We went to his favorite Mexican restaurant, where the staff wore sombreros, and troubadours strummed guitars and sang songs of their homeland. We had been there so often we knew the menu by heart, always ordering the same favorites. I tried to make small talk while we waited for our food to arrive, but our conversation was one-sided and flat. We ate in silence once our food was delivered.

"Would you like to talk about it?" I asked.

"No." His eyes focused on the food left on his plate.

I reached across the table for his hand and pleaded with him not to feel as if he had been the cause of our breakup. "Look, your dad and I are divorcing each other, not you. You are, and will always be, his son and my baby boy." The baby-boy crack usually made the pink creep up his neck and brought a sloppy start of a grin to his face. But I got nothing—no pink neck, no sloppy grin, no words. I couldn't tell if he was angry or sad. Did he think we'd betrayed him by not working harder on our marriage? I was afraid to ask.

I paid the bill, and when I turned around, Jackson had already walked out. He sat behind the steering wheel of the truck and looked impatient to get back to Seattle. We rode the short distance to my apartment in silence. Jackson parked close to the entrance, but we remained in the truck. Unspoken words created a chasm miles wide and just as deep.

Looking straight ahead, my voice but a whisper, I tried to close the space between us. "I'm here when you want to talk about what happened to your dad and me. We both love you, Jackson, more than you know." Tears wet the edges of my eyes and threatened to spill over onto my cheeks.

"Thanks, Mom, but I'm good."

I slid across the seat and gave him a long hug. "Thanks for your help today." I spoke into his ear and then slowly slid back over, opened the door, and stepped out. He was gone before I reached the door of my apartment.

I stood in the dark parking lot. One dim streetlight spread onto the pavement the mystical shadows of the tree branches that rustled in the wind as I watched the red of his taillights slowly disappear.

Chapter 8

There are wounds that never show on the body that are deeper and more hurtful than anything that bleeds.
—Laurell K. Hamilton, *Mistral's Kiss*

The days went by like shadows with nondescript edges to define them. I'd wake in the mornings to a hangover and a flood of memories of my now gone family, the kind of memories I wanted to wrap myself into and never let go of, along with a deep sense of loss. My chest ached—or was it my heart? Everything I loved had faded away. My family. My dream home. My mother's love.

I kept the rest of the world out of my practiced state of self-loathing. The drapes remained closed day and night to shut out the beauty of the marina and the bustling life of a small town. I didn't belong there; I belonged nowhere. I didn't answer the phone unless the caller ID indicated it was Jackson.

I glanced over at my desk, and a twinge of guilt took hold. Once again, I had missed the last deadline for my current project. I was only a few days late. I'd hit it tomorrow. Dang, I'd emptied the bottle of wine.

I sighed and stumbled into the kitchen for another bottle. Just as I pulled the cold bottle of golden refreshment from the fridge, I heard an unfamiliar knock on my door. I stood, mind-numbed from the wine, and pondered who it might be. The knocking grew louder, which gave me the impression the person would not be going away. I put the bottle of wine back in the fridge, straightened myself up, took a few deep breaths to work myself into a sober state, and walked to the door.

"Who's there?" I tried to keep myself from slurring.

"It's Carol. Let me in."

Shit. I looked down at my rumpled sweats and glanced in the mirror on the wall. I was a frigging mess. "I'm not feeling well, Carol. Can you come back some other time?" That time, I was sure I slurred.

"Nope. Let me in, or I'll get your landlord to let me in."

That was Carol—blunt, to the point, and unwavering. And my best friend.

"Hi, Carol." I opened the door and forced a lopsided smile.

Shock registered on her face at her first look at me in months. She stared and appeared speechless.

"Come on in," I murmured as I stumbled out of the way to give her room to pass.

I staggered through the room, quickly gathering papers, old mail, and paper plates encrusted with food, and with arms loaded with the trash, I offered her the now cleared chair to sit in. "Would you like some coffee, water, or maybe some wine?" I said as she sat down.

"Sara, it is one o'clock, and you already smell like a winery."

I plopped myself onto the cluttered couch, fearing what she might say next. She could be blunt to the point of being cruel sometimes. We had been friends for a long time, had worked together, and still volunteered with the same nonprofit group. I knew how her comments could slice through me like a knife and leave familiar emotions of guilt and blame.

"What a pigsty," she said in disgust, and I winced as the knife in her voice pierced my skin. "Sara, what's going on with you? You've missed our nonprofit group meetings for months now. I've never seen you look so unkempt. What has happened to you?"

I clasped my hands in my lap, studying them to avoid Carol's penetrating glare, much as a scolded child would have. I couldn't speak. The pain of lifelong hurts, guilt, blame, and self-loathing boiled up from deep within, stopped in my throat, and threatened to choke me.

Carol moved next to me on the couch and put her arm around me.

That one act of kindness burst the dam that had been leaking one tear at a time. I leaned into her arms desolately and sobbed on her shoulder. Finally, I lifted my head and sniffled. My puffy eyes felt as if pepper spray had been sprayed into them.

"You okay?" she asked.

I took a big gulp of air, wiped my nose on my sleeve, and let out a nervous laugh with a nod of my head.

"Sara, your life is a mess and sliding further downhill with each passing day. You need to put your head on straight, get back to work, and take part in activities I know are important to you. Living and not molding. You know what I mean?"

She was right, but I didn't want to leave the safe, secure cocoon I had wrapped myself in. Even if I had fooled myself into thinking

I didn't care what others thought, I was petrified to face those who knew me, who I thought would judge me or, worse, pity me.

She didn't wait for me to respond before leveraging her demand. "I've made you an appointment with Dr. Tracey to prescribe happy pills. So I suggest you get a move on, jump in the shower, put clean clothes on, and fix yourself up, because we leave in thirty minutes."

I froze and stared at her while the meaning of her words crashed into my wine-numbed brain.

"Now!" she yelled.

I jumped off the couch and ran for the bathroom with panic starting like a cluster of firecrackers in my stomach.

After my shower, I heard bottles clanking as Carol emptied my wine and dropped the empty bottles into a garbage bag to drop into the dumpster on our way out. *Shit, shit, shit. Now I have to get more wine.*

Chapter 9

I can feel a phoenix inside me. I can see the heavens,
but I still hear the flames calling out my name.
—Katy Perry

Months had passed since Carol's visit and Dr. Tracey's prescription
of the antidepressant we called happy pills. A few weeks had gone
by before I noticed a difference, but soon the urge to get myself back
into the world had started to motivate me. I had been meeting my
deadlines, and I went to my volunteer meetings and participated in
a few activities. Thomas and I spoke on the phone regularly, and
instead of waiting for Jackson to call, I reached out to him. They were
short calls to let him know that I loved him and was interested in his
day and that I was okay too. Life was much better and had promise.

The day came when Ray and I met with our lawyers to hash out the separation agreement and the property settlement. He and his lawyer sat across the table from my attorney and me. We were close enough for me to see the ice in Ray's blue eyes again. I once had loved looking into those blue eyes. They had given me peace and comfort. I looked away, swallowed hard, and wished we could rewind the time to five years ago, before we grew apart.

Our attorneys did most of the talking while Ray and I nodded in agreement. The meeting didn't take as long as I expected. When we got up to leave, my nervousness suddenly increased with the realization I would be walking out of the office with him. Maybe we would exchange pleasantries and at least keep the friendship we once had had, I thought. But his attorney called him into his office to sign the paperwork, and I left the building alone.

I felt a sense of finality. That day was a separation, not a divorce, but in ninety days, the divorce would be final—twenty years erased, as if our marriage had been chalk on a chalkboard to be permanently rubbed out.

I surprised myself by smiling on my way to the car. Maybe the happy pills worked better than I'd imagined. My life was getting back on track. I had purpose and meaning, a direction, and a few friends around who cared enough about me to hold me accountable and make sure I kept moving forward. I was not as alone as I'd thought during those bleak, lifeless, lost months.

While work and volunteering kept me busy, one thing had not changed. Every evening at five o'clock, I turned the television on and poured my first glass of wine. It wasn't noon, or even earlier, so in my mind, that was an improvement. And now, when I went to Walmart to replenish my stash, I was showered, with hair combed and makeup on, looking presentable in jeans and a T-shirt instead of sweats. It felt good to look people in the eye again. I had nothing to hide or be ashamed of. Divorce happened. Few knew it was my second time, and I committed to keeping it that way. I'd chat with people I ran into and get caught up on the island gossip. Then I'd pack my precious cargo into my car for my evening ritual of wine, popcorn, and mindless television.

There was a new confidence about me. Carol even remarked on my change. My mother's haunting voice telling me I was no good and not deserving of success in any part of my life appeared less often. I began to believe it was possible to accomplish my dream of owning a successful business, albeit with lots of hard work and opportunity. I would do the hard work; the opportunities were what I needed to create.

Thomas had begun to feel the pressure of meeting with our clients alone. I joined him in conference calls, but as we got deeper into the projects, I had more questions, and our clients wanted face-to-face meetings. The closer we got to our deadlines, the more we had to reassure them we were moving forward at the pace we had promised.

"Why don't you come to London, at least until Phillip's project is complete?" Thomas asked during one of our phone calls.

Doubts filled my mind. I had been to London several times for our initial meetings with clients but had never stayed for more than a few weeks. I could stay home and work with clients on Whidbey Island, I thought, but I wasn't sure if local clients would bring in any real money to support myself without Thomas. An average website netted me less than a thousand dollars. It would take a lot of work and energy to build my business up by updating my website and doing some extensive marketing, but did I have the energy for that? If I continued to partner with Thomas, I would move closer to my dream of becoming financially independent. The obvious solution was to go to London and work with clients Thomas procured for us, who paid well. I was afraid to leave all that had been home to me, yet I was scared to stay, unsure of my financial future if I did.

If I was to be the woman I wanted to be and fulfill my potential, there was only one answer.

"When do you want me in London?"

TWO

London

Chapter 10

**Every new beginning comes from
some other beginning's end.
—Seneca the Younger**

Relief washed over me when I saw Thomas at the welcoming gate outside customs. I was bone-tired from the journey, and my computer bag was so heavy I figured it had gained twenty pounds since I left home. Thomas gave me a warm, welcoming hug, after which I handed him my computer bag and the cart loaded with my luggage.

"Good flight?" he asked, leading me to the car park.

"It was great. Nine hours is a heck of a long time to be in the air. I'm sore from not moving as much as I should have."

"Good. I booked your hotel room a short walk from Phillip's office; all you have to do is give them your credit card when you check in."

"Aren't my expenses covered by Phillip's company?"

"Not yet. You'll send Phillip an invoice, and he will reimburse you, okay?" His voice was all business.

I was surprised the hotel wasn't billing Phillip directly, as we had agreed. "Um, well, sure," I responded, a little unbalanced by the news. I would be there for three months. Three months in a hotel in downtown London would massively crash my credit card if Phillip didn't come through.

"I'm completing the details on renting a flat in Enfield, a borough north of London. It has two bedrooms and is within walking distance of the Gordon Hill train station. I thought sharing a flat would be less costly than your being in a hotel room. What do you think?"

"Wow, that's great. When do you think you'll sign the lease?"

"Next week, by the looks of it. The apartment isn't much, but we can use the furniture I kept from my divorce. Guess we'll have to get you a bed." He grinned.

Thomas's long legs outpaced mine, and I lagged behind him as we entered the parking garage. He was on his phone talking with someone—I assumed a client or his good friend Jon, whom he always chatted with. It didn't bother me that he was on the phone so soon after I had arrived; I was lost in the sensations of the London air and smells.

"Here we are." Thomas popped open the boot after he put his phone away, and he carefully arranged my luggage.

"So where did you get the car?" I knew that Alice, his ex-wife, had gotten their one car in the divorce, which had left Thomas without one. They'd only been divorced for about six months and remained friends. Over the past several months, Thomas had listened to me complain about my soon-to-be ex's hostility. He'd related to me how pleasant his relationship with Alice had become since their divorce. They even went to dinner together on occasion. I could not imagine sharing a civil conversation over a dinner table with Ray, a thought that made me a little sad.

"Alice lent the car to me to come pick you up. You can come with me to meet her when I drop it off later if you like."

"Thanks, but I think I'd like to get settled and explore around the hotel before work starts. Is Alice driving you back to your mom's?"

Thomas had told me he'd been staying with his mum since the divorce. "Yes, sure."

We got in the car, and he pulled out of the parking garage. Thomas filled me in on our work schedule on our way to the hotel. I was only half listening, mesmerized by the grand city that seemed to swallow us into it. Sara, a girl from a small island who'd never been anywhere significant, was there in London. It was almost like a fairy tale.

I pressed my nose to the car window to take in as much as I possibly could. I saw no pastoral fields or blue water sparkling in the sun. Instead, there were lots of narrow streets and monolithic buildings, people walked everywhere with purpose, and black cabs darted in and out of the mess they called traffic. I was alive with the sights and sounds of a busy, bustling megacenter of humanity.

"Here we are," Thomas said, pulling into the Strand Palace Hotel's valet lane.

The hotel looked expensive. The porter loaded my luggage onto a cart, and visions of dollar signs floated by my eyes. Phillip would eventually pay the bill, but the charges would be on my credit card, which already had a high balance, until then.

The porter followed us into the lobby and patiently waited for me to check in. He then escorted us and my luggage to my room.

I was surprised but grateful when Thomas tipped the man after he deposited us and my luggage in my room. I turned around to face the room and grimaced. It was tiny. I opened the wardrobe and heaved a big sigh. Where would my clothes fit? Had I made a mistake in coming there? First, I'd have to front the hotel bill, and now I had a tiny dollhouse of a room.

"Let's leave your unpacking for later and walk to Phillip's office so you can learn the way."

I looked forlornly at the cramped room; the only empty space was the top of the bed. "Okay, let's do it. How long of a walk is it?" I gathered up my purse and a light jacket.

"Not far. The walk will give you a chance to see some of London and pick out some landmarks for walking to the office on your own tomorrow."

Lord, he knew how geographically challenged I was. I'd have to pay attention to landmarks, and because I walked slower than he did, I hoped I wouldn't lose him in the crowds.

Chapter 11

Don't panic.
—Douglas Adams, *The Hitchhiker's Guide to the Galaxy*

On our way to the hotel elevators, our footsteps were muffled by the thick oriental-style red carpet. The few people we passed spoke in whispered conversations, as if the reverence the hotel demanded would be shifted if they spoke any louder. The golden doors of the elevator opened, and we were quickly transported to the lobby.

The warm, humid day assaulted us as we walked out onto the sidewalk. Thomas turned left after leaving the hotel, and we made our way along the Strand, one of the major thoroughfares of Central London. I tried to keep up with Thomas and avoid bumping into people. They all seemed to be more interested in their phones than in where they were walking. Buildings towered above me like giant glass-encased monoliths, reflecting the gold from the sun. They provided shade for us while trapping the humidity. My pace slowed as I gawked at the buildings. People jarred into me. I smelled exhaust, curry and spices from Indian cafés, and the skunky odor of the sewers under my feet.

"Hey, you coming?" Thomas yelled at me from a good way ahead.

"Sorry. I feel like the country bumpkin on her first trip to the big city." I laughed.

Running to catch up to him, I caught a smile on his face. *Do Brits ever laugh? Really laugh until their bellies hurt?* I'd never heard him laugh during our phone conversations. *Brits are so reserved and hard for me to read.*

Thomas started walking again, and his long, lean legs outpaced me until I had to jog to keep up with him.

Getting winded, I yelled, "Hey, can you slow down a little, please?"

He turned around and waited for me to catch up with what I thought was a frown born out of irritation. "I thought all you country girls were huge walkers. You know, strolling through the countryside, chasing cows."

"We drive cars. We don't walk unless we go from our car to where we are eating or shopping or visiting," I panted, hot and sticky from the humidity.

We left Strand Avenue and walked along Wellington Street, past Covent Garden. Covent Garden had been the first piazza in London. I later learned *My Fair Lady* had been filmed there. Lots of fabulous shopping and dining among the gardens brought crowds of people to it, and at that moment, it seemed all of London were in the gardens, doing just that. As we walked by, my pace slowed once again while I gawked at the street performers who entertained the crowds.

"Didn't you say the office was close to the hotel?" My tiredness from the nine-hour flight started to settle in.

"Yep, it's right up here."

How far "right up here" could it be? He outpaced me, and the gap between us had increased. The familiar sensations of a panic attack crept into my body. I wrapped my arms around my middle to stop the cluster of spark plugs that fired off one by one in my stomach. I began to pant, and sweat trickled down my neck. I kept my head low and concentrated on putting one foot in front of the other. The buildings and the mass of people closed in on me and threatened to suffocate me. Desperately, I tried to maintain my focus. *Keep walking. Do not look up; do not look around. Just keep walking.*

Absorbed in my effort to control my panic attack, I almost knocked Thomas down.

"Watch out," Thomas said as he turned to face me. His eyes widened when he saw me. "Wot's wrong?"

I wet my lips and tried to breathe deeply to clear my head but didn't have much luck. "I don't think I can walk this alone tomorrow," I whispered, every word an effort to speak. In my panicked frenzy, I'd already forgotten the landmarks I'd identified along the way. Claustrophobia had me in her grips and brought confusion with her. Crowds of people swirled about me; horns blared and sounded as if they were inside my head, echoing through my ears.

Thomas took me in his arms and rocked me gently. Hours seemed to pass before I emerged from the panic attack that had paralyzed me.

"There's a wine bar just over in Covent Garden. Let's walk there and have a nice glass of wine, and we can talk this over."

"Is it far?"

He gave me a wide grin. I looked up at him just then, and the shiny points of gold in his eyes mesmerized me. *Almost shaped like swords*, I thought absently.

"Not far. I promise."

"Yeah, that's what you said the last time," I muttered as we started to walk again, this time with Thomas's hand in mine.

Thomas was right; the wine bar was just across the street and down a block. We soon arrived at the Crusting Pipe, a grotto wine bar situated in the basement of the busy and vibrant Market Building in Covent Garden. As we entered the meandering path through it, we passed cubbyholes in which tables gave the patronage an intimate space to dine or share a glass of wine. Hushed voices whispered through the cave-like atmosphere.

After we were tucked away in a corner, the waiter served our wine.

Thomas reached across the table and covered my hand with his, and his soft brown eyes gazed into mine. "How about telling me what that was all about?"

A softness in his voice threatened to release the lump in my throat into a torrential storm of tears. The genuineness in his voice made me more emotional. I began to believe he was really interested and really cared.

I raised my eyes to meet his, intrigued by the candle's light on the table, which made those golden swords dance, and then pulled my hand back and rested it in my lap. He was quiet and sipped his wine while I mulled over whether I could trust him.

I wet my lips and, with a shaky hand, reached for my wineglass, took a large gulp instead of a delicate sip, and hoped for courage. I told him everything about what my stepfather had done to me.

I paused, unsure what to say next. There was much more to say, but I tried to gulp down that damn lump, even while tears wet my cheeks. Thomas sat quietly, as if he knew more would be coming.

"Today the buildings and the people were closing in on me,

suffocating me. It was like he was on top of me again, pressing against my ribs. I couldn't breathe. It's just that what he did to me came back again, and I feel he is—you know."

We were silent. The hammer in my heart still pounded out its heavy beat.

"That isn't the worst of it," I said, and I took another drink of wine, this time a sip. "The worst was that she didn't believe me."

"Your mum?"

"Yes. I mean, you go to the one person in the whole world you think will protect you and keep you safe, and she calls you a liar and makes you apologize to him for telling her." My voice shifted from a soft whisper to an angry tone. "It wasn't the molestation that changed me as much as her accusation I had lied about what he had done. Because she didn't believe me, he kept molesting me for seven more years." My eyes narrowed, and heat crept up my neck to meet the hot tears that fell.

"Bloody hell." Thomas reached for my hand.

I relaxed a little at his touch, but the anger remained and ate holes in my soul. "She told everyone I was a liar. She humiliated me every chance she got. Always told me I would never amount to anything, and I might as well hope someone married me, so I wouldn't be living on the streets."

I wiped more tears away. Thomas, ever patient, looked at me with soft brown eyes filling with his own tears. After another sip of courage, I continued, my anger softening.

"It didn't matter what I did in my life; I never got her approval. I excelled at many things, but she and my stepdad would tear me down, always finding fault. My entire life up to this point has been spent trying to make them proud of me, and for what? More humiliation and more desperation for them to be proud of their daughter. And you know what? I am almost fifty, so no more of this crap. From the moment I decided to come to London, I decided to live my life for me, whether they like it or not." Those were brave words since I didn't have a clue how to break free.

Thomas moved his chair next to mine. "They are both wankers, love. You know it, and now I know it. You are brilliant, beautiful, and the best business partner. I am proud of you. We'll walk to the office together in the morning."

I looked at Thomas, and for the first time in a long time, I felt safe.

Chapter 12

Let me wake up next to you, have coffee in the morning
and wander through the city with your hand in mine,
and I'll be happy for the rest of my fucked up little life.
—Charlotte Eriksson, *Empty Roads and Broken Bottles:
In Search for the Great Perhaps*

True to his word, Thomas stopped by my hotel each morning to walk with me to the office. We'd stop at a tiny café along the way, where we'd get a cheese bun for me, a bacon sandwich for him, and coffee for us both. Work consumed us from early morning until darkness fell. Dinners were mostly a quick pizza, after which he'd walk me back to the hotel and then head to the train to go to his mum's house.

Three days into our routine, Thomas gave me some good news. "We can move into the flat tomorrow."

"Wow, that is great news." I was relieved to be leaving the expense of the hotel after just three days. My credit card would be happy too. "How much stuff do you have to move?"

"Not too much—a sofa, a bed, a dinette with a couple of chairs, and a telly. Jon will come help. He also thinks he has a spare bed for you."

I'd met Jon once before while in London. He was a pretty successful photographer. Once we were done with Phillip's project, we would start work on an asset-management system for him if another more lucrative project didn't come up first.

The next day, Jon and Thomas picked me up at the hotel, and after I checked out, we drove to our flat. A steep flight of stairs within an enclosed entry took us up to the front door. At the top of the stairs, I noticed one flat directly across the hall from ours. *Nice. We'll have neighbors.*

Our flat was lovely. Two bedrooms and a bath were along one side of the entry hall, and French doors led to the living room and dining room on the other side. Large windows in the living room brought in the brightness of the day and made the rooms all look cheery. I wandered into the tiny kitchen, with its tiny refrigerator, tiny dishwasher, and tiny stove with an oven. The kitchen was compact but was well designed for space.

"Hey, love, Jon and I are going to my storage unit to pack up my things. Mind if we drop you off at Tesco on our way so you can shop for food? We'll pick you up on the way back to the flat."

"Um, sure. Anything special you want me to get?"

"Not really. Bacon, bread, milk, coffee, and whatever else we might need."

"Like toilet paper maybe?" I said with a grin.

He laughed, and we made our way out of the flat, down the stairs, and into Jon's truck.

"How far is Tesco from here?" I asked.

"Not far."

It seemed like ages before we got to the store. The roads wound around each other with roundabouts, and I got so confused I wasn't able to identify any landmarks.

"Here we are," Jon said, pulling up to the entrance of Tesco. "Wait out here for us when you are done. We won't be long."

I jumped out of the truck, waved them on, and wandered into the cavernous building. The store was the same as supermarkets in the States, with rows of shopping carts, smaller baskets on the floor beside them, cashiers, and baggers loading groceries into plastic bags. Carpet steam cleaners were to the left as I walked in, and beyond them were lotto machines.

I grabbed a cart, threw the items we needed into it, and noticed differences in foods available there. Biscuits were cookies, and in the meat department, I was lost with the names of the cuts offered. I got to the checkout, when I realized with a jolt that Thomas hadn't given me any money. *Fuck. Another dent to my credit card.*

Jon and Thomas pulled up just as I walked out of the store. Thomas got out and put the bags in the back of Jon's truck while I slipped into the middle seat.

"Thanks for sticking me with the bill," I said.

"Bollocks. I forgot all about the money. Look, I'll buy the next bit of groceries," Thomas said, brushing me off.

"Where's all your stuff? I thought you were going to move it out of storage and then come pick me up?"

"We dropped off everythin' in the bloomin' flat before comin' to pick yer up." Jon spoke with a cockney accent, words and cadence I found funny sounding and difficult to understand.

We drove to the flat in silence. I couldn't shake the worry I had over the credit card used for daily living expenses. Months were left in this project. My hotel bill and payment for the project would not be paid until all work had been completed. I would have to have a serious talk about financials with Thomas once we were alone.

Jon helped us lug the groceries up to the flat. I was amazed when I walked in; there were beds in the rooms, a sofa and dinette with chairs in the living room, and a few boxes on the counters in the kitchen.

"You boys did a great job in such a short time. Thank you so much for your help, Jon."

"Aw, it wasn't nuffink! 'Ave a look over 'ere. Yer can watch them play tennis, and over there, yer can see the bleedin' cricket games."

I went to the large windows in the dining area and looked out. Sure enough, a tennis game was being played on the courts below our windows, and farther over was a cricket match. "Yeah, but I know nothing about cricket," I said, laughing.

"It ain't that 'ard ter catch on. Yor'll be callin' the bloody games before yer know it!" Jon showed himself as the optimist he was.

"How about I buy you a nice glass of wine for all your help today?" Thomas asked Jon in his upper London accent.

"Naw, right. I'll let yer settle in and unpack. I'll go on with yer tomorrow."

"Okay then, thanks for the use of your truck and your brawn. I couldn't have moved all this without you," Thomas said, walking Jon to the door.

"See ya, Jon, and thank you!" I yelled after them.

"How about a glass of wine to celebrate?" Thomas asked when he came back into the room.

"How about we talk about finances first?"

"Fine. Just let me pour us some wine first. You got a bottle, didn't you?"

"Yep."

When we were settled at the dinette with glasses of wine in front of us, I began. "Thomas, I can't afford to keep subsidizing our expenses. I have no cash until the divorce settlement comes in, and my credit card is quickly reaching the limit."

"Yeah, I've been thinking about this too. I think the best solution would be to open a business credit card with me as a second cardholder. Then we can deduct our business expenses easily."

"Deducting is not the problem, Thomas. Paying the charges off is the problem." With hesitation in my voice, I asked, "Do you think Phillip would give us an advance based on the work already accomplished?"

Thomas downed half his wine in one gulp and said, "I'll ask him in the morning."

He emptied his glass and walked into the kitchen to pour himself another.

I had trusted him with my story. Why didn't I trust him now?

Chapter 13

Deceiving others. That is what the world calls a romance.
—Oscar Wilde

Riding the underground, or the tube, was a fascinating, in-depth look at humanity. Almost everyone wore black, and no one made eye contact, nor did they chat with each other. Even Thomas and I were silent. He talked on his phone, and I studied people, trying to guess where they came from, where they were headed, and what they did in life.

To catch the Piccadilly line to Covent Garden, we transferred from the overground Gordon Hill train to the underground at Finsbury Park. We descended three levels on steep, serpentine steps. Going down was easy, but going back up would be a bitch—no wonder I hadn't seen many obese Londoners.

That day, when we reached the platform and waited for the train to arrive, I thought about how the underground had stood in for bomb shelters during World War II. What was Thomas's education about the war? Would it have been different from the United States' perspective? Everything about his upbringing was different from mine—the formality of his culture, the size of his family, his passion for his country. I wanted to learn everything about him, but his past had remained a mystery to that point.

The Piccadilly train pulled alongside the platform, and we boarded into the cramped standing-room-only compartment. I stood behind Thomas and gazed at his back, admiring his physique for the hundredth time. He was taller than I was. I had always been attracted to tall men. But he was thin and, more importantly, thinner than I was. I felt like a walrus next to him. Yet I couldn't deny my attraction to him. Maybe his intelligence, along with his height, attracted me.

It took about twenty minutes to arrive at Covent Garden. A recording on the train announced that we were at our station and advised us to mind the gap as we disembarked.

Puffing my way up the unforgiving, steep stairs to street level, I noticed trash littering the walkway and streets. "Why aren't there trash cans to put litter in? I imagine there would be far less trash about."

"Trash cans make a great bomb receptacle for the IRA," Thomas responded in a flat voice. Another difference in our lives based on the countries we were from.

I loved the walk from the Covent Garden station to the office. Thomas took my hand, and every morning, we stopped at our favorite café for coffee and a breakfast sandwich to go. It had become a ritual for us to stop there. After the first few times, the owner noticed us and treated us like long-lost friends. A warm rush filled my heart as

I began to think of the café as our place. *Sara, stop. Just stop. You are business partners, not lovers.*

The walk to the office was wonderful. I felt I truly belonged in the world of London. I wasn't a tourist; I was part of that magical, swirling, fast-paced city. More importantly, I was part of something of my own making and not there to please anyone else. Goose bumps prickled my body as self-pride soared inside me. I loved being in London and riding the tube. I loved being Thomas's business partner. I loved being his flatmate. I loved saying *the tube* and *flat* and hearing, "Mind the gap." *I love—*

I stopped short and pulled my hand away from Thomas. What had I been about to think?

Thomas turned toward me with his brows knit together. "Wot's the matter?" he asked with a look of concern. He probably thought I'd had another panic attack.

I had surprised myself by what I had been about to say to myself. Had I really been about to say I loved him?

"A huge rat ran down the sidewalk," I quickly lied.

He grinned his magnetic grin and took my hand again. "I will be your knight against all rats, big or small," he promised.

Phillip's company occupied an entire two-story historic building that had been renovated to modern requirements yet still held the charm of its historic features. Our workspace was located on the second floor, with windows that overlooked the cobblestone street, our favorite pizza joint, and the Royal Opera House.

I'd just finished my cheese bun and stood at the window, watching the street scene. Below, men with push brooms sprayed small patches of the cobblestone with water from a tank truck blocking the narrow street. After they sprayed the water, they scrubbed the road with their brooms before stepping two feet to the right, as if cleaning a square, and began the process over.

"What are they doing?" I asked Thomas.

He came over to where I stood and said nonchalantly, as if what they were doing was as regular as rain, "They are cleaning the streets. Friday is the queen mother's birthday, and she'll be going to the opera."

"So they scrub the streets for royalty?"

"Sure. Don't want their royal tootsies to get dirty, now, do we?" He laughed and then bent down and kissed me.

The rest of the world fell away. His kiss was slow and soft, comforting in ways that words could never be. The kiss lasted only seconds, but it contained an eternity of warmth and security. I quickly pulled away from him and turned back to the window.

"Couldn't help myself. You look fetching this morning," he said softly with the gold swords in his eyes laid to rest.

Heat crept up my neck and reached my cheeks. I couldn't help but think the kiss was sweet, but what he said was more delightful.

Just then, the door opened, and Phillip walked in. "Good morning, you two," he said in his normally booming voice, and the spell was broken between Thomas and me. "How's the project coming along?" he asked as he strode over to the deep blue velvet plush couch by the window.

I don't think he came in while we were kissing. Oh Lord, I hope not.

Thomas updated him while I busied myself with our newest coding problem, which had threatened to delay the project. Phillip was tall, with dark hair in a stylish cut and blue, almost violet, eyes. He was handsome in a polished sort of way and dressed in expensive-looking suits with silk ties. He owned the largest direct marketing firm in London. While friendly and respectful of our knowledge, he had an all-business air about him that told me there would be hell to pay if we came in late on our work. I kept quiet and focused on the code in front of me, but my ears had been pulled into their conversation.

"All is on track. We should meet the deadline and go live when we agreed to. Your account managers have been great, giving us the information we need, and Sara is flying through the coding work."

I couldn't believe what Thomas had told Phillip—he had lied to him.

"Once she completes the coding, she'll develop the training at the same time I test the system out with a few account managers. I think there will be few problems, if any," he said.

I must have gasped. I turned to look at them just as Thomas stole a quick glance my way with cold, hard eyes I took as a warning to keep my mouth shut. Fear clutched my gut as I turned back to my work.

"That's good news. Well, I'll leave you to it then. Good to see you, Sara." Phillip waved, and then he was out of the room, and the door closed behind him.

My shock was replaced by anger. I moved within an inch of Thomas and said, my voice low and seething with rage, "What the heck, Thomas? This coding problem is huge, and I don't know how to fix it yet. Why did you lie to him? Why didn't you give him a warning that we might not meet our deadline?"

The golden swords of his eyes, previously at rest, were now at full attention. His eyebrows knit together, and he pressed his lips together so tightly their natural pinkness turned to white. Surprise replaced my anger. While Thomas could be quiet, moody, and even distant at times, I'd never seen such a quick change in his demeanor. I backed away from him and put distance between us.

He poked his finger into my chest and snarled, "Look, don't you ever question me. I know how to handle Phillip. You just worry about getting that coding right—and fast." He walked out the door without a glance back.

I stood in the middle of our office, too confused to move.

I fell onto the plush blue velvet office sofa and tried to sort out Thomas's abrupt change. He'd never shown me that side of himself. He had always been kind and gentle with me, even loving at times. The tone of his angry voice sent pinpricks racing up my spine and brought back bad things I didn't want to hear that others couldn't.

My eyes darted around the empty office, looking for her. "Are you here, Mom?"

No answer. No silky, smooth voice threw darts into my heart with her hateful words. I wondered if she'd finally left my mind. I laughed bitterly, knowing she had much more work to do to drag me down into a dark well with no escape. I wrapped my arms around myself. My fingers were icy against my skin—a warning sign I had recognized when my stepfather and I were alone.

I glanced at my watch, frustrated that too much time had slipped by while I recovered from Thomas's outburst. I slowly rose from the couch and walked over to my desk. The code on the screen taunted me. I needed to solve the coding problem fast. Defeated and unsettled, I sat down to troubleshoot the code. The pressure was on to deliver on time.

God knew what Thomas would do if we didn't.

Chapter 14

Authority without wisdom is like a heavy ax
without an edge—fitter to bruise than polish.
—Anne Bradstreet

Fixing the code was hopeless. I pushed my chair back from my desk and stretched out the kinks from having sat hunched over the computer for hours. Thomas was excited about the new software we had been coding, which returned a high-resolution image on the computer screen in nanoseconds versus long minutes.

"Sounds good in theory," I said to what I thought was an empty room.

"What sounds good in theory?" Thomas had walked into the room.

"I didn't hear you come in." I hadn't noticed the shift in the air, which underscored the uncertainty I experienced about him now. "I haven't cracked the code," I said in a flat voice.

"Not to worry, love." He circled his arms around me and whispered in my ear, "Let's go for a pizza and then to our flat."

Who is this man? Not four hours ago, he had lied to our client and threatened me to keep my mouth shut, and now he was once again the old Thomas—like Dr. Jekyll and Mr. Hyde.

"Sure," I said with a wary smile.

I closed down my work and the office and met Thomas at the elevator. He chatted with a few of the employees we had become friends with. Bethany was young and excited to be working for Phillip's company; Paul, like Thomas and me, was middle-aged. While he loved his creative work, he was well past the youthful exuberance of Bethany.

"Hey, want to join us across the street for pizza and pints?" Thomas asked Bethany and Paul. I silently groaned with disappointment. I'd wanted the time alone with Thomas to talk over what had happened that afternoon.

Bethany giggled and said sure; Paul thought it was a brilliant idea.

Once we were seated with our drinks in front of us—pints for the guys and wine for Bethany and me—and had ordered our pizza, we fell into a conversation about work. It was about the only thing we had in common.

"How's the project coming?" Paul sipped his lager from a mug that looked larger than a pint.

"Brilliantly. Sara gobsmacks me with how quickly she has detailed the requirements identified by you and your team and coded them into the database."

"Thomas—" I hesitated. I wished I were brave enough to tell him to stop lying.

"We'll be populating the assets and images soon. Afterward, we can start testing." He shot me a look with the golden swords pointing at me. I sat back and sipped my wine.

"I can't wait to use it," Bethany bubbled excitedly. "Sara, when will the training begin? I'm ready." She laughed.

"Sara should have the training developed when we start the testing," Thomas said. I took my cue from him and remained silent.

Our pizza arrived, and Thomas ordered another round. I could only guess who would pay for the dinner, and it wouldn't be any of them. Thomas had invited Paul and Bethany to join us, and hadn't paid for anything since I'd arrived. Why couldn't I stand up to Thomas? Not just about my paying for everything but about lying to Phillip and now to Paul and Bethany?

I had never been assertive in my relationships, but I always had been more comfortable in being assertive at work—until now. I usually could stand up for myself and colleagues, but with personal relationships, I turned into a submissive doormat who deferred to others, afraid to swim against the current. I understood where that fear came from: Mom had punished me most times I stood up for myself. She had called me naive. I probably was naive, but mostly, I trembled inside with indecision when faced with a significant life decision. Had I been gullible in my relationship with Thomas? Even Mom had said he was right for me. Had I deferred to the opinion of a ghost?

Our conversation drifted away from work, and we chatted about families, London, and movies.

"So tell me—you two are shacking up together, right?" Paul asked in between bites of pizza.

"I wouldn't call it shacking up," Thomas said. "We both have our own bedrooms and share expenses."

I almost choked. *We share expenses?*

Paul turned to Thomas. "So you aren't shagging?"

Thomas looked as uncomfortable as I felt. "Well, no, we aren't." He looked at me with his lopsided grin, the golden swords sheathed, and said, "Not yet anyway."

Chapter 15

Time they said…Time will heal all wounds, but they lied.
—Tilicia Haridat

"How dare he?" I sputtered to Thomas after we left and headed for the station. "What business is it of Paul's what we do in the privacy of our flat?" My cheeks burned while I tried to calm myself.

Thomas grinned at me as if I had made a mountain out of a molehill. "Haven't you ever considered it? Us making love?" His grin had vanished and been replaced by a look of longing. His brown eyes had softened.

I became confused. Love was hard to define, yet when he looked at me with soft and dewy eyes, my pulse quickened, and an electrical jolt took my breath away.

"Um, well, no," I lied.

"Never?" he said, his eyebrows raised in surprise.

"Never," I lied again.

At Gordon Hill station, we turned silent on the short walk to our flat, where Thomas didn't miss a beat and poured us glasses of wine and Pernod. We sat at our dinette; both of us remained quiet. I studied the top of the table while I tried to figure out what was happening between us. The air had become as still as my breathing. Confused and scared, I questioned the turn of events. Hadn't it been just an hour ago when we were only friends and business partners? Even if I'd tried, I wouldn't have been able to define what our relationship was now. I was not yet divorced and was still in love with my soon-to-be ex-husband, so what the heck was going on with me? Could I be falling in love with this man who had confused me and lied to Phillip?

Then, in his soft British voice, Thomas blindsided me even more. "Love, I've loved you since the beginning." He stood, came to my side of the table, and knelt in front of me.

"Wha—"

His hand went behind my head and pulled me closer to him. Suddenly, his lips found mine. The kiss was as soft and gentle as our morning kiss had been. Oh God, it had been so long since a man had treated me gently and lovingly. I didn't want our kiss to end. I wanted to stay and float in that warm, loving cloud forever. But instead, I pushed him away—a little too roughly.

"Thomas, we can't do this. I'm not divorced, and I don't want anything to come between us and our business." I sounded brave and matter-of-fact, yet my insides had turned to mush.

"I've loved you for so long. I've longed for you forever," Thomas whispered. His eyes were pleading. In those earthy hues, I saw his soul. I saw a beauty that expanded in a moment into a personal eternity, a heaven I wanted to be part of.

My hand caressed his face, and I felt the stubble of his five o'clock shadow rasp against my soft skin. I whispered in return, "I can't. Not just yet. I need time."

We both stood, and I hugged him tightly.

In a serious tone, he whispered into my ear, "Until you are ready then. But don't take too long." He pulled away and held me gently by the shoulders. He gave me a light kiss on the cheek and then walked into the kitchen to pour himself another glass of Pernod. I went into my bedroom and softly closed the door behind me.

I lay in my bed, unable to sleep. It wasn't the new development with Thomas that made me restless. The movie of my life played before my eyes. It would not detour to anything pleasant: I saw my stepfather, my mom, and my most well-kept secret above the other memories. I wanted to curl up and die when I thought of the promiscuity of my younger years. I had searched for the elusive and fleeting concept of love by giving of myself to the men I was with, having learned from my stepfather that sex was how I would find love. The film clips floated across the ceiling in full Technicolor while I relived every humiliating episode.

"Oh, I remember that part—I made you apologize to your stepfather. What a good time that was!" There she was, towering over me as I sat on the bed, with her ever-present cigarette in her ghostly hand.

"Just go away, Mom." I pulled the covers over my head as if I could block out her voice by blocking out her vision.

"Why, darling, I'm here because I care." Her silky, smooth voice was full of deception.

"Yeah right," I murmured, and I rolled over to face the window in an attempt to tune her out.

"Turned him down, did ya?"

God, I wanted to block out her contemptible voice forever.

"Look, sweetie," she said, her voice dripping with fake honey, "you screwed everyone in town. Why stop now?" She ended with her self-righteous, long, drawn-out sniff that drove me up the wall.

Anger roiled up in my gut, and I rolled over to face her ghostly image. "You're right. I screwed everyone. You wanna know why?" I said in a measured voice, keeping my volume low so Thomas wouldn't overhear us.

My mom sighed and flicked her curls aside. It appears her hair had grown since her last visit. She never had had long hair when she was alive, but I supposed in death, you could do whatever you wanted. Or maybe there weren't any hair salons in hell.

"I suppose you will tell me anyway, so go for it, darling, if it makes you feel any better."

"You denied the truth, and because you did that, your husband raped me for seven more years." The anger in my voice changed to melancholy. "When I finally moved out, I was lonely by myself. I felt no one loved me. Definitely not you." I shot her a look that would have killed if she hadn't already been dead. "Every man I met wanted the same thing your husband took from me. I desperately wanted love, and I thought screwing was love."

My movie began again and brought to life memories of the humiliating things I had done with and for men. I hugged myself tightly and rocked back and forth, numb to the emotions that ached to be released from my soul.

"Well, sweetie, guess my work is done here for tonight. But don't worry; I'll come back for a visit soon."

I watched with an intense, angry stare as she faded away to nothingness.

I pulled the blankets up over myself again and curled into the fetal position as self-pity wrapped me in its arms like an old friend.

A few minutes later, I heard a tap on my door and then Thomas's whispered voice.

"Are you okay, love?"

Instead of answering, I snuggled deeper into the blankets with my back toward him. I heard his slippers pad closer to the bed. "I'm fine." I wished he'd go back to his bed. He sat down on my bed next to me and softly rubbed my blanketed shoulder.

"I thought I heard voices. Are you sure you are okay?" His voice was soft, almost lyrical, and threatened to break through my shell of self-protection.

How could I ever tell him about my mother and her visits? If he knew I talked with a ghost, would he still want to be with me? I rolled over to face him and almost got a lie choked out to explain what he might have heard. The unspoken words died in my throat. The look of genuine concern on his face stopped them from being said.

"Sara," he whispered, tenderly touching the tears that rolled down my cheeks. "Oh, darling, wot's wrong?" he said while he reached for me and pulled me into a gentle hug.

His comforting touch was all it took for the decades of emotion stuffed deep into the recesses of my soul to erupt in a hurricane of self-anger and self-loathing and a river of tears. Through it all, Thomas held me gently and patiently and let me thrash out my demons through unintelligible words and tears. Finally, my storm subsided, and I lay exhausted against his chest, soaked by my tears. His arms still held me. Shouldn't my heart have felt lighter after that release?

Then it hit me. I'd blubbered my way through stories of my stepfather, my mother, men, Ray—all who had taken my love and thrown it away. My facade of being the perfect person had crumbled. In its wake, it had left someone who forever disappointed her mother and would screw anyone for the unachievable prize of being loved.

Chapter 16

They say a person needs just three things to be truly happy in this world: someone to love, something to do, and something to hope for.
—Tom Bodett

The next morning, movement next to me in bed startled me into groggy wakefulness before the alarm jarred me awake.

"G'morning, love." Thomas pulled me closer to him and nuzzled my neck, spooning. "How did you sleep?"

I rolled over to face him and was surprised to see he had dressed. "Have you been up already?"

"Nope. I lay right here beside you to make sure you were okay through the night. That was a pretty intense breakdown you had."

His soft breath on my neck and his empathy made me feel safe and loved. I closed my eyes, never wanting the feeling to go away. I prayed the pain of the past never became a pain in my future.

"Thomas, I'm so sorry I dumped on you last night. You don't deserve—"

He lifted my chin and looked me in the eyes. "Stop right there. Sara, I love you. I meant it when I said it last night, and I mean it today and will mean it forever. I want to know everything there is about you so I can love you even better. So no regrets. You didn't burden me; you helped me love you more completely."

He gently pulled me into him, and our parted lips kissed softly at first and then passionately. His kiss was not the same as those of the other men in my life but was steeped in a passion that ignited. It was the promise of everything I had dreamed of having in my life, of the primal desire that lived in everyone. The kiss ended too soon and left me breathless and wanting more.

"Go jump in the shower while I get the coffee started," Thomas said, breaking the spell. "We've got time for a cuppa before we have to catch our train." With a quick peck on my cheek, he jumped off the bed and made his way to the kitchen.

I stretched out the kinks that lying in one position gave a body. It amazed me I had been so open and emotionally vulnerable with Thomas. Then guilt came and took me down the old familiar, well-trod path that I wanted to refuse to walk again. *I shouldn't have told him anything. It was supposed to be our little secret between my stepdad and me. I promised. I promised him, and I promised Mom I'd never tell.*

What if I broke down like I had last night and told Jackson my story? He had a close relationship with my stepdad, whom he called Boppa; they were buddies. I slumped over as my body caved in on itself. If Jackson ever found out, it would ruin his memories of Boppa. My mind screamed silently, thinking of what my son would think of me if he ever found out.

"Are you there, Mom?" I asked to the empty room. The silence that answered brushed my skin like sandpaper scraping against my limbs; Mom's silence was probably punishment for my telling. I rose from the bed and slowly made my way to the bathroom, filled with guilt and remorse, to start my day.

Last night had been tough at the office, and that morning was as well. The problems I'd discovered with the code were unrelenting and kicked my butt. The network was down, and then the coding issue I'd thought I fixed was once again breaking. Only this time, it was taking hostage the rest of the code. I dreaded when things didn't come together as they should have or as quickly as I thought they should have. Thomas always got angry and mean with me more so than anyone else at the office. While working on that project, he'd yelled, called me stupid, and told me I couldn't code my way home and back.

That day was different. He sat beside me without a tinge of tenseness leaking from his body while we reviewed the code byte by byte and brainstormed possible fixes. I glanced aside at him and marveled at how good we were with each other right then, as if we were indeed partners. My dream of success with a business of my own felt once again within my grasp. Thomas's kindness and understanding the night before and that day helped me feel hopeful that my dream would be within my grasp. But something teased the back of my brain: Could I trust him?

Thomas caught me looking at him. "Wotcha lookin' at?"

"A handsome, smart man who helped me climb out of a deep well last night." I smiled back at him. He leaned toward me and landed a wet peck on my cheek, which raised my heart rate.

"Let's knock off early today and go back to our flat, have a nice supper, and relax for a while. We can connect to the network from there and work on it some more after we eat. I think a break will do us both good—clear our heads."

He surprised me with his offer. We usually stayed at the office late and were the last ones to leave.

"Sounds too inviting to pass up," I said, and I gave him a wink and a smile. Even though the coding problem frustrated us, Thomas made me feel loved, accepted, smart, and equal. Maybe I could phone Jackson after supper before we started work again, I thought.

Thomas caught my wink and, with a mischievous grin and a wink of his own, said, "Who knows? There may be more behind that invitation."

Chapter 17

What good is intuition if your heart
gets in the way of hearing it?
—Shannon Adler

Paul looked up from his computer screen as we walked by his desk on our way out. "Hey, where ya goin'? It isn't quittin' time. Off for a shag?"

His comment mortified me. I felt as if someone had turned my internal heat system to full blast.

"Some of the code is being persnickety, so we're gonna take a break and work on it from our flat," Thomas said with his hand pressed on my back to keep us moving forward. "But maybe." He grinned over his shoulder at Paul as we stepped out onto the cobblestone street.

"Damn, I wish he'd quit already about shagging," I said.

"He's just teasing us, love. Don't let him get to ya." Thomas squeezed me as we headed toward the tube station.

I didn't like that kind of teasing by Phillip's account handlers. It felt demeaning.

We stopped at a fish-and-chip takeout shop and took food home.

"I want to call Jackson after eating," I told Thomas in between bites. "It's been so long, and I want to check in to see if he's managed to come to terms with the divorce."

"There won't be time, love, and we have to fix that code. Besides, won't it be early in the morning there?" Thomas responded.

It was three o'clock in the afternoon London time, which made it seven o'clock in the morning at home. I was disappointed, but Thomas was right; it was too early to call. I didn't want to take the chance of waking Jackson up if he had been up late studying for a test.

Guilt settled in, and I pushed the rest of my food away. How long had it been since I'd spoken with Jackson? I felt as if I'd deserted him after I dumped the divorce on him—just one more thing to feel guilty about.

I cleared the paper containers off the table and then opened my laptop to work on the broken code.

⊶⊰⊱⊷

I thrust my arms in the air in a sign of victory. "I think I cracked the code!" I screeched excitedly from my chair in the dining room, which served as our makeshift office. I heard ice clink in a glass as Thomas walked over to me. It could have been orange juice at six o'clock in the evening—after all, Pernod and orange juice were the same color—but it wasn't. The closer he got to me, the stronger the licorice smell got.

He leaned behind my chair and said, "Show me."

It took a half hour to guide him through the code. I showed where I had gone wrong and the fix to make it right. I ran it through several tests, and the code performed precisely as it should have every time.

"Bloody hell, you are brilliant!" he cried out happily as he picked me up out of the chair. His strong arms held me tightly.

The hug was a simple enough gesture, one that many people did when celebrating a solution to a tough problem. However, the feel of his body close to mine started a whole new problem—a problem with only one solution. The smell of Pernod wafted up into my nostrils as he bent down and landed a victory kiss right on my lips. We pulled back and stood facing each other, our eyes searching to read the signals our bodies were sending each other. With one touch, it would be all over. It always had been that way for me. I had always submitted to a man because he desired me and told me how beautiful and smart I was—at least for the five minutes it took him to get his job done. I no longer wanted that kind of love, if anyone could have called it that. With Thomas, I saw the chance of the type of love I had searched for all my life. The kind Mom had told me would never exist for me.

Thomas's tongue worked to pry my lips open. I wanted to pull away, but my body betrayed me, and I drew closer to him. Our hands explored and caressed each other. Thomas's touch was not demanding, unlike the touches of my stepfather and the other men I had given myself to. Soft, gentle hands caressed me, teasing and inciting, not insisting.

We broke away from our kiss, and he led me to my bedroom, where he had held and comforted me the night before. The lights were off, but the brightness of the full moon shone through my window and gave his face an ethereal glow, softening his angular jawline. We stood next to the bed, searching each other's eyes, before he pulled me closer to him again and pressed his hard body next to my softer one. I reached up and unbuttoned his shirt while his hands caressed and teased my body, and he landed wet kisses on my neck. He eased me onto my bed and pulled my jeans off while I yanked my top and bra off, exposing my breasts. He stood above me and gazed at my pudgy body, which glowed in the moonlight. I feared my not-so-perfect physique disgusted him, and he'd walk out of the room, rejecting me, but instead of turning away, he leaned onto me with his breath ragged and his eyes bright and hungry.

His mouth explored the curve of my breast, trailing down to the inside of my thigh, igniting and unleashing passion I had thought was all but dead. I traced and caressed his body with my fingers, exploring every crevice and muscle. He growled with an urgency that burned fingers of need deep inside of me. Urging him to go faster and harder, I gave myself into my desire, into him.

We lay facing each other while recovering from the most exquisite lovemaking I'd experienced in a long time. Our bodies were still intertwined; my fingers nestled into the soft hairs of his chest. It had been so long since I had felt so content. We spoke no words; we simply relaxed into each other's arms. I listened to the rhythm of his breathing as it changed from panting to normal. Soft snores told me he had drifted off to sleep.

My body was spent, yet I felt an unexplainable energy. I watched him as he slept, and my heart grew tender at his hair boyishly falling over his forehead in contrast to his strong jawline. A strange feeling eased through my body. *Is this what others call love?* I thought I had been in love before, but this felt different. I didn't feel used, as I usually did after sex; this feeling was a whole different experience I couldn't put a name to.

The morning sun crashed through the curtainless window and landed on my closed eyes. *My wake-up call*, I thought, groaning inwardly. I stretched, and awareness of our lovemaking the night before crept into my sleepy brain. I turned over to snuggle with Thomas, but he was gone. Just as I pulled back the covers to get out of bed, he came into the room, dressed, with his hair combed and a massive smile on his handsome face.

"Good mornin', love," he said in an unusually cheery, crisp voice, handing me a steaming mug of coffee. "I thought we'd share our first cuppa in bed before you get your shower."

I took the mug filled with hot coffee and said, "Coffee in bed? Thomas, you spoil me."

Thomas bent down and kissed me tenderly on my forehead. "Nothing is too good for you, love."

Thousands of butterfly wings fluttered in my stomach, and my heart jumped with pleasure at his touch. He sat on the bed next to me and outlined our workday ahead as we sipped our coffee. It had been a relief for both of last night to get the fix to the code completed.

"All we have to do now is ramp up, work a little quicker, and meet our deadlines—which means I won't have to tell Phillip about the code problem and delay," he said.

The bile in my stomach threatened to erupt at the lie Thomas was keeping alive. "Thomas, what happens if the code breaks again or we run into some other unforeseen problem? We can't lie to Phillip again." My tone was accusing.

He turned to face me, his eyes dark. "Leave Phillip to me; you just do your work, and we will be fine. Time for you to get your shower and dress." With that, he was off the bed and left me stunned at how quickly he had gone from sweetness to controlling.

I'd seen hints of Thomas becoming controlling before, but I'd always brushed it off as how he showed his stress. I had a hard time brushing it off that time. There was something in his eyes that had set me on edge.

It was a quiet ride to the Covent Garden tube station. I tried to make conversation, but Thomas only grunted in response to anything I said. Once we got off the train, he walked well ahead of me and didn't stop at the café for our usual coffee and breakfast. This was a side of him I had not seen before. I was confused about what had brought on his behavior. Surely it couldn't have been my calling out his lie.

Thomas arrived at the office well ahead of me. I didn't see him in the lobby, so I asked Paul if Thomas was upstairs in our office as I passed his desk.

"Naw, I think he is with Phillip. Phillip has been asking for him all morning. How come you guys are so late this morning?" Paul asked with a sly grin and a wink.

I didn't respond to his question. I thanked him over my shoulder as I continued to the office I shared with Thomas. I heard muffled voices through the closed door of Phillip's office. They were not loud enough that I could have understood the words spoken. I hurried to get to my office before Phillip's door opened.

I grabbed a cup of coffee at the kitchenette outside our office before unlocking the door and preparing for the day. That day, we could work ahead in the project plan, having solved the code problem last night. It would be a good day, I thought, while I fired up my computer.

"Oh no," I whispered to the empty room. "No, no, no, it can't be!" I screeched while I scrolled through the code on the screen.

Thomas chose that moment to walk into the office. "Wot do you mean 'Oh no'?"

"The code," I responded in a crackled, strangled voice, my eyes glued to the screen. I scrolled down, then up, and then down again, trying to find the break.

Thomas leaned over me to focus on the screen, as if he would have known a correct code against a broken code. I felt his warm, Pernod-scented breath on the back of my neck. Had he been drinking already? It wasn't even nine o'clock in the morning yet.

My neck hairs stood at attention, and I had a strong impulse to bolt out of the chair. Unexplainable fear seeped into my veins. Fear of Thomas?

Chapter 18

**The trouble with scary people is everyone's too
scared to tell them how scary they are.**
—Janey Colbourne

"Wot happened?" Thomas remained leaning over me with his eyes glued to the screen and an icy edge to his voice.

"I don't know yet." I desperately scrutinized the code line by line. I struggled to keep panic from squeezing the clarity from my brain. I needed to focus, and Thomas's questions were distracting me and increased my level of fear.

"Well, wot could have happened between last night and now? Wot did you do?"

"Thomas, I didn't do anything but open up the code to retest before moving to the next phase," I said with a low, guttural voice.

"You had to do something to break it again, you stupid cow."

My head shot up, and my eyes blazed as heat rushed to my cheeks. "Stupid cow?" I asked incredulously. "What the hell, Thomas?"

The adoring look he had always shown me was now a twisted, angry look with the golden swords at full attention. "You didn't get it right last night, and now we are even further behind than we were." His eyes still flashed swords at me, but his voice got softer, with just a tinge of anger. "Look, I had a meeting with Phillip this morning, and while he doesn't know how far behind we are, he is concerned he hasn't seen any results yet. I reassured him, but we need to start meeting our deadlines and show him we are capable of delivering on time."

"Did you lie to him again?" I whispered, not wishing to anger him again.

Thomas noticed our office door was open and strode over to close it before he answered me. "Look, Sara, I didn't lie—not really. It's good business to help the client be confident in his project's progress. I simply told him we had a problem with the code last night, but we fixed it, and the project is on track."

My heart hammered small nail holes in my chest, but I put my best poker face on so as not to start an argument, suddenly fearing the outcome of such an argument. Thomas's anger earlier had thrown me off balance and revealed a part of him I had not seen before. I knew he had lied to Phillip and then to me about lying. The bottom line was that Phillip was not happy with our slow progress.

"I'm going to get some coffee," he said. "You can work on getting that code right while I'm gone." Why did he sound as if he were talking down to me?

After Thomas left, I focused on the broken code and pushed the morning's argument to the background. It was after lunch before I discovered where the code had broken and made a fix that—knock on wood—would be permanent.

I stood. My butt felt dead from having sat on a hard chair for hours. I realized Thomas hadn't come back. I took the stairs down to the plush lobby of the office building to look for him.

He lounged in the overstuffed blue velvet chair with a glass of wine in his hand, entertaining the receptionist with stories that were most likely lies. She laughed and obviously enjoyed his tales, which struck a pang of jealousy in me. I'd noticed he had started to drink earlier and earlier each day. How could he drink all day and still look and act sober?

"Where's my coffee?" I didn't try to keep the sarcastic tone out of my voice.

He looked at me quizzically, as if experiencing memory loss regarding why he had left the office in the first place. Instead of answering, he took a sip of his wine and said, "Get the code you broke fixed?"

I flinched and glanced at the receptionist while she looked back at me with a slight "Gotcha" smile. My mind raced. I couldn't believe he had said that in front of her.

"Yes," I said, trying to keep my voice even.

"Brilliant. Better go catch up to our next milestone then. Phillip is expecting a demo of our progress in a few days." He dismissed me with a toast from his wineglass before he took a sip and returned to his conversation.

I turned around with my lips tight and my fists clenched at my sides and walked back to our office. I felt like a reprimanded child with figurative angry smoke blowing out my ears.

"Hey, Sara, how's it going?" Bethany called out to me as I passed her desk.

"Don't even ask," I fumed, and I didn't stop to chat.

I stepped inside the office and slammed the door behind me. Anger was replaced by the old familiar sense of betrayal. *Why couldn't I stand up to him? He doesn't treat me like his partner, more like his flunky.*

"You can't stand up to him any more than you could stand up to me, dear daughter of mine."

Mom—just the person I didn't need right now. She sat on the arm of the couch with her legs crossed and her familiar cigarette smoke curling up from her fingers.

Ignoring her, I made my way to my desk, sat on the familiar hard chair, and turned my computer on. "How about you go back to heaven, or is it hell where you were sent? You, dear mother, are the last thing I need in my day right now."

"I am exactly what you need right now, young lady."

Here we go—another lecture from the woman who failed to protect me from one of the worst things that ever happened to me. I kept my back to her and concentrated on the project plan.

"You are such a wimp. You know that? How do you expect ever to make anything of yourself if you can't stand up to bullies? You are still, and always were, my biggest disappointment. You know that?"

The smoldering fires of fury and hatred exploded into a million buzzing bees in my stomach. I spun around to face her taunting voice and tried to swallow the rage down a few decibels.

In a low, controlled voice, I asked, "Don't you remember, Mommy dearest? You taught me that bullies win. Go away. Just go away." I turned back to my desk and slumped down with my head in my hands. The waterworks that had threatened to fall since Thomas humiliated me finally broke their dam. "I'm sorry. So sorry, Mom," I whispered into my tears, despising myself for apologizing. But she was gone. Again.

I was tired of feeling like this. Like crap. Like the lowest human form on earth. I'd spent all my life in tears, hiding the person I was, the person my past had made me. I was getting damn tired of it.

I wasn't sure how long I drowned my desk in years' worth of tears, but soon guilt over wasting time when I should have been working sobered me. I straightened up and bolstered myself to quit feeling bad over my outburst to Mom's ghost. After all, she was a ghost and not real. I wiped the wetness from my face and desk and started to work on fixing the code. The last thing I needed was to have Thomas walk in and find no work had been accomplished by a weeping female. His anger always translated into sarcastic put-downs that cut right through my soul.

Then a weird thought stopped me short. The code had been working last night. Was it possible Thomas had gotten up while I slept and broken the code himself? Why would he have done that?

Chapter 19

The more I see, the less I know for sure.
—John Lennon

The idea that Thomas would sabotage the code shook me to the core. Why would I even consider he'd do anything to the project that would jeopardize our success? Had he told Phillip that morning that the code had broken and that it was my fault? Had he been undermining my progress? But why would he do that?

The idea that the code had broken because of Thomas was too far-fetched for me to believe. He had as much at stake as I did to deliver the project on time. I shook it off and, sniffling, turned back to my work.

Deep in concentration, I didn't hear the door open.

"How's it going, love?"

With narrowed eyes, I tried to figure out if he remembered how he had treated me earlier. The fragrance of chardonnay entered the room with him and gave a hint of how much work he had not gotten done that day. Blood rushed to my head, and sparks fired up in my stomach, but I swallowed my anger. "The code seems to be holding up to the fix. I'm halfway through the next phase."

"Brilliant," he said in a flat voice.

Where had his enthusiasm gone? Wasn't he happy I had been moving forward and wasn't behind?

"Let's knock off for today and go have a wine at Crusting Pipe to celebrate," he said.

"It's early afternoon. I can't make progress by drinking wine at the pub, and besides, I want to talk about how you treated me earlier. If it's okay." Why was I asking his permission? *Damn.*

"We can chat about it later. I'll go get a table, and you join us when you're ready to knock off for the day." With that, he left. No kiss. No goodbye.

And who was *us*? The giggly receptionist who looked at him with google eyes? I didn't like doubting Thomas, but it seemed that day I had questioned him in ways I never had thought I would.

Obviously, Thomas was more into drinking and socializing than working that day. I hoped the *us* referred to future clients he was pitching our business solutions to, but I had a feeling he would be with Paul and Bethany. I turned back to my computer and vowed to catch us up to where we needed to be before I left to join them.

Darkness came as early in the day in London in the winter months as it did on Whidbey Island. That day, the darkness caught me by surprise. Where had the afternoon gone?

I stretched to work out the kinks and felt particularly pleased with myself. I not only had solved our code problem but also had made significant progress on the project plan and moved us ahead on our milestones.

The office lacked the normal daily sounds of phones ringing, printers humming, and account handlers chattering. The silence felt a little eerie. The only light came from the glow streaming in the windows from the streetlamps. I relished a few moments of peace in the semidark office. I shut down the computer and picked up my purse and jacket, and the dim light guided my way through the darkened office building.

The walk to Crusting Pipe was pleasant. The December sky was starless, hidden by the light of the streetlamps. Shadows of people, some arm in arm and some hand in hand, walked all around me, and their chatter and laughter lightened my mood. I supposed they were making their way along the cobblestones to their favorite restaurants before going to the theater. I strolled along and savored the smells and the sounds, reluctant to end that brief moment of solitude before joining Thomas. I always had looked forward to being with him in the past, but lately, his moods had become unpredictable. I missed the old predictable Thomas.

I saw them at their table as soon as I walked into the wine bar. Rather, I heard loud laughter, and my curiosity led my eyes to see where it was coming from. Shedding my jacket as I walked to the table, I noticed Paul, Bethany, Phillip, Thomas, and an empty chair, which I guessed had been saved for me.

"Cheers, Sara." Thomas spotted me, stood, and wrapped me in a huge hug. He pulled the chair out and said proudly, "Sara fixed a bugger of a break in the code that had hampered our progress the past few days."

Our coworkers raised their glasses to me and hollered, "Cheers to Sara!"

I quickly sat in my chair, mortified. I snuck a glance at Phillip to see what his reaction was and was rewarded with a half smile. "Thank you, guys. Hello, Phillip. I haven't seen much of you around lately," I said in a quiet voice. I hoped to instill some decorum in the wine-happy group and keep the other patrons' eyes off our table.

"I took the family on a little holiday to France for a couple of weeks. It was relaxing and good to recharge those creative brain cells." Phillip smiled and took another sip of his wine. "What do you do for fun, Sara?"

I realized I didn't know Phillip very well. Thomas knew him from previous employment and had negotiated our contract. As soon as he asked the question, my mind went blank. What did I do for fun?

"She reads a lot, and we enjoy going out to our favorite pub for trivia night and dinner," Thomas said. He then ordered two more bottles of wine for the table with an extra glass for me. "And she loves her wine."

The others laughed, and I bristled at his audacity in speaking for me but kept my mouth shut. It was, after all, a table full of Brits, and I was the outsider.

"Thomas gave me an update on the project this morning," Phillip said. "And, Sara, I must say, I am gobsmacked at your talent and skills. I have to admit I was worried this morning you wouldn't meet our deadline."

Did that mean Thomas had told him I had broken the code?

I rarely received compliments and wasn't good at handling them. Everyone at the table turned to look at me—everyone but Thomas. I looked down, hiding behind my lashes; cleared my throat; and whispered a thank-you to Phillip.

"So Thomas said we are on schedule, but I want to hear what you think." Phillip settled back in his chair with his glass in hand and waited for my answer.

I snuck a glance toward Thomas, who wore a scowl as if he were upset Phillip had asked my opinion. I was pleased to be asked but confused at Thomas's response. I gave Phillip my update, and all the while, I felt Thomas seething beside me.

"Brilliant!" Phillip clapped his hands in excitement and turned to Thomas. "You chose your business partner well. You make a great team."

Thomas relaxed. A grin replaced the scowl. "Yep, we do."

We spent the rest of the evening sharing stories, eating tapas, and drinking the bottles of wine. Relief washed over me when Phillip called the waiter over to get the bill, for two reasons: one, I wouldn't be stuck with the bill, and two, I was dead tired. It had been a stressful day, not to mention confusing with the changes in Thomas's behavior earlier. I wanted to get on the train, get home, and lay my head on my pillow.

Once the check had been paid, we stood, said our goodbyes, and gave Phillip a huge thank-you. I reached for Thomas's hand, but he surprised me by jerking it away from me. I watched the others for their reactions, and by the looks on their faces, they were surprised by his action. Embarrassed, I shrugged and fell in step behind him as we walked out of the grotto to the tube station.

The train ride home was a quiet one. Theaters had not let out yet, which made the passenger load light. I was glad for the quiet time and allowed myself to relax. Phillip's compliments about my work played over and over in my head. It was odd for me to receive compliments and to know someone appreciated what I did. A smile snuck onto my face, and I let go of a deep, satisfied sigh.

"We're at our station." Thomas's announcement pulled me out of my starry-eyed dream world back into reality. I couldn't tell if he was still put off, but the smile stayed with me as I followed him down the hill to our flat.

There was just one more thing I needed to do, and I had to do it while the day's events were still fresh in our memories.

Chapter 20

It hurts the most when the person who made you feel so special yesterday makes you feel so unwanted today.
—Unknown

"How come so quiet?" I asked Thomas, still on a high from Phillip's positive comments about my work earlier that evening.

He stared at me, his eyes slit with sharpened swords; turned; and casually walked into the kitchen without a sound.

What's up with him? It doesn't matter; nothing will ruin this sense of accomplishment. Phillip's words had been a gift, and I wouldn't let Thomas ruin it.

The sound of ice clinking in a glass made me look toward the kitchen. He poured a drink for himself and wine for me and then came to the dinette, where I sat, and placed the drinks on the table.

"Cheers," he said in a flat voice as he lifted his glass toward me. He took a large sip. His eyes put me on edge; the golden swords were pointed right at me.

I picked up my glass, returned his cheers, and sipped my wine. I ignored what appeared to be his lousy mood and watched a couple who played tennis on the lit court below.

"I don't appreciate your taking the credit for our work," Thomas said in a cold, expressionless voice.

My attention flipped back inside the room, and I looked at him. He took another long draft of his drink before he continued.

"We are a team, and we both take credit for our work, no matter who does it. Get it?"

Fingers of ice crept up my spine; adrenaline pumped into my veins. I was not sure why I felt threatened. Was it the menace in his voice?

"But you didn't help today, Thomas," I said in a whisper-thin voice. I sat up straight in my chair and, with my normal voice, tried to sound confident and keep the sarcasm out of my tone. "The progress made was because of me. All the while, you were entertaining the receptionist and drinking the afternoon away."

Thomas glared at me from across the table, gulped down the rest of his drink, and slammed his glass down. I jumped, and he rose from his chair and came to my chair, looming over me. He grabbed a clump of my hair and jerked my head backward while I desperately clawed for his hands to get him to let go. The chair tipped over, and he slammed me onto the floor on my back. The air flew out of my lungs as I let out an "Ufff." Before I could recover, he raised both of my legs until he had them pressed to the floor above my head, doubling me over. The pain was unbearable; a sharp stabbing sensation ran up my legs. I struggled to get out of his hold on me, but the more I struggled, the harder he pushed my legs down, until my toes touched the floor. He sat on them, cutting off my breath. The muffin top I had never been able to lose didn't help with the pressure. Gasping for breath, I begged him to stop, but the words had no air to speak.

He bounced on me; with each upward bounce, the pressure on my diaphragm eased. I could grab a quick, small breath before he pounced down onto me again and pushed the air I desperately needed out of my burning lungs. Panic struck me motionless as I realized I was going to die.

"You are never to do what you did today, bitch. Got that? You're a dumb, ugly bitch who would be nobody without me and whom nobody wants."

Adrenaline rushed through my veins and pushed the fear aside. Anger replaced the fear. Anger that he was doing this to me. Anger that he had taken away the good feelings Phillip's praise had given me earlier. The anger gave me new strength, and I tried to push back, but my legs didn't obey. Confusion muddled my brain; my lungs were close to having no air at all. Why had I ever come to London?

"Who do you think you are? Where would you be if I hadn't gotten Phillip as a client for us?" His voice constricted, and he pushed harder against my feeble attempts at getting him off of me. "You forced me to do this. This is all your doing," Thomas gasped, out of breath. His bounces on my legs had become weaker.

I kept trying to swing forward and shove him off me. My arms became free, and in a frantic last-ditch effort to get air into my lungs, I pummeled his sides, trying for his ribs. But in my confused mind, any place would have done.

It was as if he didn't feel the pain. Either that, or I was getting weaker. The pain that had burned in my legs like claws of fire faded away to a cold numbness; gray shadows filled the corners of my vision. The only thing I heard was the slowing of my heartbeat. Darkness surrounded me. Then there was nothing.

∞

I came to on my back on the floor with my legs relaxed in front of me. I didn't know how long I had been out. An uncanny silence muted my ears. My brain slowly brought back bits and pieces of what had happened. I struggled to sit up, and the ache in my legs and hips confirmed each memory that flooded back into my consciousness. My God, he was a Thomas I didn't know. What else didn't I know about him?

The room spun like a merry-go-round, and the acid from the glasses of wine I'd had that evening burned my throat. I panicked when I remembered Thomas was still in the flat somewhere.

I collapsed when I stood and leaned on the table for support. Fear spurned me to hurry to my room and lock the door. It was a slow walk; each step was filled with pain. I passed by his bedroom and saw him in his bed, sleeping off a full day of drink. I continued to my room, relieved he had passed out. Upon reaching safety, I slowly closed the door and turned the lock. For extra measure, I leaned a chair under the doorknob to keep him out. I fell onto my bed, drained, with a hazy notion I should have a hot bath and soak my hip bones to soothe them. Fear kept me from going to the bathroom, which was next to his room, and running the water. What if I woke him up out of his stupor?

Jackson. Oh God, Jackson. I couldn't allow him to know. He would look at me differently; probably as a week and foolish woman After I left his Dad, I didn't even know if he loved me now or not. Thomas always came up with a reason why I couldn't call him. I hadn't talked to him since I had arrived in London. I swore to myself that Thomas would never again keep me from my son, and my son would never know what Thomas had done to me that night.

My last thoughts were of my day, a typical day in the story of my life. A day when I'd felt good about myself, only to be ripped apart by someone I loved and who I believed loved me.

Chapter 21

Reality is merely an illusion, albeit a very persistent one.
—Albert Einstein

The December morning sun peeked through the window shade; our flat was quiet. The nightmare of last night felt surreal. It had happened. Thomas had attacked me, right? I moved a little, and the pain in my hips and legs was a sure sign it had happened. He had said it was my fault, but what had I done to deserve being attacked by him? I lay on the bed, reliving last night's events and trying to figure out where it all had gone wrong. A dry mouth and thirst beyond belief prompted me to reach for the water glass on the nightstand. It slipped out of my hands and shattered on the wooden floor.

There was a timid knock on my door, which was still locked and fortified with the chair against it.

"You okay in there? I heard some glass break." It was Thomas, with just a hint of concern in his voice.

"I'm fine. Just dropped my water glass." The sound of his voice sent ice through my veins.

"Look, love, can we talk about last night?" His voice had become softer, conciliatory.

"Thomas, I don't want to talk about last night right now. I hurt from last night and will be staying home to work. Would you please go to the office and leave me alone?"

There was a moment of silence, and then Thomas whispered through the closed door, "I'm sorry, love."

Was that a hint of sadness and maybe even tears I heard on the other side of the door? Last night, he had shown me a side of himself that I had never dreamed existed in him. Had I made a mistake in coming to London? Worse, had I made yet another fatal mistake by yielding my heart to Thomas? I had to be alone that day to figure things out.

Another knock on my bedroom door brought me out of deep thought.

"I'm leaving now, love, but I'll call later to see how you are getting on," Thomas said through the still-closed door.

"Just go," I wanted to say, but instead, I said the only word I could speak to him now: "Goodbye."

"Not even a goodbye kiss?" he said lightheartedly.

"Just go!" I wanted to yell, but instead, I said, "Have a good day."

Confusion overtook my mind. That morning, Thomas had turned into his old self, and all resemblance of the monster he had been last night was gone. Even though my pain reminded me it had happened, my brain struggled against dream or truth.

There was a quiet pause on the other side of the door before I heard him shuffle to the front door, unlock the dead bolts, and quietly close the door behind him. I painfully rose from the bed to look out the window and watched him walk up the hill to the Gordon Hill train station. I breathed a sigh of relief, and my body slowly stopped its trembling.

I was safe until he came home that night.

Chapter 22

**Everything was perfectly healthy and
normal here in Denial Land.**
—Jim Butcher, *Cold Days*

A great rush of relief washed over me when I heard the front door click and watched through the window as he made his way up the hill. The threat would be gone for at least eight hours, hopefully longer. Last night seemed like a C movie, with actors who didn't understand their roles or their lines but got to walk away whole at the end. Except we hadn't walked away whole; it felt as if we were breaking. I hadn't done anything to deserve what he'd done to me, or had I? What could I have done differently not to trigger his anger? The knowledge of domestic violence I had received as an advocate for abused women reminded me of the abuse pattern. I knew I was in denial and helpless to pull myself out of it.

The more I turned options over in my brain, the more I convinced myself I had done something to make him angry; I just didn't know what. It couldn't have been that Phillip praised my work in front of our friends, could it? I hoped Thomas would be in a receptive mood that night to talk it through. Never did I want another night like last night. My life had been one abusive relationship after another, and I was committed to ending the cycle I'd been in forever.

Was I just fooling myself with my newfound confidence to confront him? Would I have the strength to follow through when he got home?

The bedside clock said it was ten o'clock. "Holy crap," I said, and I tried to jump out of bed. The pain brought waves of nausea and kept me from standing until it passed. No quick shower that morning—a nice hot bath was in order.

It was noon when I sat at the dinette, opened my laptop, and connected to the network. I gave my phone a quick look and noticed voice mails had come in—thirty-five of them, all from Thomas, all that morning. Fear traveled through my veins until my heart throbbed in my ears when I heard his voice.

"Hi, love. Just checking on my girl to make sure you are okay. Call me when you get this. Love ya."

Most of them were the same message, spoken in a soft voice full of caring, until the last one: "Sara, call me back right now!"

With hands shaking, I dialed his number. I didn't want to talk to him yet but was fearful of what might happen if I didn't.

"Where have you been? Are you okay?" he said instead of the usual greeting of "Hello." His voice sounded a little frantic and a lot annoyed.

"My legs and hips hurt from what you did to me last night, so I took a long, hot bath," I responded in an emotionless voice.

"I'm sorry, love. I don't know what came over me. I've never done that before to anyone. I promise it won't happen again. Forgive me?" His voice softened somewhat, and he sounded genuinely sorry.

"Sure," I half lied as denial started to creep into my truth. I feared if I held him accountable, it would trigger another argument and possibly lead to a not-so-good ending for me. *Trust—isn't that what good relationships are built on? I need to trust what he says. Until I can't trust anymore. Shit, why did I think that?*

"I was getting worried about you. Haven't seen you on the network yet this morning. How come?" All sense of an apologetic voice was gone, replaced by a "Let's get down to business" voice.

"I told you. I soaked in a long bath to help the pain, but now I'm ready to work." I was surprised at the smallness of my voice. I sounded like a scolded child.

"'Bout time. Tomorrow is our demo with Phillip. You going to be ready?"

I quickly looked over the project plan while answering, "Sure, I only have a few things to button up before tomorrow. I can easily get them done today for tomorrow's meeting with Phillip." I didn't tell him it would be a long day to button up those few things. I changed the topic and asked what was going on at the office that day.

"Not much. I've chatted with a few of the account handlers and spent some time verifying the database. Kinda slow here without you."

"Look, I'd better get crackin', or I won't be ready for tomorrow. Chat later?"

"Later then. I'll call you in a bit to see how it's going. Cheers, love." Then he was off the phone. I didn't realize how tense every muscle in my body had been while we talked until I felt myself start to relax.

The rest of the afternoon was consumed with work and stretching out my sore legs and hips. If I didn't get up every thirty minutes or so, the pain from sitting too long became unbearable. Despite the many breaks, I made progress. I leaned back in my chair, confident the demo with Phillip tomorrow would go brilliantly. It was time for a reward for all my hard work: a nice glass of pinot grigio.

Pouring the wine into my glass, I noticed the kitchen clock: 7:00 p.m. I wondered where Thomas was. It wasn't that I missed him; I was relieved he was not home yet. It was peaceful in our flat with just me there. I was unsure of him after his temper being unleashed on me last night. He was hard to read, and half the time, I didn't know where I stood with him. I anticipated his temper lashing out at me out of the blue for no good reason.

I leaned against the kitchen counter and sipped my wine. I looked out the kitchen window into the darkness of the night. It was a clear sky, with no moon; the stars were once again overtaken by the streetlamps, which gave off an eerie orange glow. There was no full moon, so I couldn't blame Thomas's rage toward me on a full moon. So what had made him snap? The only reason I kept coming back to was Phillip's praise of my work.

My body suddenly felt like a downed electrical wire flopping in water. Electrical shots went through me when I realized tomorrow might bring more of the same if Phillip said nice things about my work during our meeting. Shit, how would I make sure Thomas received more of the praise than I did? *Hopefully no more anger bubbles up before I leave for Whidbey in two days.*

In two days, I would be home, and I couldn't wait to talk to Jackson again. We hadn't been in close communication since I came to London, and I missed him terribly. Christmas, my favorite holiday, was just a few weeks away, and I already imagined how I was going to decorate the apartment. Joy filled my heart as I thought about finding just the right present for my son and watching the happy look on his face while he opened it. I always gave a lot of thought to each gift I gave; I wanted it to be just the right thing. I'd already gotten

Thomas his present and had it hidden away to give to him before I left. I could almost smell the turkey in the oven as I thought about being with my son again.

Lost in thought, I didn't hear the key turn in the lock. When I heard an "Ahem," my gaze shifted from the window to the kitchen door. Thomas stood there with a tiny poinsettia plant in one hand and a dozen deep red roses surrounded by dainty pure-white baby's breath in the other. Dumfounded by his generous gifts, I just stood there and stared at him.

"Hullo, love. After what happened last night, I wanted to let you know how much you mean to me." Thrusting the roses toward me, he said, "These are for the rest of my apology. Words can only touch the surface of the guilt I have, sweetie. I'm so very sorry."

I took the bouquet from him and buried my nose in the roses to fill my lungs with their heavenly scent. I softened a little, and with gentle Thomas and not the monster Thomas, my panic subsided a little. I thanked him and then looked for a vase to put them in.

"I know what the Christmas holiday means to you, and because you are leaving before Christmas, we don't have time to get a tree. I hope this little poinsettia makes it up to you."

I stopped looking for the vase and turned to look at him with tears in my eyes. Either he was playing me, or he genuinely meant what he said. Anyone who knew me knew Christmas was a sacred holiday for me, filled with magic, family, surprises, and love. I was not religious but was spiritual, and during the Christmas holiday, I hoped to create enough magic for all I loved and cared about. For him to remember and celebrate that part of me melted some of the misgivings I had begun to have about us.

"Oh, Thomas, it's beautiful!" I gushed, and I reached for him to give a tender kiss of thanks, wincing from the pain from my legs, a reminder of the result of his anger. "Thank you for remembering." I limped into the living room and placed the plant on the dinette table. "It makes it look festive in here, doesn't it?" I asked. Several times, I had looked throughout the flat to find something Christmasy to decorate with but hadn't found anything. Either Thomas didn't think of the holiday as special, or his ex-wife had kept all their decorations. I folded my arms across my chest and felt the Christmas spirit take hold as I looked at the little plant. Such a big feeling from such a small thing.

I stiffened a little as he came up behind me, wrapped his arms around my chubby body, and nuzzled his nose in my hair. His nuzzles soothed my fear from last night—fear he would snap again. "I want to talk about last night, Thomas." My voice was a shaky whisper.

"Love, I'm so sorry I hurt you, and I can't tell you how much it hurts me to know that what I did made you afraid of me." He turned me around to face him, and his eyes were deep and sorrowful, with no signs of the swords. He held me close and said almost wistfully, "I love you. I promise you right here and now I will never hurt you again."

I stepped up on tiptoes and kissed him tenderly. He returned my kiss with passion. As he led me to the bedroom, I knew there would be no more talking that night. It felt as if he had blown off my concerns about last night. But there was always tomorrow. We would talk tomorrow.

Chapter 23

Never was anything great achieved without danger.
—Niccolò Machiavelli

Thomas's lovemaking was even more passionate than before. Still, his passion didn't erase the images of last night that ran through my head as we made love. I had accepted gifts—which I probably had paid for on the business credit card—from the man who had terrified me the night before. I gave myself in the most intimate way to the man who had demonstrated that he could and would unleash his anger on me.

Thomas fell asleep as soon as he was done. I wished I were so lucky. I tossed and turned for the rest of the night and kept beating myself up for enduring his treatment and still making love to him. *Who am I? Who am I that I survived his physical and emotional attacks and still lay in bed next to him?*

Morning finally came without a minute of sleep for me. I groaned and remembered we had the presentation for Phillip that morning. Our morning went by as it routinely did, only that morning, Thomas was cheery, and I was sullen.

"Cheers, you two," Paul said as we walked by his desk into the office. I still had a prominent limp. "Blimey, Thomas, you look like the mouse that ate the cheese. What's up?"

Thomas just smiled and shrugged as we continued to make our way to our office.

"So how do you feel about this morning's demo with Phillip?" Thomas asked as he chucked his jacket and draped it on the back of his chair.

"Pretty good. I ran through it several times to test everything before you got home last night, and not a problem arose, so I think we are okay," I responded as I waited for my computer to boot up.

"That's brilliant. We are on the home stretch now. When does the training start?"

"I figure the training will be completed and tested next week when I am back home. Once you are done with the beta testing, I will be ready. I'm connected to the network now. Why don't you come over here and watch as I run through the demo?"

Things felt tense between us, but maybe it was just me. I couldn't wait to get home to Whidbey to think through our whole relationship.

We had just enough time to run through the demo once before we met with Phillip. With the history of the code breaking, I worried something might have broken between last night and that morning. If it had, it would prove Thomas had had nothing to do with the first code break, because he had been with me all night.

As it was, I was worried for nothing, as the demo went as it should have.

"Brilliant work, love! I'm so proud of you," Thomas said as he bent down to kiss my forehead.

"I am proud of the team of us—we both created this," I said. I had done 90 percent of the work. Still, I did not want Thomas to think I would take all the credit, especially if Phillip credited me with the job once again.

As the time for our meeting got closer, thoughts began to accelerate and jumble inside my head. I wanted them to slow, but no matter how hard I tried to focus on other things, they wouldn't. I felt as if I would black out, and my heart hammered so loudly it was all I could hear. The room spun, and I fell to the floor. Thomas, watching me dissolve into a panic attack, magically produced a brown paper bag from the kitchenette and knelt next to me. I looked at him as if he were an alien from a strange planet while he placed the open end of the bag, crumpled to capture my breath, against my mouth.

"Breathe," he said.

I gasped at first and grabbed the bag from him to hold it tighter against my mouth. Slowly, my breathing returned to a normal cadence, the room slowed its spinning, and my lungs relaxed and filled with oxygen. The thoughts inside my head slowed, and focus returned.

"You okay?" he asked.

How could he be so caring and tender and then dissolve into a fit of rage?

"Yeah, I think so. Thanks for the bag trick. It worked." I looked up into his soft eyes; the swords were at rest.

"What brought that on?" he asked, still kneeling beside me.

"I guess the meeting coming up with Phillip. I worry the code will break again, or I got the code wrong, or it doesn't match what his vision was when we started this project. What if he doesn't like it?"

Thomas rubbed my shoulders. "What if he doesn't like it? Sara, you captured excellent requirements from him. We developed it into a plan, then a database, and now a brilliant platform. He will be gobsmacked at what we show him this afternoon. You scared me just now. You weren't breathing and gasped out words that didn't make sense. Please, love, relax. You have this. I promise."

I sighed and whispered, "Thanks for your vote of confidence," although confidence had not seeped into my skin yet.

"Time to head to Phillip's office. Are you sure you are okay to run him through the demo, or do you want me to?" Thomas asked.

If I let Thomas run the meeting that afternoon, any bit of self-confidence I had gained would evaporate. "No, I need to do this. But please pitch in if I forget something, okay?"

"Okay, if you are sure. You still look a little pale—don't push yourself into another one of those attacks."

Funny, his words showed concern, but his face showed something different—as if maybe he had wanted to run the meeting himself.

I rose from the floor and straightened my clothes. "I'll be fine," I said, hopefully with a tone of confidence. Anyone could playact. Heck, I'd been playacting all my life to be the person people wanted me to be. With my mom, stepfather, employers, friends—anyone and everyone. I could surely do it in the meeting with Phillip.

The meeting went better than I could have hoped, especially after my panic attack. Sara, the Academy Award–winning actress, gave yet another award-winning performance as a professional confident in her work. The platform performed well, with no code breaks, and the look of the system matched Phillip's business branding perfectly.

"This is brilliant!" Phillip exclaimed, clapping his hands in appreciation.

"There are just a few tweaks we need to make, but we are ready for beta testing with a few of your account handlers," Thomas said in a pleased, almost arrogant tone. "Sara is leaving to go back to the

States tomorrow, but she will work with those who volunteered to help with the testing over Skype."

"Sara, I hate to see you leave. You and Thomas have done a tremendous job here for us. The work you both have done will support our business for years and years. How's the training going?"

I had been silently praying he would include Thomas in his praise, and when he did, I quietly released my breath. "Almost complete. Just have a few additions to make, and then I will meet with our testers to go over it all and answer any questions. Thomas and I will start the testing on Thursday—I need a day to recover from jet lag." I spoke with confidence and authority. Who knew where I pulled those out of? Part of my acting bag of tools, I supposed.

"Testing should take about a week. Then another week to perform any fixes needed that come out of that." Thomas retook control of the discussion. "So in two weeks, we can train the rest of your staff, and after that, we can go live. Sara will work with me during testing and training."

Ha! Work with him? He'll act like he is in charge, as usual, but I know who will be doing most of the work. Gawd, he is so narcissistic.

"She'll be back in London before we know it," Thomas said.

"Well, you mates have delivered exactly what I wanted and met your deadline too. Thank you." Phillip stood, then Thomas and I stood, and we all shook hands.

As Phillip walked us to the door, the conversation switched to mundane topics. Did I look forward to going back home? What would Thomas do while I was gone?

On the other side of the door, Thomas and I looked at each other with big grins, and relief poured out of our muscles. My smile wasn't due to the outcome of the meeting. Instead, I was relieved Phillip had included Thomas in his compliments, and I was smart enough to let it be. I had learned my lesson.

We made our way back to the office, giggling and teasing each other. Life looked much brighter. I was an intelligent woman. Why had I allowed my life to revolve around Thomas's mood?

Back in our office, I opened my laptop, anxious to finish up the training for the testers.

In a low, seductive voice, Thomas, bending to nuzzle my neck, said, "Hey, babe, how about we go home and spend the rest of the night exploring each other's body?"

I closed my eyes as my body yielded to his warm breath and soft, wet kisses. It was all I could do to decline—for now. "Give me an hour to finish up the training, and I'm all yours." I grinned as Thomas left the office.

My last night in London would be full of love and lust. Or so I hoped.

Chapter 24

Happiness is when what you think, what you say, and what you do are in harmony.
—Mahatma Gandhi

Thomas left the office before I did. I was disappointed he didn't stick around and plan goodbye drinks with Paul and Bethany. I knew I'd be back in London soon, but it would have been nice to have a send-off anyway.

I looked around the office to double-check if I had forgotten anything I would need back home. *Home.* I could almost smell the salty air brought by the ever-present breeze that gently blew off the water. I could hear the squawk of the seagulls that woke me up in the mornings. I ached for the slower pace of island life. But the best part about being home again would be seeing Jackson. I missed him terribly and made a mental note to make a date with him first thing back on the island.

I strolled over to the large office windows to look out into the eerie streetlamp-orange world of London, and my thoughts shifted to Thomas. It would be good to have some time apart; it would give me time to sort out my feelings. I still questioned whether this relationship was healthy for me. All my life, I had searched for love, the kind that was forgiving, passionate, and complete. All my life, my relationships had turned into disasters. *Is this the beginning of another disaster? Do I even know what love is? Someone once told me I wouldn't be able to love until I love myself. How does one go about loving herself?*

It was time to go back to the flat to pack for my trip home tomorrow.

The train trip home was uneventful. I spent the time watching the other passengers and realized Brits were no different from Americans. Some were reading books, others played games on their cell phones, and others rustled their newspapers. They all had somewhere to go and someone who loved them.

"Gordon Hill Station. Mind the gap." The automated voice transcended my thoughts.

I hopped off the train and made my way down the hill to the flat. As I climbed the stairs to the flat, the aroma of something delicious awakened the hunger pangs that had somehow lain dormant for most of the day. The scent had to be coming from our neighbors' flat, I thought—Thomas didn't cook.

The soft sounds of Eva Cassidy greeted me as I entered the flat. The table had been set for two, with the poinsettia as the centerpiece and lit candles. Thomas stood in the middle of the room in an apron, with two champagne flutes and a big grin.

"Thomas …" My voice trailed off. I was speechless.

"Love, tonight we celebrate two things that have been made possible because of you."

"Two things?" I stammered in bewilderment.

He handed me my champagne flute and raised his in a salute. "Yep, two things. First, here is to us, to the wrapping up of our first phase of a major project." He clinked his glass against mine, and our eyes locked as we sipped. "Second, I am coming to Whidbey Island in a week to be with you."

My mouth fell open, and my heart began a slow drop to my stomach. "Whidbey? You are coming to the island?" I asked incredulously.

"Yep, isn't it wonderful, love?"

He was obviously excited about coming to be with me, while I was not excited. I had been looking forward to time with my son and time by myself to sort out how I felt toward Thomas. He was moving way too fast for me, which made me a little nervous about his direction. I wasn't even divorced yet, and he'd indicated he wanted us to be a couple permanently. I wasn't sure if I was ready for that kind of commitment yet, and his anger scared me away from even thinking about it. After being married to Ray for twenty years, I kept hearing my inner self tell me now was the time to discover who I was, what I was capable of, and what I wanted out of life. I wouldn't be able to do that if Thomas was with me, stealing all my time.

"Oh, I thought you were going to stay in London to find more clients," I said in what I hoped was a noncriticizing tone.

"I thought we could explore possible clients on Whidbey Island," he said with a smug smile.

I lowered my eyes, seemingly fascinated by the champagne's bubbles in my glass, and murmured, "Good idea, I guess." At that moment, I realized I was afraid of his moods and helpless to understand what would or wouldn't set him off into another rage. Instinctively, I knew to agree with him.

"Anyway, love, I've fixed us a nice salmon en croûte for dinner, and it should be almost done. All you have to do is sit down and enjoy."

"I didn't know you could cook. And a gourmet meal at that." My mood lightened somewhat.

Thomas laughed and walked back into the kitchen. "Tesco has them all prepared and ready to pop in the oven."

I laughed with him and raised my glass to cheer him, determined to keep the mood light.

Dinner was delicious, even from a preprepared meal. We lingered over a dessert of store-bought crème brûlée and more champagne. Thomas was relaxed and witty, with no resemblance to the monster he had turned into the other night.

"Dinner was lovely. Thank you, Thomas. I didn't realize what a good and resourceful cook you are, but I will remember from now on. But sadly, I need to go pack."

Thomas's eyes danced lovingly in the candlelight; the swords were at rest. "I understand. You go pack, and I'll do the cleanup."

We both stood, and Thomas gathered me in his arms and landed a warm, delicious kiss on my forehead. I couldn't help but think that one kiss was a promise of more to come.

"Oh, Thomas, I hate for our beautiful evening to end," I whispered.

Pressing his fingers against my lips to shush me, he said, "Who says it is ending?"

With that, he picked up the remaining dishes from the table and strode into the kitchen. I dreamily left to pack, with all my concerns about Thomas already packed away.

I just hadn't closed the suitcase yet.

THREE

Whidbey Island

Chapter 25

The ache for home lives in all of us. The safe place where we can go as we are and not be questioned.
—Maya Angelou

I took a deep, soul-feeding breath of the fresh, salty air from my patio; looked out over the water; and marveled at the paradise where I lived. After the cramped, overpopulated city streets and steel-gray buildings of London, the open spaces of the island felt like heaven. I hadn't realized how much I had missed home over the last three months. Boats soundlessly bobbed in the water at the marina. Traffic moved slowly, instead of frantically, along the street separating my apartment from the harbor. Even the gray skies of December felt welcoming to me. I had a sense of permanence in a welcome home.

I would meet Jackson in Mukilteo, just across the Clinton ferry, for dinner that night—another welcome sign that I was home. It had been a long three months of nothing but short emails, which hadn't given me much to gauge how he felt about the divorce and the huge change to his life.

My phone rang. It was Thomas. Again. It was his fifth call that morning, and it wasn't even ten o'clock.

"Hello again, Thomas."

"Hullo, love. How ya doin'?"

"The same as thirty minutes ago." I figured he could hear my annoyance, but I was thousands of miles away from him, where there was no need to walk on eggshells with him.

"No need to get snarky. I was just missing you—that's all. I'm looking forward to being together again and not having to rely on phone calls. I just want you to know I'm thinking of you and miss you, love."

"I know. Me too."

In reality, I wasn't looking forward to his arrival. He was coming supposedly to contact potential clients, even after I'd explained over and over again that Whidbey was an island with small-time clients. I wished I had the chutzpah to tell him to stay home. But I didn't.

"So what are you going to do today?" he asked.

I swallowed another snarky answer and repeated what I'd told him thirty minutes ago. "I'm going to test the training platform to make sure all connections are good for tomorrow and run through the training a couple of times so it all goes smoothly tomorrow. Then tonight I'm meeting Jackson for dinner."

"Well, I've got a few calls to make to potential clients."

I could hear the clink of ice in a glass, just as I had during the last four calls. "Okay, I'll let you go for now. I need to get to work on the training so I'll be done by the time I'm to meet Jackson. Good luck with your calls." We both said our goodbyes. I hoped it would be the last call until that night.

The rest of the day sped by, and before I knew it, it was time to get ready to meet Jackson. I glanced over at my phone, which I had put on silent while I worked. I opened up the phone and gasped at the nineteen voice mails from Thomas. *Holy crap!* I decided I wouldn't listen to them until later that evening, after my dinner with Jackson, and closed the phone. *No sense in spoiling my evening with the possibility of an argument with Thomas.*

Ha, how did I know there would be an argument? Was I projecting my fears onto the relationship, based on what had happened before I left London? Well, he could wait until I was back home. *Strange, isn't it, Sara, how much more assertive you are when not in Thomas's presence?*

The drive to the south end of the island, to the ferry connecting Whidbey to the mainland, was one of my favorites. The two-lane road required traffic to move at a pace fitting for island life: slow and unhurried. Thick forests opened up to farms and prairies along the way. The ferry crossing only took fifteen minutes and ended in Mukilteo on the mainland. Many islanders commuted to Boeing in Everett or one of the tech companies in Seattle daily. I tried to avoid the morning rush hour going over and the afternoon rush hour coming back home.

That day, the traffic was light on the Whidbey side, and I was fortunate to drive right onto the ferry. Once parked on the car deck, I looked around and saw a few people I knew. We waved hello to each other. Normally, we all left our cars and climbed the stairs to the upper deck to have some coffee and a snack and catch up with each other, but that day, we stayed in our cars and out of the icy December winds that blew in from the north.

My cell phone rang, and the caller ID told me it was Thomas. I swore under my breath before I sent the call to voice mail, turned off my phone, and made a promise that I would call him when I got home. I was looking forward to a lovely, calm evening with Jackson, and nothing would ruin that for me, not even Thomas. There had been so many calls from him today. Did he want to make sure he was on my mind every minute of every day?

Thomas was showing red flags of an abuser. I knew what an abusive relationship was. I had worked with abused women through the nonprofit I belonged to. Abusers had two sides to their personality; they showed others the charming side but were angry and aggressive behind closed doors. Thomas had done that several times. I would never forget when he'd scolded me in the office after wooing the receptionist with wine and tall tales. Other red flags were his violent temper and quickly changing moods. Was he trying to control me with all his daily calls, or did he really love me so much that our being away from each other was painful for him? Another red flag. He had been verbally abusive. Another red flag. So many red flags to warn me.

I shook my head. Of course I would never fall into that trap. I had listened to many women's stories. They'd told me how the abuse had started, and in many cases, they'd said they felt fortunate to escape with their lives. I would never allow myself to enter that kind of relationship.

But some thoughts niggled in the back of my brain. He never had given me time to call my friends and family and even had limited my contact with Jackson, effectively isolating me from everyone. He had physically and verbally hurt me. If I thought I had been in denial, I quickly denied it.

Butterflies swarmed in my stomach and seemed to multiply the closer I got to the restaurant. I was nervous—or was I fearful?—to see Jackson again. I didn't know what to expect. Would he still be moody and uncommunicative? Was he angry with his dad or me? Did he still love and respect me?

Chapter 26

Occasionally we must disconnect to reconnect later on.
—Dominic Riccitello

Jackson and I hadn't spoken while I was away. The pang in my heart brought back guilty feelings of not insisting on calling my son. I wondered if Jackson had come to terms with the divorce. He had been withdrawn and didn't want to talk about what was happening to our family. I hadn't been there for him as he wrestled through this life-changing event. Guilt and shame stabbed me in the heart with the knowledge I had let Thomas interfere with my relationship with my son.

Jackson hadn't arrived yet, so I found a table and ordered a margarita. As I sipped my drink, memories of my precious boy blurred my vision. An only child, he had been an easy boy to raise.

We had been close until puberty hit, when his closeness with me had been transferred to his dad. I supposed that was normal, but I missed the special connection I thought we had had. Memories of the way things used to be—*We used to be a family*—brought tears that threatened to roll down my cheeks. Nothing ever stayed the same when I was happy in life. Things changed; people changed. I had been happy with my little family, and then it all had changed when another woman entered the scene. I had been happy with Thomas, but even he had changed from the person I'd thought I knew.

I sighed. *Sara, get off your pity pot.*

"Hey, Mom," Jackson said, sitting down across from me. "You look great!"

"Thanks. You don't look so bad yourself." I always marveled at Jackson's good looks. He was tall, with a dark complexion, dark hair, eyes that drew a person in, and a physique that wowed the girls. And he was smart. He had joined ROTC and had earned a full-ride scholarship to the University of Washington from the air force. How I had given birth to such a bright, good-looking young man was beyond me.

"I see you started already," he said, pointing to my margarita.

"Yep, pretty tasty too. Let's order so we have more uninterrupted time to catch up." I handed him the menu the server had dropped off.

The server arrived, took our orders, and asked if we needed more tortilla chips after watching Jackson wolf them down.

"Yes, please," responded Jackson.

"So tell me how you've been. How is school going?" I asked when the server left.

"School is fine—well, except for physics and calculus," he said, diving into the fresh bowl of chips and salsa.

"Wow, you are taking physics and calculus at the same time? That's a tough order," I replied.

"Yeah, I don't understand the professors; both are from India and don't speak English very well. I've emailed them with questions, but I don't get my questions answered fully. I think I'll be okay with physics; it's calculus I probably will flunk out of."

We talked a little more about his options to bring up his grades until our food arrived. I changed the subject as we settled into our high-carb dinner.

"Have you seen your dad lately?" I said, keeping my voice light and my eyes focused on the bite of chimichanga on my fork as it headed for my mouth.

"Nope." The finality of his answer told me he wasn't interested in talking about his dad. "Look, Mom, I don't talk about you to Dad, and I'm not going to talk about Dad to you."

"Good, I guess. I just miss the connection you and I had. Everything has changed, and I feel a little lost; I don't know how to be with you. How are you coping with the divorce? The last time we were together, you were pretty moody about it."

"Mom, just be yourself with me, like you always have been. I'm better about the divorce, but I miss our family too. It was, well, my normalcy, and now I'm searching for what the heck is normal for me."

"I guess the timing wasn't the best, with you just starting at the university. I don't suppose there is a good time for a family to break apart. But remember, your dad and I are divorcing each other, not you. I think I can speak for your dad here: we both want you in our lives forever, and if there is anything I can do to support you, I'm just a phone call away. Just promise me one thing: you won't come to the island without giving me a call."

"Promise."

Our conversation turned to lighter topics while we finished our dinner. I told Jackson about my time in London, my work, and the flat but left out Thomas's abuse. I would have been humiliated for my son to know about it. He grimaced at the news that Thomas would be there next week. I didn't pursue asking how he felt about him.

We finished dinner, I paid the bill, and then Jackson walked me to my car.

"Thanks for dinner, Mom," Jackson said, and then he grabbed me for a big hug. Tears wet my eyes as I felt his heartbeat next to mine, just as I had so many years ago when I carried him in my womb. Just for a moment, I thought I had my baby boy back again, and the tears began to roll.

Our hug ended, and I swiped the tears away before Jackson could see them. That was all he needed—his mom sobbing in the parking lot.

"You're welcome, sweetie. Let's do this more often, okay?" I said as I choked back the lump in my throat.

"Yeah, just you and me, okay?"

I knew what he meant: without Thomas. "Okay, deal."

We said our goodbyes, and then he got in his car and headed south to Seattle, and I headed north to the ferry. It had been wonderful to spend time with him, albeit a short amount of time. New memories of that night began to heal some of the old ones. New memories—maybe that was what it would take for all of us to find ourselves again or to find our new normalcy, as Jackson had put it.

I arrived back at the ferry landing just as they were loading the cars on. Parked in my lane on the ferry, I rested my head on the headrest and allowed the pleasant memories of that night to heal my heart.

I reached for my phone as it rang and then jerked my hand away. I wouldn't let Thomas interfere in that evening until I was home.

Why was I so hesitant to answer his calls? A man I said I loved called me, and I didn't respond with eagerness in my heart—only dread.

Chapter 27

The most courageous act is still to
think for yourself. Aloud.
—Coco Chanel

Back home, I settled into my apartment with a glass of wine in hand
and snuggled into the soft sofa. The warm memories of the evening
wrapped around me like a familiar, soft, worn blanket. I supposed I
should listen to Thomas's voice mails.

As I listened to them, my breath came in short puffs while I heard
his anger escalate. I was grateful he wasn't there. Who knew if he
would have allowed his rage to become unleashed? I was afraid to
return his calls and afraid not to. It was 10:00 p.m., which made it
6:00 a.m. London time. He'd be up, I reasoned; he was usually an
early riser.

My fingers shook as I dialed his number, and then I heard the familiar *burrr-burrr* of his phone. *Why do London phones always ring twice?*

"Good of you to finally call," he said in a voice loaded with sarcasm, bypassing the usual greetings.

"Hi, Thomas. I'm sorry I didn't return your calls sooner, but if you remember, I was having dinner with Jackson, and I just now got home." My voice was soft and shaky and gave away my fear of his anger.

"That's no reason to ignore my calls, Sara."

Something in his voice made the hairs on the back of my neck stand at attention. "Did something happen?"

"Only that you didn't answer my calls. What else were you doing besides having dinner with your son?"

"Thomas, I was with Jackson the whole time, except for driving there and back. What do you think?" My tone showed my annoyance at being questioned. *What is with this guy anyway? He's insecure in our relationship—that's obvious.*

"Love, I get worried when I can't reach you." His tone became softer and gentler. "I miss you and can't wait until next week when we're together."

"I know. Me too," I lied. Well, it was half a lie. A big part of my heart wished he was not coming. I could have used the time to get my head and, more importantly, my soul together.

Our conversation turned to the training set for tomorrow, and as usual, the call went on for a full two hours. He rambled on and on about databases, which nearly put me to sleep. After a bottle and a half of wine for me and an unknown amount of Pernod for him, we hung up.

Why had he called so much? It felt as if he needed to know where

I was and what I was doing every second. *Control, Sara. It is his way of controlling you. A red flag, remember?*

I had been quiet on the call; all I could think about was what our relationship had formed into. I questioned why I stayed with him, especially after he had physically hurt me. Had my desperate need for someone to love me made me ignore the red flags? But then I remembered the kind, loving, gentle side of him, and my body craved him physically. His strength, hardness of body, and soft touches always made me feel safe within his arms. Safe and loved. His love made the other side seem inconsequential in comparison.

After we ended the call, the apartment was quiet. Neighbors had long ago gone to bed; it was just the rats on the patio outside and me inside. I welcomed the peace and sat on the sofa in my living room, which was lit only by the streetlights outside. The events of the evening ran through my thoughts. I recalled a sense of contentment with my son, the fear of returning Thomas's calls, and my annoyance at his jealousy.

The morning broke as another gray December day on Whidbey. It had been a restless night while I mulled over doubts about Thomas and his constant calls on top of his quick rises to anger. Last night, he'd confused me. At first, he had been angry, and then, just like that, he'd become gentle and loving. Why had he called so many times to check in on me? I felt smothered by him, so why hadn't I broken it off with him? Was I so insecure that I needed a relationship just because Ray had one—and had had one even before we separated? Or was I really in love with Thomas? Maybe I had wanted to love and be loved for so long that I had fallen into the trap of being with someone just to be with someone. That strategy had always proven disastrous in the past.

"Shit," I muttered as I looked at the clock and panicked at the late hour. I threw my bedclothes off and ran to the bathroom for a quick shower. Training started in one hour, at 3:00 p.m. London time and 7:00 a.m. my time. I had one hour to get dressed, have coffee, and get in the training mind-set. Thank goodness the training session was over the computer, so as long as my hair was combed and I had a little makeup on, no one would know I was in my sweats.

I showered and walked out of the bathroom with hair combed and sweats on, when my phone rang. It was no surprise that Thomas was on the other end.

"Good morning. Everyone there in London ready for the training?" I asked.

"Cheers, love. We are ready here. How are you getting along there?" Thomas sounded bright and happy, which was a good sign.

"Yeah, all set here. I did all the prep yesterday, so all I need to do is connect to WebEx and start. Has everyone logged into WebEx at least once to make sure they have no problems connecting?"

"Yep, all the trainees connected without an issue. So we have thirty minutes before we go live with the training—what are you going to do?"

"Finish my coffee, go pee, and then connect." I wondered if my bluntness would throw him off guard.

He laughed. "TMI. Okay, love, I'll be sitting in on the training, so go break a leg!"

I stifled a groan at the old-fashioned term. Did actors really want their fellow actors to break a leg?

We said our goodbyes, and I finished my coffee. I found it weird that I was more comfortable talking about business versus personal stuff with Thomas, as if I was confident about my skills and knowledge but was a confused, unsure mess when it came to my feelings and what I wanted from life—a holdover from my childhood, I supposed.

The cliché old tapes of my mom's put-downs told me what I could and could not do, should and should not do. When would I have the courage to burn those tapes?

With an empty bladder and a fresh cup of coffee, I sat at my desk and started the training. It lasted for three hours, with lots of questions and suggestions for increased efficiency. I hoped Thomas took accurate notes. That was his one job during the training: to take down ideas. I recorded it all so I wouldn't need to train again with the rest of Phillip's staff; the recording would do that for me.

I closed down the WebEx and decided to go back to bed for a few hours, but before I did, I sent an email to Thomas to let him know we could talk after my nap.

The bed felt like heaven. All of last night's worries were gone, replaced by a high I always got after I led a successful training.

I had just nodded off, when my phone on the nightstand buzzed. I wanted to ignore it, but the thought that Jackson might need me made me pick it up.

The caller ID told me it was Thomas. I placed the phone back on the nightstand and rested my head softly on the pillow as sleep overtook me.

Chapter 28

Burning bridges behind you is understandable. It's the bridges before us that we burn, not realizing we may need to cross, that brings regret.
—Anthony Liccione

It was midafternoon when I woke from a restful nap. I stretched luxuriously in bed and then remembered Thomas had called just before I fell asleep.

"Well, hell," I muttered resignedly, and I sat up in bed and reached for my phone. I had received three more calls from him and had three more voice mails, and each one escalated in frustration and anger.

I paused before I called him back. My confusion over our relationship churned inside my head. I thought about not returning his calls, hoping more time would help him to cool off, but I knew more time would only make him angrier. I dialed his number.

"Damn bitch, where have you been?" he said in a tense, low-voiced, controlled snarl.

"Don't you read your emails?" I tried to keep my voice steady and assertive.

"Yeah, I did read that email, but you napped for so long, for Christ's sake?"

I was relieved when our conversation turned to lessons learned from the training. Two hours later, we hung up.

"Does this man ever sleep?" I muttered on my way to the kitchen for a cold glass of pinot grigio. It was late afternoon, but as the saying went, it was five o'clock somewhere.

I hadn't thought it weird then, but Thomas had slept for only a few hours a night the whole time I had been in London. I'd heard him pace in the wee hours of the morning with his companion Pernod and the familiar chinking of ice in his glass. I'd assumed nervous energy kept him wired through the night.

I took my wine into the living room, plopped onto the sofa, and sipped the golden nectar. My thoughts stayed with Thomas. After Ray and I had broken up, I had been hesitant to start a romantic relationship with anyone, especially my business partner, but Thomas's attention, pampering, and proclamations of love had lured me into his arms and crept into my heart. All I had ever wanted was someone to love and protect me and not betray the trust I had given him. Thomas's love gave to me what I had been searching for forever. Or was I so needy that I was blind to what real love was?

Ray had been loving towards me for many years. My place in his heart had been my safe harbor where nothing could break the trust we had for each other—nothing but another woman. I knew I'd had a role in our breakup, but I hadn't brought another man into our marriage. Had I always looked at my relationships with rose-colored glasses? Had I ached so much for someone to love me that I couldn't see reality from my fantasy? It must have been so, because why else had every relationship, starting with my mom, ended up in the trash heap?

"Hello, dahlin'." There she was again, drawing out *dahlin'* in that fake way she always had, perched on the arm of the chair that faced the sofa. She wore her favorite wispy negligee; her cigarette dangled from manicured fingers. She had never had manicures when she was alive. Hell must have received a few manicurists recently.

"What are you doing here?"

"Don't be like that, sweetie. I'm here because you seem to be conflicted about Thomas, and I want to help."

I snorted my disbelief and said, "Like you helped with your hubby the molester?"

It took a nanosecond for her to change the subject. "I don't know why you are so confused about your feelings for Thomas. He's the best man who has come your way in forever. You want someone to love you, don't you? Well, whether you deserve it or not, here is the guy who claims he does." She tossed her head back, took a long drag off her cigarette, and tried and failed at blowing a smoke ring. "You are one unlovable girl, and here comes Thomas, proclaiming his love for you. Are you going to throw away the one chance—and probably the last chance—you have at love?"

"Mom, I've started to feel like his possession, not his partner in business and life. He calls an ungodly number of times a day, and if he can't reach me, he gets angry with me. It feels like he is jealous when I do things without him; it is suffocating at times. I don't want that kind of relationship. I want one with love and trust. With Thomas, I feel like I have to account for every minute of my day and night."

"That, my dear girl, is love. He loves you so much he can't stand being away from you. Pay attention, or he will be gone, and you will be alone once again, yearning for the love you will never have."

With that foreboding message, she evaporated.

Maybe Mom was right. Perhaps this would be my last chance at love, and wouldn't I be a fool to let it slip through my fingers because of these silly doubts? *Give love a chance, Sara. Just give it a chance.*

Chapter 29

We don't even ask for happiness, just a little less pain.
—Charles Bukowski

It had been a good two weeks since Thomas arrived on Whidbey Island and back into my bed. I had introduced him to a few of my friends and showed him a tour of the island from north to south. We met with a few potential clients, but Whidbey didn't have clients with deep pockets, as London did. Thomas didn't seem interested in pursuing smaller-revenue clients. He quit meeting with any new potentials after the first week.

Christmas, my favorite time of year, was just a week away. It would be my first Christmas with Thomas, which was exciting to think about at first. But my excitement switched to anxiety when I remembered Jackson's grimace when I'd brought Thomas up to him during our dinner. I worried he would cancel spending Christmas with me when he found out Thomas was there and would spend the holiday with his dad.

Jackson and his girlfriend were coming for Christmas Day. After he'd learned of the divorce, he'd promised we would spend all our Christmases together. He knew how magical that time of year was for me. It wasn't the presents that made it magical for me; it was the traditions I'd grown up with and made my own throughout the years. My artificial tree always went up on December 11, exactly two weeks before Christmas and my birthday. The ornaments I'd managed to take from the family home were not commercially bought ones. They were the snowman Jackson had made out of clay when he was in second grade, the paper bell with his fifth-grade picture on it, and others he had made throughout the years. Those ornaments were priceless to me, and the memories they brought flowed through me like warm maple syrup. The most critical tradition was the sense of family, no matter how small, around the tree to share the sounds and joy of the season.

Thomas didn't share my feelings about the holiday. Still, he put up with my feverish activities to make everything perfect for everyone in my world.

It was a lovely day, the best day I'd had in a long time. Jackson's girlfriend was friendly and fit right in, and she was smitten with him. I couldn't tell if her feelings were reciprocated. He and Thomas were civil to each other, which left me to breathe a sigh of relief. We shared our presents in the morning, oohing and aahing over each one and passing them around so everyone could see what we had gotten.

Thomas went into the bedroom to call his mom to wish her happy holidays while Jackson and his girlfriend watched the game. I prepared dinner for an early afternoon feast. I knew the kids wanted to get on the road back to Seattle early to spend some holiday time with his girlfriend's parents. Thomas had been drinking Pernod one glass after another, and I worried if he'd be awake for dinner. I wished he wouldn't drink so much, especially that day, a day that was so special.

Thomas had two extra bottles of Pernod in the pantry. Did I dare hide one? Would he notice? I took a deep breath, grabbed one of the bottles, and hid it in a drawer, tucking it underneath the kitchen towels.

It was a lovely family dinner. I looked across the tiny dinette and glowed with happiness as I watched Jackson enjoy his dinner. His girlfriend was obviously happy to have been invited. The conversation was lively; we talked about school and what my plans were, and Jackson filled me in on some of the shenanigans his friends had pulled. I smiled contentedly. I knew he'd had a part in those shenanigans too, but I didn't mind; he was living his life, making his way, with adventures along the way. I glanced over at Thomas, who had been quiet throughout the meal and wore a scowl on his face.

"How's your dinner?" I tried to engage Thomas in the conversation.

"The beef was too bloody rare," he said with an edge to his voice.

"Oh, you should have said something; I could have zapped it in the microwave a few seconds for you."

He looked up from his plate with the swords at half-mast. "How could anyone get a word in edgewise with you two blabbering away?" He took a long swig of his drink and then banged his glass down on the table.

Jackson looked at me in surprise. Thomas's angry outburst stupefied us all. Fear clutched at my throat. *Not in front of Jackson. Please, not in front of my son*, I begged silently.

After a few silent and uncomfortable moments, Jackson cleared his throat, glanced at his watch, and announced it was time for his girlfriend and him to head back to Seattle.

"What about dessert?" My hopes for a happy, family-centered holiday had been ruined.

"It's okay, Mom; we planned on dessert with her family." He got up from the table and began to gather their gifts to take them to their car.

I didn't want him to go. It had been a wonderful day with him there.

They said their goodbyes with a lot of hugs and a few tears sneaking down my cheek.

"Take care of yourself, Mom," Jackson whispered. Then they were gone, with full tummies and the car loaded down with presents and leftovers from dinner.

"I need a drink," Thomas muttered when I closed the door. I watched him pour the last of the open bottle of Pernod, which didn't even wet the ice cubes in his glass. He bent down to reach for one of the extra bottles under the sink.

I held my breath as blood rushed through my ears like waves in a hurricane, hoping he didn't notice there was only one extra bottle, not two.

"Where's the other bottle?"

I tried to swallow, but my throat had suddenly gone dry, and I was sure he could hear, if not even see, my heart jumping through my chest.

"I think you drank the other bottle." I didn't know why I lied. I knew it would only make the situation worse for me when he found the other bottle. And he would find it.

He lunged for me; grabbed at my blouse, the one I had splurged on especially for Christmas; and pushed me hard up against the wall. "Where is it, bitch?"

"It's in the towel drawer," I whispered, gasping to get air back into my lungs.

"Go get it, and pour me a drink." He released me, popping the buttons on my blouse as he did.

I walked the few steps to the drawer, pulled out the bottle, and filled his glass with shaky hands.

"Hand it to me."

It was another order I knew to obey. I handed him his glass; my hands shook, so the ice clinked as I did. Our eyes never left each other while he sipped his licorice liqueur. It felt like an eternity before he set his half-empty glass on the counter beside him. Without warning, he slapped me with the vengeance and strength of a boxer. My hand automatically went to my hot cheek, and I looked at him in disbelief.

"Don't ever take it upon yourself to hide my alcohol again, slut, or the next time will be worse—trust me. Now take your sorry self to bed."

Another order. This one I was happy to obey just to get out of his presence and the unknown of what he might do next.

I ran into the bedroom, gently closed the door behind me, and threw myself onto the bed. Tears stung my newly bruised cheek; he had struck me hard.

It was Christmas, the most special day of my year. He knew how important that holiday was for me. He knew how important Jackson was to me. How could he have ruined it for me?

I cried until only dry tears were left. A man who proclaimed his love for me had hit me and then ordered me to bed. What kind of love was that? *Another betrayal. Just like mom, just like her husband, just like Ray, and just like every other fucking person in my life.* Anger boiled up from my gut and into my throat, burning. Whom was I most afraid of: Thomas or myself for continuing to stay with him?

Tomorrow I would tell him our relationship was over. I wanted him out of my apartment and my life.

Merry fucking Christmas.

Chapter 30

**If you do not change direction, you may
end up where you are heading.**
—Siddhārtha Gautama

Sleep wouldn't overtake the thoughts that whirred in and out of my mind. The anger that had been on Thomas's face haunted me. He had hurt me more than once. His strength was unimaginable for a skinny, lanky guy. It was futile to fight against him. I couldn't match his stronghold on me when he became that way. His mood went from mellow to frightening with a snap of the fingers. I tried to figure out what his trigger was, but there wasn't anything I could think of. But one thing was for sure: hiding his booze was a surefire way to provoke his anger. He both scared and angered me. When I closed my eyes, I saw his angry face: empty eyes, stony facial expression, and a black hole where his mouth should have been.

It must have been three in the morning when I heard the bedroom door open, and he stumbled in. I froze, lay as far on my side of the bed as possible, and slowed my breath to quiet, shallow breaths. He didn't bother to take off his clothes before falling onto his side of the bed. His soft, alcohol-induced snores told me he had fallen asleep. Pernod's sweet, sickening odor permeated the room and churned the bile already bubbling in my stomach.

I got up and crept out of the room, away from him, away from the licorice stench. I stood outside the closed door and listened to see if he had woken up, but all I heard was my own heart thumping against my chest walls.

I lay on the sofa, but sleep still evaded me, replaced by the night's events. Every time he drank, he lost control of his temper. I didn't think he was an alcoholic, but the amount he had drunk that night pointed to his being one.

Denial. You are in denial, Sara.

I knew people drank for all sorts of reasons. Escape and emotional pain were mine. What were his reasons? He appeared to be a together guy—that was what had attracted me to him. So why did he depend on alcohol so much? What had growing up as Thomas been like? I hadn't met his mum, and his father was dead. His past was a mystery to me. More of a mystery to me was why he was still there in the apartment.

Dawn peeked through the blinds; a new day was about to emerge. Tired of thinking and tired of trying to sleep, I rose off the couch and headed for the kitchen to start the coffee. On my way, I stopped by the bedroom door, pressed an ear against it, and listened. Relief washed over me when I heard no sounds of Thomas waking up, just a thick silence.

The smell of coffee brewing in the pot lulled me into a sense of normalcy. Yet that day would be far from ordinary. The dark bruise on my cheek, whose blue color snaked up to my eye, reminded me of my promise to send Thomas back to London.

"Good morning, love," Thomas said, startling me out of my deep thought.

"Good morning," I replied coldly as he sat in the chair across from me at the dinette.

"Look, love, I'm sorry about last night. It won't happen again. I promise. I mean it. If you hadn't hidden my booze, I wouldn't have had to do what I did. I'm very sorry for both of us for having behaved as we did."

My brain stuttered, and my breath went on pause for a moment before I blurted out, "You make it sound like it's my fault you hurt me and treated me like crap." I braced myself for a physical or verbal blow. Instead, he responded calmly, void of any hints of anger.

"Well, you have to admit none of what happened would've happened had you not hidden my booze." He reached over and covered my hand, which rested on the table, with his. A warm, familiar sensation settled me into a state where I could illogically accept his logic. But no, I wouldn't be that illogical.

"What happened last night was because you drank too much, plain and simple. I worry about the amount of alcohol you drink. You drink all day and into the night, and what is really scary is you don't seem to ever get drunk, except for last night."

"Look, I will slow down on the drinking if you forgive me for last night." His apology sounded a little off-center.

Gazing into his sad brown eyes, I remembered what my mom had said about Thomas. He loved me and was the best thing that ever had happened to me and what my heart had been aching for my entire life. Why would I throw away what I'd always dreamed of having?

Because he hit you! He treated you like his slave! my inner voice screamed. I took my hand away from his and kept my eyes on his, searching for any indication he understood how deeply he had hurt me, not just physically but also emotionally.

"Look, love, I don't know why I get so angry. You just push my buttons, and my anger starts boiling up inside of me until I explode."

There it was again. It had been my fault.

"It's not my fault, Thomas," I said between gritted teeth.

The silence that followed created a chasm between our understandings of each other. Convinced he would never accept that his anger was not my fault, I prepared to deliver on my promise to myself to break up with him.

"I get it, Sara," he said before I could speak. "I know deep inside that it isn't your fault, but it is easier to blame you than to blame myself. I've always had a problem admitting when I was wrong and even taking responsibility for the hurts I give others. That was the main reason my ex and I got divorced. I never hit her, but I wasn't always nice to her. Look, I will slow down my drinking and keep my anger in check. I promise. I don't want to lose you."

He looked sincere while he talked. Tears had softened his eyes. I'd never heard anything that close to genuineness from him before, and it moved me. I heard my mom whisper, "He loves you." What if he was my last chance at love?

"I don't trust you, Thomas, not even a little bit. But everyone deserves a second chance. We have so much to lose business-wise if we don't remain partners. Maybe we take it one day at a time."

And just like that, I broke my promise to myself.

We stood and, with tears in our eyes, hugged. He wouldn't know my tears were from the disappointment I felt in myself.

Soon the day came when Thomas had just one more month to go on his visa before he had to go back to London. I worked on Phillip's project and finalized loose ends while Thomas spent hours on the patio on his phone. He was secretive about his phone calls. I was curious whom he talked to for hours at a time but decided not to ask to prevent a possible argument. While he hadn't quit drinking altogether, Thomas had kept his word and hadn't drunk as much as before. I suspected he'd become a closet drinker and hid the amount he drank from me. He went on errands as a ruse to buy more Pernod—on our business credit card. The monthly statements proved how much he purchased. Yet I never confronted him about it. I was afraid to stir up his anger again. He hadn't lost control lately, but deep inside, I suspected his anger was on simmer until the next time.

One day in January, Thomas came back from his errands and sat on the arm of the chair next to my computer.

"Hey, did you get everything done?" I asked, not looking up from my work.

He leaned over and planted a wet kiss on the back of my neck, partially waking up my desire for him. Things had cooled off considerably since the night he hit me, but I couldn't help the lusty feelings his kisses aroused.

"Love, can you stop work for a sec? I have something I want to talk with you about."

I stopped my typing and saw an unusual look on his face, as if he had a happy surprise he was about to spring on me. I hoped it was news of a new client signing on. I turned away from the computer and said, "Sure, what's up?"

"Well, let's take a look at our schedule. Because of the visa waiver, you can be in London for just three months, and I can be here for just three months. We have a small flat in London and a smaller one here. I've been thinking this over and cannot think of one good reason we shouldn't buy a house here on the island for when we are here. It would give us more room and a dedicated home office. Eventually, I'll apply for a work visa, which would allow me to stay here longer."

I stared at him as if he had just produced a hippopotamus from his pocket. The words *house* and *work visa* pierced my brain like electric jolts. *No, no, no.* How could I live with him 24-7 for the rest of my life?

"What did you just say? How can we afford to buy a house? Phillip hasn't paid us yet, and there's no new job in the pipeline. With you here instead of networking with your contacts in London, we aren't likely to get a client any day soon." My voice was a higher octave by the time I finished. My mind raced. What was the chance I could put him off until he forgot the whole crazy idea?

"I've got my retirement pay from British Tel. I took it all in one lump sum. Plus, you are getting a nice settlement from your divorce, which we can use for the down payment. Between the two of us, money won't be a problem. Can't you see what a great investment this would be for both of us?"

"Thomas, I struggle just to pay the rent here, plus the credit card charges. My divorce won't be final until next month. Can we at least wait until then?"

"We can start looking at houses now, and if we find something, I'll make the down payment, and you can pay me back when your divorce settlement comes in."

He gave me his winning smile, the one he used to charm me when he wanted his way. Usually, it worked on me, but this was a huge step. I wasn't sure I wanted to spend the rest of my life with him, much less make such a substantial financial investment with him. I didn't know what I wanted after divorce. Maybe I wanted to travel or use my settlement to support myself for a year while I lived out my lifelong dream of writing the novel locked up inside of me. The house idea was a new thought for me, and I was not warming up to it.

"I'm not so sure I want to get locked into a house purchase right now. There are so many what-ifs. What if we don't get another project and then another one after that? What if you decide to stay in London and not come back here? What if we don't make it as a couple?" My mind raced and tried to make sense of his proposal.

"Look, why don't you take a few days to think about it, and in the meantime, we can drive around to see what's on the market? Hey, why don't you phone your Realtor friend and have her send you some listings of homes for sale?" There was no mistaking the eagerness in his voice. He was like a child who couldn't wait for Christmas morning.

"Slow down a little. Please give me time to think about it." I sounded like a woman burdened with a decision she wasn't prepared to make.

My mom's voice whispered in my ear, "He's all you ever dreamed of, sweetie. Don't throw it away."

Chapter 31

"Contrariwise," continued Tweedledee, "if it was so, it might be; and if it were so, it would be; but as it isn't, it ain't. That's logic."
—Lewis Carroll, *Through the Looking-Glass*

A house. He wanted us to buy a house together. We didn't have a new client, and we hadn't been paid for the work we'd completed for Phillip. I hadn't been reimbursed for my hotel in London. The credit card charges increased with each bottle of Pernod he drank. And he abused me—probably the most important reason to say no to him.

Practicality, not to mention maturity, would dictate we penny-pinched until we were paid and signed on another client. I had always lived safely and always had a little nest egg of my own, even when married to Ray. It had given me a sense of security and independence to know I had money to back me up in case of an emergency. Life was different now. There was no nest egg. It had been spent on flights to London; kept the credit card at a manageable balance; and paid the rent, utilities, and groceries. Could I trust him to pay his fair share if we bought a house? He wasn't paying now—what made me think he would in the future? All the years I'd known him, had I really known him? If I was honest with myself, which most times I wasn't, I guessed our relationship wouldn't last, no matter how much I wanted it to. It was probably not in my best interest to lock myself into a partnership on a house with him.

Saying no to Thomas would be a wise decision for me. But what if this was my last chance for love? I wouldn't have called Mom's feelings for me love. She'd created a woman who lived to please anyone and everyone. A woman who put on a facade and hoped no one uncovered the real person underneath—the stupid, clumsy, fat, and worthless one. Thomas saw through all that and loved me anyway. But what if I tied myself to this significant financial investment, and he continued to abuse me?

A house was an investment, and real estate on the island was one of the best investments anyone could make. If things continued to go wrong because of his abuse, I could get an excellent return on my part of the investment. That line of thinking seemed less threatening to my financial future. I'd still have a nest egg to fall back on if we parted and if he reimbursed me for his part of the credit card. That was a big *if*. The fact that he hadn't helped pay and the times he had struck out at me niggled at the back of my mind. But not enough to dampen my growing excitement at the prospect of owning a home, with room to stretch out, a real kitchen with a dishwasher, no gold shag carpeting, and no funky-smelling bathroom.

I poured another glass of wine. My trepidations about going in on a house with Thomas were fading. I wasn't surprised by my quick decision. At least I had allowed myself to think it through.

"Ah, you are off the phone," I said as Thomas came in from the patio. He always made his calls outside, which gave me the impression he didn't want me to listen in on his conversations. Should I have been suspicious? Ray had carried on with his girlfriend long before I found out about his affair. Had my naivete blinded me to yet another reality? I shrugged off the idea. After all, Thomas was loving toward me compared to Ray, who had turned cold toward the end.

Thomas strode over, gave me a wet peck on the cheek, and handed me his empty glass. "Cheers, love. I see you have some more wine. Be a dear and get me another Pernod while I go to the bathroom."

I got up from the sofa to fetch him his drink and had just sat back down when he came back into the living room and took a seat on the chair next to the sofa.

"Have you heard anything about when Phillip is going to pay us?" Even I heard the faint note of desperation in my voice.

"He will direct-deposit the payment into my account. Then we will deduct all expenses, pay taxes, and split the rest."

"What about my reimbursement for the hotel? That is reimbursable, not income and not split between us," I said nervously.

"Well, it will be included in his payment; we can separate that out."

"Also, you owe more than I on the credit card. I've itemized each purchase, and your liquor bill is higher than even our business expenses." Saying it out loud started to make me doubt my decision to buy a house with him. Jitters ran up my spine and made their way to the part of my brain responsible for common sense.

"Cheers, love. Don't worry. It will all be sorted fairly," Thomas replied.

I still didn't trust him. *Shake it off, Sara. It'll all work out.*

"Did you think any more about us going in on the house?" he asked, switching the subject.

My mind had been deep into our finances, so it took me a moment to catch up to his question. The strength of my decision made earlier waned. The pros and cons ran through my mind, lightning-fast. I was aware there were many more cons than pros, but the courage I needed to say, "No, not now," was nonexistent.

"Well, yes, I thought quite a bit about it. So I would pay half the down payment and half the monthly payments once my divorce settlement is finalized?" I wasn't sure. My heart was all for it, but the logic center in my brain screamed no.

"Yes, a true partnership in business and life," he said with a smile.

I looked at my almost empty glass, and my eyelashes shaded my eyes from him. Did he mean marriage? A house was one thing—granted, a pretty big thing—but marriage? I wasn't sure I wanted to get married again.

I swallowed a deep gulp of air and, in a timid voice, said, "Well, sure, let's go for it then. I'll call Carol in the morning to have her search for some properties for us to look at." I couldn't believe I had agreed.

We talked a little longer about price range, location, and what we'd like in our new home. The more we talked, the more we drank and the more excited I became about the possibilities. Thomas moved over and sat next to me on the sofa while we dreamed and schemed like two kids planning what we wanted for Christmas.

Hours later, we were talked out. We had recorded on paper our dreams for the house we wanted. Content to be alone with our thoughts, we silently finished our drinks. I laid my head on the back of the sofa and closed my eyes, partly due to tiredness and partly so I could imagine a home with all our dreams tucked into it. With each glass of wine, my doubts became fewer.

I felt Thomas move next to me, and before I could open my eyes, his warm lips were on mine. His kiss wasn't one of the closed-mouthed kisses we had shared recently. It was a full-mouth, open kiss, with his soft, velvety tongue exploring. My body melted into his while one of his hands played with my hair and the other lightly touched my breast. The rest of the world evaporated. All my worries about our finances and buying a home dissolved into a soft whimper. All that existed between us was his kiss, which became more and more sensuous. His touches awakened hot, longing desire. We broke apart and looked deeply into each other's eyes, which spoke what our bodies told us. He took my hand as we rose from the sofa and led us into the bedroom.

Chapter 32

**Follow your heart, listen to your inner voice,
stop caring about what others think.**
—Roy T. Bennett, *The Light in the Heart*

I woke to our legs tangled together and my head on his chest, and listened to the soft and steady beat of his heart. His arms held me close; fingertips like feathers ran up and down my arm draped over his body. There were no words to describe the feeling I had. *Warm*, *fuzzy*, and *content* didn't even come close. *Love?* I hadn't felt so wonderfully in love since my early days with Ray; how I had missed that feeling.

"You awake, love?" Thomas whispered, stirring a little.

"Um, yes. Your fingers tickling my arm woke me up," I replied, lost between wakefulness and dreaming.

He rolled over to face me; cupped my face in his hands; and landed soft, warm kisses on my cheeks, forehead, and neck. He drew me into him as his kisses made their way to my mouth and turned sensual and then demanding. His fingers recorded every curve and teased my nipples until they were hard and ached for more. He was gentle and then demanding and had me begging for release. His mouth was on mine; his tongue explored every part of my mouth. I desperately wanted him inside me, bringing me to the edge of ecstasy.

Our passion quieted to a sense of euphoria and then contentedness as we lay naked on the bed, spent from our morning lovemaking, entwined in each other's arms. Our breathing slowly came back to normal.

"I suppose we should get up," I said.

Thomas gave a grunt, untangled himself from me, and rolled over. Within seconds, his soft little snores told me he had fallen asleep. While he slept, I could have a long shower and take my time in the bathroom. I half smiled, and butterflies fluttered in my stomach; I hoped it wouldn't be long before we had two bathrooms.

Thomas was at the dinette and had the coffee on when I walked out of the bathroom refreshed and ready to start my day. I walked over to him, leaned down, and kissed the back of his neck.

"G'morning, love. Sleep well?" I asked as I poured two cups of coffee and then got the milk for his. *Strange. Americans say "coffee with cream"; the Brits say "white coffee."*

"Slept like a baby or a man who just had the best sex ever." He smiled up at me and reached to take his mug from me. "And you, love?"

Heat traveled up my neck and warmed my cheeks. With eyes downcast to avoid his sexy grin and dancing eyes, I responded, "The best ever."

"You're so cute when you blush, you know," he said as he reached across the table to take my hand. "I mean it, you know. Last night was heaven on earth."

I wished he would quit talking about our sex. It only made my cheeks hotter. "Do you still want me to call Carol today to put together a list of homes for us to look at?" I said, changing the subject. I still had many doubts, and with my luck with men, I worried Thomas would not be with me for the long haul. *Stop it, Sara. You'll jinx it all, and then what?*

"Sure, why not ring her now?"

I grabbed my phone and mug of coffee and went into the living room, where the list of wants we'd talked about last night lay on my desk. I glanced over at Thomas for reassurance that I was doing the right thing and dialed Carol's number.

"Hi, Carol," I said, sounding bright and cheery to extinguish the doubts from my voice. "How would you like to be Thomas's and my Realtor?"

"What?" Carol said, clearly surprised. "You are buying a house with Thomas?"

"Well, yes. We decided that our flat in London was small, and my apartment is even smaller, so we want to have a house here that would give us more room."

"Why don't you just rent a bigger apartment or house?" she asked quickly.

Frankly, I had not thought of that, but when I looked over at Thomas, I didn't know if he would go for renting.

"Sara, please tell me this is a joke. You aren't even divorced yet, for God's sake, and you and Thomas just a minute ago became romantically involved. This will be a mistake—one of your biggest." Carol always had been a blunt, tell-it-as-she-saw-it friend, which I had always appreciated—and she was usually right.

That day, I found her bluntness annoying. I wasn't in the mood to have more doubt planted in my brain. I picked up our house wish list, walked into the bedroom, and closed the door behind me. If our conversation continued with her disapproving comments, I didn't want Thomas to overhear.

"Do you want to be our Realtor or not?" Annoyance seeped through my tone.

"If you are sure, but I'm on record as saying this is a big mistake for you," Carol said. "What are you looking for in a house?" Her tone was terse.

We spent the next half hour talking through the list Thomas and I had put together, which included price range. The more I shared our wants, the more excited I became again.

"Sara, you know I think this is a huge mistake you're making, but I won't say any more about it. From what you've told me about your ideal house, I've already thought of a few we can see tomorrow if the owners give the okay. What time in the morning is good for you and Thomas?" There was an icy edge to her voice.

We didn't have anything planned for the next day, so I told her we could meet her at the real estate office at ten o'clock to review the listings before we toured them. I wanted to get started right away and get out of that apartment as soon as possible. My lease on the apartment ended next month, so the timing couldn't have been more perfect.

True to her word, she did not bring up again that she thought I was making a huge mistake. But disapproval was evident in the tone of her voice. Maybe I filtered her voice through my lack of confidence in my decision.

Chapter 33

See the world as it is, not as you wish it would be.
—E. Lockhart, *We Were Liars*

The next morning, Carol called to say she had five houses to look at and confirmed we were to meet her at the office around ten. Thomas and I finished our coffee and then, with me behind the wheel, drove the ten miles south to Coupeville, where her office was located.

Of all the cities on the island, Coupeville was my favorite. The town was in the center of the island and located on Penn Cove, with magnificent views of the water, the cove on the west side, and Puget Sound on the right. A population of just one thousand or so community-minded residents called it home. The outlying area was rural, with farms, forests, prairies, and rocky beaches. Ray and I had bought our first home there.

As I drove down Sherman Hill to the only stoplight in the town, the loss of Ray and the life I had known for twenty years tugged at my heart.

Carol greeted us at the office door and looked at Thomas expectantly. I realized that while she had known about Thomas as my business partner all those years, she had not met him in person.

"Carol, this is Thomas. Thomas, this is the number-one Realtor on the island and my best friend."

They said their greetings on our way to the conference room where we would review the listings. Two out of the five listings didn't meet our requirements, so we set them aside, leaving three houses for us to look at. The three of us loaded into Carol's car. Thomas climbed into the front passenger seat, which left the back for me, and the search for our new home began. The thought set off a few butterflies in my tummy again as I fastened my seat belt. Life seemed perfect at that moment. What could go wrong?

We toured one house after another, and with each one, there seemed to be something wrong with it. It needed too much fixing, the price wasn't right, or it didn't have a water view. My philosophy was "Why live on an island if you can't see the water?"

Upon my first step inside the last house on our tour, contentment surrounded me like a security blanket, as if to tell me I had come home at last.

The house was beautiful and overlooked Penn Cove, with the rafts of the mussel farm below. It had three bedrooms, an office, a gourmet kitchen, two roomy bathrooms, a deck on the back, and a massive deck on the front to watch the whales and eagles from. The best part was that it was in Coupeville, the town I loved.

Ray still lived and worked there, and the sudden thought I might run into him dimmed my excitement for a moment. How would I respond if we met each other at the market or the post office? How would he react? It would be uncomfortable, but we were two adults; we could manage the chance encounter maturely. Couldn't we?

Thomas and I stood in the living room, which faced the expansive windows that framed the fabulous view. Carol must have sensed we needed privacy to talk it over and left to stand on the front deck. That was what made her good at what she did: her ability to read people so well.

I looked at Thomas, hesitating to say anything. I tried to read whether he liked the house or not.

He turned to look at me. "Well, what do you think?"

"I love it. It has everything on our wish list and then some, and the price fits into what we figured we could afford. What do you think?" All my doubts from earlier had been forgotten in my excitement.

"I think if you love it, we should put an offer on it. Don't you think?" He had a sly smile on his face and a twinkle in his eyes.

I couldn't believe he had said yes. I threw myself into his arms and hugged him tightly as tears spilled over onto his shirt. "Thank you," I whispered in his ear.

"Let's get Carol and get the paperwork started," he whispered in mine.

When we told Carol, she gave me a less-than-happy look; nodded; and, with teeth clenched, walked toward her car. We followed, but her lack of enthusiasm troubled me. The doubts crept back one by one. What would I have told the women I had counseled if they'd told me they were buying a house with their abuser?

On the way back to the office, Carol congratulated us half-heartedly. She and Thomas discussed what a reasonable offer would be and terms. I bowed out of the conversation and, true to my lifelong behavior of keeping myself on the sidelines, preferred to let Thomas handle the details. On the short drive back to the office, I looked out the window at the pastoral scene that characterized Coupeville.

"Bollocks, all this paperwork just to buy a house?" Thomas asked once we were in the office's conference room and Carol brought in the file with the purchase and sale agreement.

Carol snipped, "Buying a house is the biggest purchase of your life, Thomas. There are many legal documents to protect both you and the seller." She then gave me a look that would have struck down an elephant. I wished she would just chill and quit showing me how much she disapproved.

In the next few hours, I watched Thomas sign his name on various documents that Carol explained to him in great detail. I couldn't sign the papers as cobuyer because I was still married. My name would not be recorded on the deed. I would have no legal right to the house. I would not be bound financially to the mortgage and other expenses. I realized I would have no liability. I had an out if our relationship turned sour.

I looked over at him, and my heart skipped a beat—he had secured our future with this purchase. Ray had done the same; the difference was that both our names were on that deed, and I would be awarded half the equity. I pushed my doubts to the back of my mind.

"Are you sure about this, Sara? Your name will not be on the deed, so if anything should happen and you and Thomas are no longer together, you will have no claim to the house. Do you understand the implications of that?"

"Yes, I'm sure, and I know what I'm doing, Carol. I'm grabbing a little bit of happiness and a lot of love for myself," I said as I reached for Thomas's hand.

Carol grimaced, stood quickly, and left to make copies of the paperwork. I felt breathless and wanted to jump out of my chair and dance around the room. I was happier than I'd been in a long time. My life was finally headed in the right direction, I thought, with a man who proclaimed his love for me, a new home in which to build our life together, and hopefully more contracts for work. The future was no longer dim; it had turned as bright as the sun.

Carol came back into the room, handed us our copies, and then shuffled the others into a file folder. Still standing, as if to send us a message we were done, she told us she would present our offer that evening.

"Thanks for everything, Carol." Thomas extended his hand to shake hers.

I reached out to hug her, whispering my thanks.

She whispered so only I could hear her, "You should not do this, Sara. This could be the worst decision you ever made."

I stiffened, broke away from her, and paused when I saw tears in her eyes. "I'll be fine. I promise."

Chapter 34

Two things are infinite: the universe and human stupidity; and I'm not sure about the universe.
—Albert Einstein

While Thomas drove us back home, I was quiet and lost in my thoughts. Carol's warning about not having my name on the deed haunted me more than I liked to admit. My gut told me I might have made the worst mistake of my life; my heart told me that buying a home with Thomas was the best decision I had made in a long time. I could always back out of the deal. We had no contract, just trust between us. Doing so wouldn't have been fair to Thomas, though, not after I had already committed to the deal.

Mom's criticisms throughout my life had turned me into a people pleaser. I always put others' needs and wants ahead of mine. Every decision was made with an enormous lack of confidence. It must have been why I allowed myself to be led by others, why I followed instead of leaving.

"A pence for your thoughts." Thomas's voice jarred me out of my thoughts.

I turned to look at him and noticed his strong jawline and how sexy he looked with his day-old beard. "Oh, nothing. Just figuring out where the little furniture I have will go, trying to picture it in my mind," I lied.

"Your furniture is crap. Why don't we go look at furniture and buy some new? You know, start a new life fresh and break free of the past by getting rid of Ray's hand-me-downs."

"What? We can't afford new furniture, and we don't even know if the seller will accept our offer." My voice was tight and high and made it evident I was shocked at his suggestion.

"Well, think about it some, okay, love?" he responded.

The rest of the ride returned to quiet, as it had started. We stopped by our potential new house on the way back just to drool some more. The sellers had already moved out, so I peeked in the living room windows. While I didn't want to admit it, I knew my furniture would look like trash in that elegant house. But I was determined not to give in; we couldn't afford new furniture right now. We never would be able to unless Thomas got off his butt and got us some new clients.

We stopped for an early dinner at our favorite pub. We chatted some about the house, but mostly, the conversation was about our next steps to sign on a new client, at my insistence. Thomas agreed to call his network in London to round us up a contract or two. While we ate and chatted, he slurped down quite a few gin and tonics to my one glass of wine. I wondered why Brits loved their gin so much. It seemed everyone I knew in London drank gin—well, except for Thomas when Pernod was available.

With our dinner eaten, Thomas paid the bill with our business credit card, which did not go unnoticed by me.

"When are you going to start paying your fair share of the credit card bill?" I asked after we got back in the car. My anger bubbled up from the depths of my bowels, ready to spill over if he said the wrong thing. I knew I sounded like I was nagging, but I was worried about finances now that he had signed the offer—a little late.

"You must be going daft. I told you I'd pay the bill off once Phillip pays us in full."

"When is that going to be?" I knew I was dealing with danger. His anger had always been trigger-happy. Even so, I couldn't help myself and added, "I need the money, Thomas. I'm tempted to pay off the bill with my settlement instead of using it to make the down payment." I watched as he turned rigid, and his eyebrows knit together as he tried to control his anger.

"Look, don't get your knickers in a twist. I told you I would call him tomorrow."

We arrived at the apartment, and after slamming the gear into park, he got out and banged the car door shut. By the time I got inside, he had already stepped out onto the patio with his phone to his ear with one hand and a drink in the other. *That was fast.* I figured I might as well enjoy a glass of wine since he continued his drinking. I wondered whom he had called. It was six o'clock, which meant it was two o'clock in the morning in London, so unless he knew some night owls, it wouldn't have been anyone from across the pond.

Instead of one glass of wine, I finished the bottle, and I was reaching for another bottle out of the refrigerator, when Thomas came back into the apartment.

"Hi. Who were you talking with?" I was in a good mood. The effects of the wine helped me let my guard down.

He shot me a snarky look and then poured himself another drink.

After a couple of sips, he set his glass down on the counter and walked over to where I stood.

"That, my love, is none of your business." Without warning, he slapped my face so hard I slid down the wall to the floor and splashed wine all over myself. I rubbed my cheek and looked up at him in shock, speechless. He grabbed my arm and pulled me up to stand in front of him. Still holding on to my arm, he reached for his drink with his other hand and threw his Pernod in my face.

"You are never to question me about who I am talking to. Got it?"

I nodded, sputtered, and wiped my eyes with my free hand. Booze dripped down onto the linoleum floor yellowed by years of wax buildup. He grabbed me by the arms and pulled me back up.

"If I say I will pay the credit card bill off, I will. Got it?" His face was just inches from mine.

Fear spread through every cell in my body. I was afraid he would do more than slap me this time. I couldn't talk; I simply nodded.

"If I say we are getting new furniture, we are getting new furniture. Got it?"

I swallowed the lump in my throat, reminded myself to breathe, and nodded.

He stared me down, still holding me in his clutches, and punched me in the stomach. Every wisp of air from my lungs was knocked out. He released me, poured himself another drink, and walked into the living room. I was left to cradle my stomach with my arms, doubled over, drenched in booze.

I sat in a deflated pile on the kitchen floor in the pool of Pernod and wine and struggled to breathe, in pain and disbelief. Stunned, I realized he had assaulted me. The man who said he loved me had attacked me. The thought could hardly fit into my mind, and I shuddered from deep within my core. Why had he punched me?

Because I'd challenged him and held the truth up to him? Who was I to him? Who was he?

I groaned, my stomach turned into knots and cramped, and rose from the floor, grabbing onto the counter for support. Pieces of my smashed Russian crystal wine glass on the floor glistened in the light of the single bulb that hung from the ceiling. A burning boil of anger replaced the stomach cramps. How dare he treat me like that? Who was he to order me to behave in only the way he approved of?

I had seen firsthand the damaged women left behind by their abusers. There was something wrong with anyone who took his or her anger and frustration out on another. I shuddered, realizing something was terribly wrong with Thomas. He was damaged. Had someone abused him when he was growing up? Rarely did I ask him about his childhood and his parents, but every time I asked him about his dad, he simply told me his dad had been a lawyer and had passed away when he was young. It felt weird that he was so closed to the conversation.

I knew the best action I could take now, besides cleaning myself and the kitchen, would be to call the cops and charge Thomas with assault. I also knew that once that door was opened, it would be tough to close. That incident was a damn good sign I should get out of that relationship—and fast.

I glanced around the kitchen in search of my phone and then realized I had left it in the living room, where Thomas was. Would he take another opportunity to cut me down again with words or his fists if I walked in to get my phone? I decided it would be safer to call the cops in the morning, when he was sober.

But if I called the cops, Jackson would be sure to find out what Thomas had done to me. Hell, the way gossip flew around the island, Ray would know by morning. I wouldn't let Jackson know how weak his mother had become. His once-successful mom had been beaten by her boyfriend. How many women's stories matched mine? No, Thomas and I needed to work things out, I thought. One thing was for sure: he needed to go back to London as soon as possible, preferably tomorrow.

Chapter 35

Facts do not cease to exist because they are ignored.
—Aldous Huxley, *Complete Essays 2, 1926–29*

Thomas finally passed out on the couch. I tiptoed into the living room and quietly picked up my phone from the coffee table. I made it to the bathroom without Thomas hearing me and locked the door. I caught the reflection of my face in the mirror and saw a character from a horror movie. My face had turned red; black and blue colored the area under my eyes from the slaps; and my hair was matted to my head. I stripped and gasped at the bruises that speckled my arms and chest.

He had done this to me. I didn't know whether to cry or be angry as I looked at the injuries. *Sara, anger will not solve this problem; violence begets violence*, said the voice in my head, which sounded like my mom's. I looked around the bathroom, but she had not appeared. I supposed she had just whispered into the room as a word of warning.

I hated to admit it, but she was right—and as soon as I admitted that to myself, my anger lessened. Tears stung my bruised face while I ran the shower. I needed the water to be hot. I wanted the heat to burn the bruises off my skin. My pain and humiliation were swept down the drain along with the stench of booze. It was too bad the bruises in my heart couldn't be washed away as easily.

After showering and getting into my nightgown, I listened at the closed door for any sounds before I unlocked and opened it. No sound came down the hall, not even the television. I tiptoed past the living room, where Thomas was still snoring loudly on the couch, and headed toward the kitchen to clean the booze off the walls and the floor. I was grateful the counter and overhead cupboards blocked the view, and hopefully some sound, from the living room. My body ached, and with each move, a groan escaped from my mouth as I mopped up the broken glass and booze with paper towels, careful not to cut myself. My tears fell to the floor, where they mixed in with the liquor. Never in my wildest dreams would I have believed I would be with a monster who hurt me. The humiliation and disbelief came back and crushed me. *Is this what those women felt after their partner or spouse beat them?*

With the kitchen cleaned, all I wanted to do was go to sleep. I decided against locking the bedroom door to keep Thomas out. What if that made him angry again?

The smell of freshly brewed coffee and bacon tantalized me awake. Still in a half-dreamy level of consciousness, I snuggled my pillow and pulled the blankets tighter around me—what an excellent way to wake up. The smell of a breakfast that waited for me while the winter sun streamed through the dusty blinds reminded me that this life was the one I had always dreamed of: a home, a family, and a partner to have breakfast with and share days and nights with. I luxuriated in my dream. Then—*bam*—the bruises on my body rebelled against my morning stretch, which woke my memory center and reminded me of the horror of last night. I wondered what kind of mood Thomas was in and if he had been drinking already that morning. The smoothness of the covers on his side of the bed made it evident he hadn't slept there.

I rose up, limped over to the door, and cracked it open a tiny bit to hear what was going on in the kitchen while I slowly got dressed. All I heard was bacon sizzling, and Thomas was humming "Hey Jude" while he cooked.

"Good morning," I said quietly when I entered the kitchen.

"Good morning, love," Thomas responded in a cheerful tone, turning away from the stove to face me. "Bollocks, I'm so sorry," he said softly, and shock registered on his face. He gently touched my bruised cheek and black eye.

"Thomas, we have to talk. I don't know why you think it is okay to hit me and treat me like you do when drinking. I think maybe we need a break from each other."

"Oh, sweetie, I am so, so sorry to have hurt you. I don't know why I take it out on you." He turned back to the stove, turned off the burner under the bacon, and then joined me at the dinette. He drooped his head and wouldn't look me in the eye.

Would this be just another excuse before moving on as if nothing had ever happened? "Take what out on me? Why are you so angry?"

He raised his head to meet my eyes. "I don't know."

We were silent; both of us looked down and studied the grain of the wood table. He slowly got up, poured two mugs of coffee, brought them back to the table, and set a cup in front of me before he sat back down.

I was the first one to speak. "Thomas, look at me. No one but you has given me a black eye and bruises. No one. Last night will be the last time, Thomas. I won't allow you to treat me like this. I'm worth more than your punching bag."

There was a long, uncomfortable pause before he said anything. What was he thinking? I worried the strength of my words would set him off again. I pulled a napkin out of the holder, began to fidget with it, and waited. Thomas hadn't moved; his head was still down, which prevented me from seeing the position of his telltale eye swords.

Thomas broke the silence between us, though not the tension. "I don't know why I'm so angry and why you seem to be the target of my anger. I guess it goes back to my relationship with my dad. He was never physically abusive. Still, nothing I ever did was good enough for him. Neither my mom nor I could do anything right, and well, by watching my dad hate my mum, I ended up hating her and treated her like Dad did. I felt in control when I did, replacing the control my dad took away from me."

I saw the hint of a tear and, with a lump growing in my throat, reached to cover his hand with mine. He had beaten me and lashed out at me for no reason, but I related to his story; it was close to mine. "I'm so sorry, sweetie."

He leaned forward, his eyes searching mine. "Look, love, how my dad treated me is no excuse for doing what I did last night. I'm deeply sorry for hurting you, more than I can ever say. I love you so much. I've never felt this way about anyone before. Please, can you ever forgive me? I swear I will never hurt you again. I promise. It will never happen again."

I had heard this story before. Abusers abused, whether verbally or physically or both, and when they saw the damage caused, reality hit, and they were sorry and swore they would never do it again—until the next time it happened. Then the cycle started all over: the abuse, the hurt, reality, and promises to never again hurt the one they said they loved. So why would I trust him? He had said those words to me before, yet now I had noticeable bruises and a black eye despite his promise to me.

He had been authentic when he told me about his parents, especially his relationship with his father, and how he had formed his opinion of women. It broke my heart to think of a young Thomas growing up in a home with so much violence and hatred. *Life is never fair; we are all dealt our lot in life, and it's up to us to make sense of it all*, I thought. I loved him, and I knew he loved me. *If I throw it all away, will love ever find me? We can help each other make sense of our screwed-up childhoods and work through what is tearing us apart.*

So I stayed with him.

Chapter 36

I wonder if fears ever really go away, or if
they just lose their power over us.
—Veronica Roth, *Allegiant*

The next few weeks went by quickly. My bruises and black eye healed.
Our offer on the house was accepted, and we bought furniture and
placed it all in storage with my old stuff until we closed on the deal.
Thomas secured a new client in London to develop a system for a
modeling agency specializing in disabled models.

Phillip finally paid us. After Britain's value-added tax and US taxes
were paid, there was not enough left over to pay off the business
credit card. From my share of the profit, I paid what I could and saved
the rest for my next trip to London. Due to unforeseen expenses at
home, Thomas's promises to pay on the credit card bill fell through,

or so he said. He promised he would give me the money on our next payday.

I decided to give him some latitude. After all, he had made the entire down payment on the house and had been patient about my paying it back. Still, it was comforting to know I could pull out at any time. In the meantime, I asked him to limit the number of personal expenses he put on the card, which meant using his own money to buy his Pernod.

"Should we ask for a deposit on the system for our new client? We've projected it will take around six months to finish, and that's a long time to go without a paycheck. We could pay some of our business expenses down," I said to him one day on our way to the pub for dinner.

"Cheers, love. Sounds like a good idea, but they are a start-up company with minimal funding. Let's just go forward and produce and take our payment when we are done."

I sat back in my seat and gazed out the car window, disappointed. We were a start-up company as well, and it sure would have helped us to ask for a nonrefundable deposit to get us through until the end of the project. With a deposit, we would have been paid something if the company decided to nix the project halfway through.

Even though I had a sound argument to ask for a deposit, I dropped the discussion. I wanted a relaxing dinner with a quiet evening afterward. I didn't trust his promise not to hurt me again.

The day came when Thomas's time on his visa waiver expired, and he went back to London. He would finalize the contract with the modeling company. I remained on Whidbey to close out the apartment, arrange to have Ray pick up the furniture I'd taken when we separated, and facilitate the move into the new house. Thomas would sign the closing papers electronically—thank goodness for technology.

The closer our move-in date came, the more excited about my new life I became. Who would have thought that pudgy Sara from an island in the Pacific Northwest would move into a new home with a water view and travel to London for work? When I'd left our home, Ray's last words, which reverberated through my mind, had been "You'll never make it without me." *Ha, that's what you think, bub. Watch me now.*

Moving day finally arrived. I woke to my last morning in the dingy apartment that had eventually come to be my safe place. I had started to heal from the loss of my marriage there and had discovered I enjoyed the bits of independence that gave me strength. But then Thomas had hurt me there, humiliated me, and turned my safe place into something unrecognizable. Still, I would miss the old place. I laughed. *Will the rats miss me?*

The movers arrived on time, which was unusual for island time, and packed my things into their truck in no time flat. I stood in the middle of the gold shag carpet in the empty living room, surveying what had become my first home after my marriage dissolved. Memories of grieving for my dying marriage clouded my eyes with tears. I turned and walked to the door and gave one last look at what had been my first safe harbor.

"Goodbye, old friend," I said, and then I closed the door for the last time.

I pulled into the driveway of our new house and stopped the car before I reached the garage. I wanted to take in the beauty of the setting and feel the joy of hope for the future as it spread through every cell in my body. That step, that moment, made the divorce and the beatings seem insignificant. I experienced a jolt of disbelief to know this was my house. *My house.* I drove the rest of the way to the garage, and the movers pulled up behind me.

The movers brought in the new furniture, along with what I'd inherited from my family and the boxes of stuff out of storage. I hummed as I unpacked my favorite knickknacks, many of which I had inherited from my grandma, happy for the first time in days. Without Thomas there, I felt free and not as tense. It had become apparent I still didn't trust him to keep his word, and that troubled me. Was I too deep in that relationship to get out? Financially, I knew I was. But what about my heart? I didn't feel my heart was in the relationship all the way. Yet there I was, in a new home I would be sharing with a man who lied to me about our joint finances and took his anger out on me. I remembered his words. *I love you. It will never happen again.*

I jumped when the phone rang. I had worked my way to the kitchen to unpack the dishes, and I quickly placed the last plate in the dishwasher to rinse clean and then picked up my phone.

"Hi, Thomas," I said, noticing his name on the caller ID before I answered.

"Cheers, love. How's the move going?"

"Well, the movers have delivered everything, and I'm unpacking. Getting the kitchen squared away and then will get the bedroom unpacked and the bed made so I have somewhere to sleep tonight. How's it going with the modeling company?"

"It's a good thing you are making progress unpacking, 'cause we need you to come to London. We are ready for you to drill out the requirements so we can get to the development stage. When do you think you can come?"

My heart sank. I'd known I would need to go back to London sooner or later, but now that the house was full of boxes, I had been hoping for later. I had been looking forward to bringing my cat, Kitty, home from Ray's. The apartment hadn't allowed pets, so I had left her with him. Plus, my hope for a few tranquil days without Thomas had been dashed.

"Any chance I could identify the requirements over Skype?" I asked hopefully.

"Naw, you need to be here to meet everyone, talk to them face-to-face, and have focus groups to make sure we don't miss anything."

I knew he was right; I was just hoping to delay leaving our new home, and I wasn't looking forward to being so stressed around him again.

I sighed with disappointment and said, "Okay then, how about the end of next week?"

"Try for the first of next week," he said in a flat voice.

"Okay, I'll check the flights." I was more than disappointed.

We talked for a few minutes longer and then said our goodbyes and hung up. I stood at the kitchen window and looked out at the forest behind the house. I didn't want to go, but it was more than that. I was afraid to go.

FOUR

London

Chapter 37

It's not fair. It's not fair that he lets his rage take over, that he lets it rule him. I don't know why he has to let it rule him. I don't know why he has to be two people.
—Amanda Grace, *But I Love Him*

After passing through customs at Heathrow and tossing my luggage into the trunk of Thomas's car, we drove to the client's office and began the long and tedious requirements work. I was committed to getting the requirements hammered out quickly and then flying back home to complete the project. There would be no need for me to stay there to do that work, and distance between Thomas and me was a good idea, I knew. I thought better of telling Thomas my plan just yet. He had been welcoming and loving since I arrived. I prayed there would be no more violence while I was there, but he was unpredictable when his anger got the best of him.

Two weeks passed without Thomas exploding into a rage. It was a pleasant few weeks, almost normal, whatever that might have been for us. I was careful about what I said and how I said it. I continuously watched him for the telltale signs of his anger escalating. But he remained loving toward me and calm even when problems in the project popped up.

After three weeks, the requirements finally were completed. I could go home and put space between myself and that complicated relationship. I had been tense throughout most of my time there while waiting for the unexpected rage to explode. Yet Thomas and I had become closer. *Strange*, I thought. I always was on edge, ready for a fight to happen, yet day by day, my heart moved closer to his. We'd had some romantic dates: dinners at restaurants with dimmed lights and soft music in the background, trips to the theater, and walks along the canal close to our flat. We made good memories instead of bad ones. The good pushed the bad further and further to the back of my mind, where they were now just faint memories.

I was packing for my trip home, when Thomas, with a twinkle in his eye, said, "Let's take a holiday before you go home—a reward for our hard work the past few weeks. We could drive down to Bath, visit Stonehenge and Bristol, and drive through the Cotswolds on the way home. Say yes."

I couldn't resist his offer. I was an adventurer at heart, so it was a no-brainer, and I immediately said yes. It had always been my fantasy to see Stonehenge in person, and now the opportunity had arrived. I was not going to miss it.

I wrapped my arms around his neck and gave him a sloppy kiss. "Thank you."

We pushed the half-packed suitcases off the bed and spent the rest of the afternoon making the sweetest love. That was what I had dreamed a relationship was supposed to be like, based on all the "And they lived happily ever after" fairy tales I had read as a child: lovemaking in the afternoons, surprises, and showing we cared for one another. My relationship with Ray had been like that, until it wasn't. Deep down inside, I hoped this wouldn't just be a fairy tale.

I hadn't even given a thought to how his surprise would be paid for. My divorce hadn't been finalized, which meant the money had not been deposited into my bank account. The credit card was limping along with the minimum payment made. I pushed all financial thoughts out of my mind; after all, the trip couldn't cost too much, because we would be driving.

We arrived at the most mysterious place on Earth to me: Stonehenge. I stared at the expanse of land before us and imagined druids roaming the grounds amid their huts, and then the stones that formed a circle came into my vision. Nobody knew how they'd gotten there, but they had lasted the ages since sometime before 2500 BC. My excitement and wonder grew the closer I got to the stones.

I listened to the recording device we'd rented at the visitors' center. Few of the mysteries that intrigued me were solved. I was disappointed we couldn't walk into the circle or actually touch the stones but understood the reasoning after I learned about how millions of touches wore the surface of stones away. Thomas and I walked hand in hand around the stones. It was a moment of shared interests and peace that I relished and hoped would never end.

It was a lovely trip, but seeing all the sights was not what amazed me. In just a week, Thomas and I discovered new things about each other; we laughed and shared our dreams with each other. The bad times between us were replaced by happy times, and I felt I was falling deeper in love with him. Everything was peaceful; everything was good between us.

Until our trip ended and we returned to our flat.

We returned to the flat the night before I left for home. We unpacked our suitcases, and I began to repack for my trip the next day. Thomas cracked open a bottle of wine and brought a glass into the bedroom for me. He held a glass of Pernod in his other hand. He sat on the bed and watched me pack.

"Love, I don't see why you are leaving. We could work together here at the flat on the programming creative parts."

"Hon, I need to get the house unpacked and things put away besides working on the project, and I have to be home to do that. Besides, I have an appointment next week with my attorney to finalize the divorce, which should make you happy. As soon as the settlement hits my bank account, I can pay you my fair share of the house." I didn't look at him but continued to pack.

He was silent for a few minutes. Then he said, "You could have at least thanked me for taking you on the trip with me." The tone of his voice brought a cold sweat to my forehead.

I stopped folding and putting clothes in the suitcase and looked at him. What I saw made my blood run cold and stopped my breathing. His jaw was set; his thin lips were pressed into a straight line. I knew where the situation would head if I didn't do something to deescalate his anger.

I put a brave smile on and said, "Thank you, Thomas. It was the trip of a lifetime, and you made many of my dreams come true." I had thanked him during our trip several times, but I didn't think it would be wise to the point that out now.

In answer to my thanks, he shoved my suitcase onto the floor, spilling its contents.

"Thomas, please don't go there. We know what happens," I begged. I didn't know what else to say. I felt anything I said would provoke him more.

He responded by tossing his drink into my face. The liquor dripped onto my once clean clothes that lay on the floor where they had spilled out of the suitcase. He shot me a look of disgust and said, "Clean yourself up. You smell like a distillery," and he walked out of the bedroom.

What happened? What had I said to set him off like that? Tears joined the Pernod dripping off my face, and I didn't stop them. With hands that trembled, I picked up the soiled clothes and my suitcase and began to pack all over again. How had my life gotten so bad that I packed wet, boozy clothes into my bag?

Thomas came to the bedroom door and leaned against the doorjamb with one leg crossed over the other at the ankle and a fresh drink in hand. I tried to read his mood, but all I saw was a superior, arrogant air that emanated from him. My eyes told me his anger was smoldering.

"You stupid cow," he said. "I can't believe you didn't wash the clothes you splashed booze onto."

My stomach boiled, seething, ready to spill over with my own anger. I wanted to scream, "It was you who threw your drink, soiling my clothes, you bastard!" But I knew damn well what his reaction would be if I did, and I would not be better for it.

"There isn't time tonight. It's late, and I have an early flight in the morning. I'll just wash the clothes when I get home." My voice was quiet and sounded timid, which angered me even more. At that point, it was a game: Could I soothe his anger and talk him down from hurting me?

That night, I lost the game.

Chapter 38

Be the reason someone smiles. Be the reason someone
feels loved and believes in the goodness in people.
—Roy T. Bennett, *The Light in the Heart*

"Open your suitcase, and get those skanky clothes into the washer
now," Thomas said. He entered the room, opened the suitcase,
and threw my carefully packed booze-soaked clothes all over the
bedroom. "Now!" he shouted directly into my face, and he walked
out of the room.

I stood there silently. My throat was parched, and heart pounded
hard and fast. His last word reverberated in my ears and finally made
it to my confused mind. I swiftly bent; picked up the clothes he had
strewn about; and, with arms full, left the bedroom and headed
for the kitchen to load the washer. I didn't see him just outside the

bedroom door; I didn't see his foot pop out and trip me. I landed hard on the floor of the living room, and the clothes flew out of my arms.

"You cheeky, clumsy bitch, what is wrong with you? I said to pick them up and get them in the washer."

Before I could get up from the floor, he grabbed me by the hair and yanked me up. I tried to stand, to loosen his grip on my hair, to get away from him. He twisted my hair; turned me to face him; and, still holding on to my hair, slapped me, first on one side of the face and then on the other hand. Again and again. I felt like a puppet on a string, only I was a real person.

Salty tears ran down and stung my already stinging cheeks. He punched me in the stomach and let go of my hair. I doubled over and clutched my stomach while I fought down nausea.

Get away from him now! The thought screamed through my head like a broken record, but he pinned me onto the floor and bent my legs over my head, making it difficult to breathe. My focus started to wane; everything seemed like a hazy dream as I fought for breath. Blackness colored the edges of the haze. I was losing consciousness.

He sat on my legs, kept them pinned to my chest, and bounced on them, effectively pumping the air out of my lungs. Frantically, despite the blackness that closed in, I reached out for him and tried to grab hold of his arms to drag him off me. Instead, my hand found his privates, and without a second thought, I squeezed as hard as I could. The threat of death gave me a second wind of strength.

But while it felt like hours of his bouncing on me and my squeezing his balls, my efforts had no effect. *Is he dead down there? Squeeze harder, Sara. Squeeze!*

Then there was blackness.

I didn't know how long I had lain unconscious. Wakefulness returned, and I realized my legs had been released. I heard Thomas in the kitchen and the familiar sound of ice cubes in a glass. *Thank goodness. Gotta get out of here before he sees me.*

I tried to stand, but my legs felt like rubber bands that had been stretched for miles. They wouldn't support me, so I crawled to the bedroom to reach my phone and then to the bathroom and locked the door. I gasped when I saw my reflection in the mirror. My face had turned black and blue, I had two black eyes and a split lip, and bruises decorated my arms. My hair stood on end. I looked as if I'd just walked out of a war zone.

How could anyone do this to someone they say they love? What had I done to deserve this from him? Why was I still there with him? Self-recrimination continued to run through my mind; my heart was broken. I picked up my phone again, called a taxi, and asked for one to be at the flat in ten minutes.

I unlocked the door and made my way out of the bathroom. Thomas was on the phone. I took a deep breath; my anger continued to motivate me. I walked into the living room, gathered up all the clothes strewn about, took them into the bedroom, and stuffed them into the suitcase. I didn't bother to fold and pack neatly. When I was done, I slammed the suitcase shut and gathered up my purse and laptop, and with all three filling my hands, I walked to the front door of the flat.

"Where do you think you are going, stupid cow?" Thomas was right behind me as I struggled with the door.

"Home," I said as I finally got the door open, and I walked to the top of the stairs. Thomas was right behind me.

"Here—let me help you," he said as he placed his hand on the small of my back and gave me a not-so-gentle push at the top of the stairs. I quickly stepped aside and struggled down the steps with my luggage and out the door.

The taxi was waiting for me outside the building. The driver helped me with my things, and I stepped into the waiting cab.

"Royal Chase Hotel," I told the driver.

He looked at me in his rearview mirror and didn't bother to hide the gasp that escaped from his lips. "Are ya okay, miss?" he said in a lyrical cockney accent.

"I'm fine," I said. His small kindness brought tears that stung my eyes.

"Did 'e do dis ter ya?" he asked, nodding toward the upper bedroom window, where Thomas hung out to watch me as I left.

"Yes, please, let's go," I pleaded. I wanted to get to the hotel and didn't want to spend time chatting.

Putting the taxi in gear, he reached back to hand me his business card. "Awright, geeza! I've got daughters, an' I would kill any bloke who did what he did ter you. Take me card, an' if i' 'appens again, dial me number anytime, day awer night, and I'll come an' get ya. Sorted, mate."

Sorted, mate. If only it were that easy.

It was a short drive from our flat to the hotel. I took my phone out of my purse and stared at it, hoping Thomas would call to say how sorry he was, promise he wouldn't do it again, and beg me to come back to the flat, but he didn't call.

During the drive, many thoughts added to my already confused mind. I'd committed myself to Thomas, if not totally emotionally, then certainly financially. I was in debt up to my ears with the business credit card, and he expected to be repaid the down payment on the house. I felt lost and confused. What was I supposed to do now? The answer was obvious and logical: call it quits with Thomas, both personally and professionally. Hold him accountable for the money he owed me. But most of all, break away from him financially, which meant I would not relinquish my divorce settlement to him. I needed every cent until I figured out what I would do for the rest of my life.

We arrived at the hotel in the blink of an eye. The driver unloaded my luggage while I got out of the car, and before I could pay him, he handed me a five-pound note, the equivalent of a little more than six US dollars. It wasn't much and probably wouldn't take me far in a taxi, but his gesture touched my heart.

"'Member wha' I tol' ya. Use this fiver to get yerself outta there. Better yet, don' go back to 'im." Then he swept me into his arms and gave me a bear hug that squeezed my breath away. This man didn't know me but cared anyway and wanted to protect me as best as possible. No one had ever been like that with me before. A stranger was the one who showed compassion toward me, not Thomas. We hugged, and I swore I saw his eyes glisten with tears.

"Thank you for your kindness," I said. "Please take care of those daughters of yours." Then, after gathering up my luggage, I walked into the lobby of the hotel. I wondered if there would ever be a kind man like the taxi driver in my life again. But how would I know if I couldn't find a way to extract myself from Thomas first?

Chapter 39

The most painful thing is losing yourself in the process of loving someone too much and forgetting that you are special too.
—Ernest Hemingway, *Men without Women*

Walking into the hotel's plush lobby, I instantly felt self-conscious. I was in my booze-soaked clothes and had bruises, a blackening eye, and hair that looked as if I had plugged myself into a light socket. The other guests looked at me with suspicious sidelong glances but said nothing and gave me a wide berth. I had no idea what they thought, but the humiliation Thomas had imposed on me was now complete, or so I thought. I stood at the front desk and waited to be registered. I just wanted to quickly get to my room and hide from the accusing eyes and whispering voices.

"Good evening, miss. How can I help you this evening?" chirped the woman at the front desk while she looked at me straight in my blackening eye.

My God, can't she see how she might help? I breathed in deeply and kept my head and voice low. "I'd like a room for one night, please." I hadn't even considered that they might be booked for the night.

"Certainly, miss. Let's see. I have a double bed overlooking the courtyard for one hundred twenty-five pounds. Would that be sufficient?"

I couldn't believe how normally she responded to me with the way I looked. "Yes, that will be fine. Thank you."

"How will you be paying tonight?"

Reluctantly, I handed over my business credit card and shuddered. I knew the balance had already gone beyond what I could pay in full. But if I hadn't had it, I'd have been either back at the flat or spending my night at Heathrow.

After I checked in, I slung my laptop bag over one shoulder, while my purse hung over my other shoulder; took the handle of my suitcase; and trudged up the stairs to my room. I kept my head down and grumbled about there being no elevators or bellboys as I made my way up a long flight of stairs. It had been a hard night, and it was made harder by the lack of conveniences that would have been standard in even a one-star hotel in the States.

It was a beautiful room, with crisp linens on the bed, a writing desk, and a bathroom with a shower. *Hallelujah. A shower.* I couldn't wait to get into it, but first, I needed to call the airline to change my flight to tomorrow morning instead of the evening.

I sat on the bed and got my phone out of my purse, when I had the crazy thought to call Thomas to let him know where I was and that I was okay. Just then, I looked up and caught myself in the dresser mirror. My battered face reflected back at me. What could he say if I did call? "It won't happen again; I promise"? "I love you; please come back to the flat"? He'd said all that before, and I had gone back. I had trusted him at his word. I looked down at my phone and dialed the airline.

Luck was on my side: British Air had a flight to Seattle in the morning with seats available. I quickly changed my reservation and paid the one-hundred-pound charge fee before I could change my mind.

My heart was heavy with conflicted feelings. The familiar sensation of fear crept into my gut. Had I made the right decision? I pushed the fear back down. It was done; I had a ticket to go home in the morning.

I stood to look at myself in the mirror carefully and noticed the broken blood vessels in my black eyes. The bruises had become a deeper blue, almost black; my split lip was still bloody. *How have you come to this, Sara? A man is never worth losing yourself over. No matter how much you crave to be loved. But this isn't love.* Fists, beatings, and humiliation were not love.

Shaking my head, I shed my clothes and headed to the bathroom. I made it just in time for nausea and vomiting to hit from the emotional trauma of the night. I slumped down on the bathroom floor; the flood of tears broke the dam; and all my fears, frustrations, disappointments, and indecision flowed onto the tile floor.

I didn't know how long I sat on that cold bathroom floor. I stood gingerly to ease the soreness of my battered body and turned the shower water on. The hot water pounded against my bruises and scrapes and made me yelp with pain. I was reminded me of why it was a good idea to leave for home in the morning and not go back to the flat. I couldn't believe I still was struggling with going home versus going to the flat and back to him. It should have been a no-brainer. Part of my counseling to victims of domestic violence had been "Once you are away, stay away. Don't go back to the person who believed he had the right to hurt you." Yet I now understood their hesitancy to stay away.

The hot water turned cold and jolted me out of my reverie. I quickly turned the water off and wrapped myself in a fluffy towel warmed by the towel warmer on the wall. *Brits sure know how to treat themselves; I'll give them that. Well, except for no bellboy or elevator.*

I spotted my phone on the bed as I walked out of the bathroom. As much as I tried not to look at it for a call from Thomas, I did anyway. There had been no incoming calls. There were no voice mails. I sat on the chair next to the writing desk and studied my phone. It would be the considerate thing to do to call and let him know I was okay and safe at the hotel, right? But why hadn't he called to find out for himself? Calling him would just invite trouble. If he knew where I was, he could come there to see for himself, and then what? More beating? More humiliation? I threw the phone onto the bed, disgusted with myself for even thinking of calling him.

I laid clothes out for tomorrow's flight and then put my boozy garments in the plastic laundry bag supplied by the hotel. I said a silent prayer they wouldn't smell up the rest of the clothes and put them in the case.

I looked up, and my reflection in the mirror haunted me again. I instantly came to the conclusion that no amount of makeup would ever cover the bruises and blackened eyes, which had deepened even more. *Maybe I should wait a few days to fly home and let them heal. But it's too late now.* I wasn't about to pay another hundred pounds for a ticket change.

All of a sudden, my phone rang. Could it be him? I hurried to retrieve it from the bed before he hung up.

"Hello?" I stammered into the phone with hope in my voice.

"Hello. Is this Sara Matthews?"

My heart dropped to the floor. I affirmed the caller was speaking to Sara.

"This is British Air, just confirming that the change you made on your ticket was made by you and not someone else."

"Yes, I made the change about an hour ago." My voice was flat with disappointment. *Oh man, I'm a sick woman to be disappointed it wasn't the man who beat me on the other end.*

"That's all I need. Thank you, Ms. Matthews. Cheers."

Was it good or bad he hadn't called?

I didn't remember dialing his number. It was as if I were in a dream and none of what had happened that night had been real. We had been business partners, friends, and lovers, and it felt normal to call him and let him know my flight had been changed to tomorrow morning. After all, he had a right to know. Didn't he?

"Hullo?" came his slurred greeting when he answered.

"Hi, Thomas. I just wanted you to know I changed my flight to tomorrow morning without a problem. I'm at the Royal Chace and plan to grab a taxi to the airport tomorrow." I knew exactly what I was doing: I was giving him one more chance to say he was sorry. One more chance to ask me to come back to him. One more chance to be in his arms again.

"Bollocks. Have a nice flight." He hung up.

No "I'm sorry" or "Come back to the flat" or "I love you."

I sat on the bed, frozen, and stared at the now silent phone. Emptiness filled me like a black hole. I was alone, a battered, bruised, brokenhearted, huddled heap sitting on a hotel bed in a strange place with strange people. Who cared? Mom wasn't there to remind me how worthless I was, yet I could almost hear her words. Thomas wasn't there to wrap me in his arms and tell me he would never hurt me again. Jackson would never know how low his mom had fallen.

Maybe by not saying he was sorry, loved me, and wanted me to come back to the flat, he had just saved my life.

Chapter 40

Home's where you go when you run out of homes.
—John le Carré, *The Honourable Schoolboy*

While I didn't look a lot better the next morning, I smelled a lot better without the unique booze perfume Thomas had thrust upon me. I repacked the few things I had taken out for the night and called down to the desk for a taxi to take me to Heathrow. With a heavy heart, I grabbed my things and stepped out of my room.

The smell of breakfast being served assaulted my senses, and my empty stomach growled in protest of not having had dinner last night. *I'll get something at the airport*, I promised myself.

I kept my head low and tried to hide my black eyes until I settled the bill at the registration desk. Just once, I looked up and caught my reflection in the mirror behind the clerk. I almost didn't recognize myself—black eyes, swollen face covered in bruises and scratches, lips split with dried blood on them. Still, the clerk treated me as if nothing were amiss.

I don't understand these Brits. I dragged my suitcase and repositioned the laptop bag on my shoulder as I made my way to the waiting taxi.

Settled into the taxi's backseat, I pulled my phone out of my purse, eager to see if Thomas had called; he hadn't. He could have at least called to check if I was all right or if I needed anything. To tell me he was sorry.

For a time, I gazed out the taxi window, not seeing and not even thinking. After a while, I looked back at my phone and then dropped my head. The silent tears broke free. Once again, I felt as if I had lost everything; my hopes and dreams had been stripped out from underneath me. There was no hope left in my soul. No new dreams replaced my dashed dreams. I wished I could just disappear.

That day's taxi driver was different from last night's driver. While I knew he couldn't have helped but notice my condition, he responded much as his fellow Brits at the hotel had and didn't ask if I needed anything. I received not even a "What happened to you?" I supposed I should have been used to that behavior. Still, it was difficult knowing I looked like a woman who had been beaten up, and no one seemed to care enough to offer compassion. I smiled a little as I remembered the cockney taxi driver who'd driven me to the hotel last night. My heart had warmed at his offer of help when he'd given me his card and a fiver. It helped to know that at least one person in the world cared and hadn't been afraid to reach out.

We arrived at Heathrow in plenty of time for me to check in to my flight, get through security, and get something to eat. I felt like an invisible woman as I walked through the airport. People looked at me and then quickly looked away, as if they recognized they had just seen a monster. It was the same at the café near my gate, where

I stopped to get something to eat. No one spoke to me; no one looked at me. The waitress took my order without a glance at me, although I was sure she'd looked at me when I walked in.

I was invisible, like I'd been all my life. The hollowness of having no one on my side chilled my insides and brought a shudder throughout my body. *Alone. Again. Unlovable and alone.*

I sipped my coffee and looked at my phone again. Damn, he hadn't called. *Maybe I should call him.* What if he had drunk himself into a coma after I left? It took me a few more minutes to persuade myself to call him. I dialed his number.

"Hullo?" came the sleepy-sounding greeting.

"Hi. I'm at the airport, waiting on my flight back to the States. How are you feeling this morning?" *Shouldn't he have asked me that question?*

"Yeah, I'm fine. Will be better after some coffee. When do you get into Seattle?"

I was surprised by his question. I was not sure why. Maybe because I could have construed it as caring about me. "Six o'clock tonight my time."

"Well, have a good trip." *Click.*

No "I'm sorry" or "I love you." No indication of remorse at all. *I suppose that clinches it. We are over.*

My breakfast arrived, but I wasn't hungry anymore. I gathered my things, paid the bill, and walked out of the café with a confused mind and a shattered heart.

The nine-hour nonstop flight to Seattle was uneventful. Exhausted from overthinking what had happened over the past few days, I slept for most of the trip. I felt fortunate to have scored a window seat, where I hid my face from the other passengers.

After I passed through customs, I dragged my heavy luggage behind me to the gates for the Whidbey Island SeaTac shuttle, which took me back to the island. The words *back to the island* wrapped me in a cloak of safety. I took a cab from the shuttle's drop-off point to the new house, the home for which I was supposed to hand over my settlement to Thomas for the down payment. How foolish I had been to promise away my money to a man who so easily abused me. I wouldn't hand over that money. Absolutely not.

The moment I stepped into our home, I felt as if a blanket of security had been thrown over my shoulders. I wandered from room to room to get my bearings back. I sat on the bed in the master bedroom while dreams of what I'd thought would have happened there—love and caring and sharing—flowed back into my heart. It wouldn't happen now. It would never happen to me. The loss of what I believed Thomas and I had had together pained me to the point of near suffocation.

I gathered myself together and made my way to the office, passing by boxes that waited to be unpacked. My cloud of sadness followed me. I remembered how excited and hopeful I had been to move in with Thomas and make that our first real home. I had envisioned us working side by side on our projects there in that room until we called it a day and shared a drink while we cooked dinner together.

I wandered back into the living room and sank down onto the brand-new overstuffed sofa we had picked out together. My mind wandered back to the days when we had been like kids on Christmas morning as we opened up our front door to a fresh new life together. Now there were no more holidays to plan for. The barbecues I'd thought we'd have to celebrate our new house would never happen. The pain of knowing my dreams were crushed like fine dust stabbed at my heart.

Hours passed by while I napped and dreamed of a future that had been forever changed. I woke to a dark living room. I went into the kitchen to check if I had left any wine behind when I left for London.

"Eureka! We struck gold!" I shouted out loud. I grabbed one of the several bottles of chilled wine and poured a nice tall glass of what I felt was my only friend left in the world. "Ah, this is just what the doctor ordered."

I decided to make a list of what I needed to do, sorted by priority: "Call regarding getting my old apartment. Get a storage unit. Hire movers." The more I wrote on the list, the more I recognized how much I would need to do. My stomach churned when I realized the cost of moving back to my old apartment, but it couldn't be helped. I'd left Thomas, but I wouldn't be leaving my stuff behind.

Then Thomas called.

FIVE

Whidbey Island

Chapter 41

Expression is saying what you really feel.
Impression is saying what others want to hear.
—Krishna Saagar Rao

I picked up my phone on the last ring before the call went to voice mail. "Hello?"

"Cheers, love. Have you made it back to the island yet?" I heard the sound of ice clinking in the background.

Drinking again? Or drinking still? "So good to hear from you," I said with sarcasm. "Yes, I'm back at the house, trying to figure out my next steps."

"Next steps?" he asked in between sips of his drink.

I was taken by surprise at his noticeable forgetfulness. "I look like a refugee caught in the middle of a war because of you. I won't be your punching bag anymore. You can't control your anger."

"Do you mean what I think you mean?"

I took a deep breath for focus and strength. "I have to walk away from our personal relationship. It's up to you if you want to continue our business relationship. Still, there need to be changes made in that arrangement too." My voice sounded strong, yet my insides crumbled. *Sara, do not lose your resolve now.*

"Darlin', you don't mean that, right?" he responded in a condescending voice.

Yes! I screamed to myself. *I damn well mean it.*

"I love you so much, more than life itself. I swear on my father's grave I will never lift a finger toward you in anger again; the only touches you will feel from me are ones that caress, soothe, and excite you." His voice softened, along with my resolve.

Oh, Sara, do you really crave love so much that you would allow this man back in your life?

"Please, Sara, don't do this to us. We are so good together. I can't live without you in my life," he pleaded.

Was he begging? Then I heard him take another sip of his Pernod and imagined the licorice aroma of the liqueur wafting through the phone's invisible line. "I can't go back to an *us* right now, Thomas. If you want to stay business partners, I will but with a contract that spells out responsibilities and obligations. I'll call the rental agency in the morning to see if I can get my old apartment back. I will make arrangements for movers to move me back and put what doesn't fit in the apartment in storage."

"Bollocks, Sara. Give yourself time to think this over. Has nothing I said made a difference in your thinking? I love you, for Christ's sake. We are so good together, in and out of bed. Don't you love me anymore?"

I couldn't answer him right away. The voice in my heart said to tell him, "Yes, I love you very much, and my dream was to spend the rest of my life with you." But if I did what my heart dictated, how would I explain to my son that I lived with a man who had abused me? The most important thing to me was to have the respect of my son.

"Thomas, your anger gets worse when you drink. You drink Pernod in the morning instead of coffee, and you drink all day into the night. I fear you are an alcoholic, and until you do something to control your drinking, I can't put myself in the way of your rage any longer. It's just that simple."

"I am not an alcoholic—that is just your excuse to shift the blame to me. If you didn't do the things you do to anger me, this whole conversation would be moot."

"What in the hell do I do to deserve the beatings you give me?"

"Don't be daft, Sara. You know very well what you do to provoke me. It's simple: stop that kind of behavior, and my anger won't be unleashed."

I knew his anger wasn't my fault, yet his words touched me in my soul. The soul that had been molded by the way my mom had treated me. "How can I stop what I'm doing if I don't know what I'm doing to make you mad?"

"I'll let you know when you behave that way the next time. Take note when I do, and we will be fine."

My anger ignited again. "Recall those times you abused me— Lord knows there are enough to draw from—and tell me now," I demanded.

I heard the clink of ice cubes against the mouthpiece of the phone before he answered, as if more booze gave him time to think and bolstered his courage. After a long pause, he replied.

"Okay, I'll concede I may have hurt you because I let my anger get out of hand, and, Sara, you don't know how much I regret that."

His voice had turned into barely a whisper. Could I trust him to live by his word?

"I don't know, Thomas. I don't think we should continue this relationship, for both of our sakes. If I upset you to the point of rage, it tells me we are not good together."

"Look, just think it over, okay, love? Stay in the house, unpack the boxes, have a nice glass of wine, and think it over. I would be lost if you weren't in my life."

I paused, not for effect but because confusion replaced the conviction I had felt earlier. *What do I do? You know what to do, Sara.* "Okay, I'll think it over."

With those five words, I had been defeated. I had caved in.

As a little girl, I'd lost myself in fairy tales in which the prince always got the princess, and they lived happily ever after. After Mom had torn me down with her harsh words, I'd gone into my room and lost myself in my favorite stories. I'd had dreams of a happily-ever-after life with every man I'd been with, a life in which love would overcome every bump in the road. So far, that hadn't happened. In the end, those men, including my soon-to-be ex-husband, had told me they didn't love me anymore.

But Thomas hadn't said he didn't love me anymore. On the contrary, he proclaimed his love for me. He wanted us to be together and to overcome the chasm that had drifted in between us. Could I be on the edge of throwing a beautiful relationship to the wind because of a few rages against me? If I read between his words, it seemed he wanted my love and help to assist him in overcoming his loss of control. Wasn't that what two people in love did for each other—support one another when one was having trouble?

Thomas and I had a growing business together, which promised to secure my financial health. It would be a long haul, but he seemed determined to make our business a success and knew all the right people through his network who could become future clients. What did I have without him? A flailing web design business on an island with a limited pool of clients, no energy to market myself off-island to gain more lucrative customers, and a mountain of debt. I was not getting any younger, and the potential for making a living for myself was limited. I had no college degree. I envisioned myself living in that dingy throwback-to-the-1970s apartment for the rest of my life. If I hadn't been depressed before, that reality alone was depressing.

I left the wine bottle and my glass where they were and made my way to the bedroom.

I had made up my mind.

Chapter 42

How 'bout a shot of truth in that denial cocktail.
—Jennifer Salaiz

The night before, I had made up my mind to stay with Thomas, but now more questions came to haunt me. How could I be sure he would change? I knew he wouldn't change overnight; it would take time. Time, patience, and unconditional love were elements he would need, and I believed I could provide that for him.

The morning was filled with unpacking and thinking. I decided to unpack my boxes. I didn't call the property management office to re-lease my apartment. It was not a conscious action; I had made my decision last night, and that day, I followed through.

As I wandered from room to room, I was pleased with how the house had transformed into a home. I loved my office, which had once been a bedroom. Windows overlooked the cove, and a thick forest was to the side of the house. I felt at peace there, a place where natural beauty was almost touchable and where my creativity would flow. The more I unpacked, the more the home became mine. I knew it was time to pick up Kitty from Ray and introduce her to her new home to complete the new feeling.

While Ray wasn't particularly happy to see me, Kitty jumped into my arms as soon as she saw me. Ray and I spoke a few words before Kitty was in her carrier, and we were off to our new home.

Everywhere I went, Kitty followed. I scooped her up into my arms, and we wandered into the kitchen together to fix some lunch. My phone was on the counter and showed several voice mails had come in from Thomas. *Crap.* I picked up my phone and, without listening to his voice mails, dialed his number.

"Hullo, love," he said cheerily. "I was getting worried about you."

I listened to his voice's tone to see if I detected any sign of sarcasm or anger, but there was none. "I just caught up on unpacking and hadn't paid attention to the time. I went to get Kitty and brought her home. What have you been up to?"

"Does all this unpacking mean what I think it means?" he asked, and I heard the familiar sound of ice clinking in his glass.

"Well, yes, I suppose it does. But hear this: I won't be an outlet for your anger anymore." I steeled myself for an angry reply.

"All I can do is promise. What I do, how I will behave, will show you how committed I am to keeping my promise," Thomas said calmly with no hint of anger. Then came the clink of ice cubes again.

"Look, why don't we talk about this tonight?" I was unsettled by the sound of the ice cubes in his glass as he took another sip.

"Good idea. Let me fill you in on the modeling project. We need you to get started with the requirements. I have an empty database to fill."

I moved from the kitchen to the office to take notes, and we talked about the project for another hour. Something bothered me about the call, but I couldn't put my finger on what it was. He was calm, even-toned, and patient. So what bothered me?

I leaned back in my chair and closed my eyes, running through our conversation in my mind. Then it hit me: the constant clink of ice coming from his end. He drank through our entire conversation, and who knew how much he had drunk before the call? Thomas could drink from morning to night without signs of having drunk at all. He also had been drinking all day every time he'd lost control of his anger.

A new plan formed for me. I'd stay with Thomas if he got help for his alcoholism. I knew his getting help would be an easier-said-than-done kind of thing, but if he genuinely wanted us to be together, he'd have to. What if he refused? *You have to be strong, Sara. Follow through with the consequences if he doesn't agree. You might not survive another beating.*

I knew that to be true, yet there was a part of me that didn't believe he would ever go that far.

I spent the rest of the day setting up my office with the technology I would need to start on our modeling company project. The room looked like a real office by dinnertime, with everything in its place and the empty boxes taken to the garage. It was a small but cozy room.

It had turned to dusk when I finally stopped working. I leaned back in my faux-leather office chair and, sipping wine, watched the headlights of cars across the cove reflect on the water. It had been a good day. I had been alone, but I hadn't been lonely. I luxuriated in my aloneness. Kitty was company enough, and we always had inspiring conversations. Maybe I didn't need a man in my life.

I hadn't called my friends to let them know I had returned to the island. I needed time alone to think through my relationship with Thomas and let my bruises and black eyes heal. I would have died of humiliation if anyone had known what Thomas had done to me. Everyone told me what strong woman I was, but they only saw the outside. I could never let them know the person I was on the inside. If they found out who I really was, my facade would crumble, and I'd be exposed as a fake.

I took one last look at the darkening sky and the headlights across the cove and then stood and turned out the lights. I made my way to the kitchen for a well-deserved glass of wine. My bruises and black eyes had better be gone soon, I thought; there were only two bottles of wine left. Dinner was a no-brainer: popcorn and wine. I was content and happy.

My phone rang as I settled on the sofa with my wine and dinner; it was Thomas. "Hello, sweetie," I chirped brightly. My voice reflected my mood. *What's wrong with you, Sara? Have you already forgotten about your black eyes and who put them there?*

"You sound cheery," he said.

"It's been a good day. Unpacking is ninety-nine percent done, and the office is ready for me to start work tomorrow."

"That's fabulous news, love. You must be tired after doing all that."

"Not really. I feel energized and ready to buckle down to work. I've been thinking about us—a lot, in fact. I think I've come up with a proposal that would be good for both of us."

"Listening." *Clink* went the ice cubes.

"Well, look, there's no other way to say it: when you drink, you get angry, and that's when you hurt me. And you drink all the time." I felt the grip of silent panic growing like a fireball in the pit of my stomach. *Panic is just a four-letter word. Panic is just a four-letter word.* I kept repeating the mantra until I felt in control again. "I think you have a drinking problem, Thomas, and I can't be with you until you deal with it." *There. I said it.* I sighed with relief and waited for his response.

In the silence that flowed through our wireless connection, I heard breathing and the clink of ice cubes in his glass. It felt like hours before he said something; in reality, it was seconds.

"Look, you cheeky bitch, I have no drinking problem. Understand?" His voice was low and measured, as if he were talking to a child. *Clink* went the ice cubes, and *click* went the phone.

My mouth dropped open, and I stared at the phone. Had I been in as much denial about him as he was about his drinking?

Chapter 43

There's a really good chance that I've confused what I "need" with what I "want." And if that's the case, I'm looking for both in the wrong place.
—Craig D. Lounsbrough

His answer was to hang up on me. I shuddered to think if I had been there with him. His anger would most likely have resulted in more black eyes and bruises. He said he loved me. Why wouldn't he want to do something about his drinking to preserve the love we had for each other? If he didn't love me enough to deal with his drinking problem, why did he want me to stay?

Logic told me he couldn't hurt me now, but I felt he had conditioned me to expect the worst even when I wasn't near him. I was consumed with thoughts about him and fear of what he might do to me next.

I knew that for my own safety and sanity, I needed to keep my promise to myself. Our personal relationship was over unless he did something about his drinking.

⚬⛓⚬

The next morning brought the promise of spring. The soft, furry pussy willows formed on the trees, and daffodils stretched for the sun from their winter's bed in the cool, moist earth. The red robins gathered their breakfast of worms, and the resident eagles swooped the cove in search of their breakfast. It was a time of renewal, a time of healing, a time for hope. There was still a nip to the air, which made my world crisp and alive.

My mood clouded when I remembered I hadn't called Jackson to let him know I was home. He'd probably want to get together. As battered as I still looked, I shuddered, knowing I'd have to decline. It broke my heart, especially after I had made him promise to call when he was on the island. I promised myself I'd call as soon as all signs of bruising were gone.

On my way to the shower, I caught my reflection in the mirror. The bruises had faded into a yellowish tint, and my cut lip didn't look as bad as it had yesterday. I'd hoped the evidence of Thomas's last beating would be better healed by then. Groceries would have to wait. I still had lots of popcorn and cereal, and there was leftover vodka that Thomas had in the house as a backup if I ran out of wine.

It was late morning by the time I settled into my office and began to work. I logged in to the network and reviewed the database Thomas had developed, which took the rest of the morning and early afternoon.

I hadn't looked at my emails since last evening and was stunned to see emails from Thomas fill my screen. There were fifteen, all in a row. I opened the first one.

Stupid bitch,

I am *not* an alcoholic, and for you to insinuate I am shows me you are using me for your own monetary gain. My drinking has nothing to do with the quality of work I do and especially nothing to do with my anger. Have you considered *you* might be an alcoholic? Your constant nagging about my drinking sets me off, and I just want to beat it out of you.

Get help for your drinking problem!

Thomas

Oh my God, he had turned this around on me—unbelievable. I moved on to the next emails; they were all the same, deflecting the blame for our problems onto me with vitriolic language. The words he used reeled me back to my childhood and things my mom had said to me when I told her about her husband molesting me. She'd used horrible, debasing names, and of course, she had deflected the blame for his molestation onto me.

With each email read, my confidence was torn to shreds. His words were worse than his fists; they attacked the very core of my being and left my soul empty, a black hole that sucked into his words as my truth.

After the last email, I knew I was in no shape to continue working with the modeling company's requirements, coding them into the database. Desolation consumed me. I felt emotionally bankrupt. There was nothing more to say or feel—nothing left but the void that sucked my mind into numbness. I'd accepted that kind of behavior from my mom because I'd believed her. But the little success I'd had with Phillip's company had shown me I was worth more than being someone's verbal and physical punching bag.

Or was I? I had allowed Thomas to treat me just like Mom

had—why? Was I programmed to be the whipping post of others? I had been defeated by those who proclaimed their love for me yet betrayed me.

There was nothing more to do but take myself to bed and shut out the rest of the world, a world that had always told me I didn't belong.

⌗

I woke to the sound of my phone ringing. I rose up on my elbow and looked at the caller ID: Thomas. I flopped back onto the bed and let the call be sent to voice mail. The phone rang again and again, but I ignored the calls. Five times he called, until I angrily picked up the phone.

"What do you want, Thomas?" I surprised myself with the strength of my voice.

"Cheers yourself, love." He didn't sound angry at all. I felt as if I were in a dream; it was surreal. He was like Dr. Jekyll and Mr. Hyde. "I have some good news for you," he said.

I relaxed somewhat, curious to learn of his good news.

"I went to the doctor today and got myself evaluated." He paused, probably so I'd ask him what he was talking about, but I remained silent and waited for him to continue. "I was evaluated for alcoholism. And guess what? His learned opinion is I am not an alcoholic."

The clink of ice cubes told me he was drinking—alcohol, I assumed. I said a silent prayer of thanks I wasn't with him. "What kind of doctor did you go to?"

"He is a psychologist specializing in addictions. He positively confirmed I am not an alcoholic."

"Did you tell him you drink all day and into the night and get mean when you do?" I felt brave with more than three thousand miles and an ocean separating us.

"Look, he said I was not. Bollocks, what more do you need?"

"Well, why don't you get a copy of his diagnosis and send it to me?" My heart beat in my throat; I knew I had pushed it.

"Bollocks, Sara, you keep moving the goalposts. What is it going to take to convince you?" *Clink* went the ice cubes.

"Thomas, I can't be with you when you drink like this. Your emails of today ripped a hole inside me. I couldn't function. And well, now I believe you are lying to me. If I were there saying these things to you in person, I would be a battered mess right now, and you know it."

"Look, love, go get yourself a glass of wine, and chill out. You are making too much out of this." His voice had mellowed and lost the edge that indicated his anger was about to explode. I almost preferred his rage over this measured, condescending tone.

"Thomas, I don't need wine; I need you to tell me the truth."

"You know I think you are a smart and intelligent woman. I just said those things in my emails because you pissed me off with the carrot you dangled that you would stay with me if I got help for what you claimed was my alcoholism. I've done that, I've been cleared, and now you need more from me. Don't you see how you keep me on a string, and sometimes that string breaks? Let's just forget all this crap and get back to work."

Once again, he blamed me for his behavior and dismissed the impact his emails had had on me. I knew I would not be in the same house with that man ever again, but how would I work with him as long as he continued to behave that way toward me?

I needed time to think. Maybe I had taken the easy way to financial health when I'd considered staying in business with him. The project for the modeling company would put me ahead financially. I'd already started on it, so I might as well finish, take the money I earned, and then cut ties with Thomas forever, I thought.

After all, he was in London and not on Whidbey Island, so I'd be safe.

Chapter 44

Ask me no questions, and I'll tell you no fibs.
—Oliver Goldsmith, *She Stoops to Conquer*

"Are you still there?" His voice brought me back to our conversation.

"Yes, sorry. I was thinking through the options. Look, you know I need the work and the money, so I will finish the development and design work on our current project. But—and this is a huge *but*—I need an advance of my share of the invoice, and you have to promise you will send me no more emails like the ones you sent last night. Also, promise you will not call so often—it disrupts my work. I will send daily updates via email." My mouth turned into a desert while I waited for his response.

"You are getting forty thousand from your settlement, right? Take fifteen thousand, consider it your advance, and put the rest in my bank account for your part of the down payment. We'll settle up the fifteen thousand when we get paid in full. You know we aren't getting paid until the work is complete, and I don't have money for an advance for you."

My blood ran cold in my veins at his response. I evaluated my options. With his plan, I would lose all my settlement. What if I promised to follow his course of action but never put the money in his account? I could tell him that a backup in the courts had delayed my divorce. What could he do? By the time he discovered I had lied, my work on the project would be completed, and my share of the invoice would be deposited in my bank account.

"Are you still there?" Impatience was evident in his voice.

"Yes, sorry. Just thinking through what you said. Okay, I will keep fifteen thousand and put the rest in your account." I lied with fingers crossed behind my back. I hoped my plan worked. Until then, I would continue to live in the house.

"Okay, deal. Look, I've got another call coming in. I'll ring you later to see how you're coming on the project. I love you, sweetie. Get crackin'."

"I love you too," I lied, keeping the sarcasm from my voice. Doubt crawled into my resolve to follow through with my plan. If Thomas found out, there was no telling what he would do to me. He could fly to the States anytime—nothing kept him in the United Kingdom—and that was the last thing I needed. *Play along with him, Sara. Don't hint at what you've really planned, or you will be a dead woman.*

I celebrated my newfound assertiveness and poured a glass of wine out of my last bottle. Raising my glass to Kitty, I said, "Cheers," and I swallowed a sip of the golden nectar. I felt different. Was that what confidence felt like?

I looked around for Mom. She always seemed to pop in when I was low so she could take me lower and put me on the path of low self-esteem again. But she wasn't there. I hoped she would stay away forever.

I wasn't in the mood for work, so what the heck? It would wait until morning. I had been on a high since my conversation with Thomas. What if I took his name off the credit card? Would he suspect my underlying intentions if I did? No, I couldn't take that chance.

I glanced out the window and noticed the vibrant sunset. Sunsets on Whidbey Island were the most beautiful in the world. I grabbed my glass and wine bottle and went out to the deck to gaze peacefully at the colors the sunset painted in the sky. I couldn't remember having had that sense of peace before; I had never felt so in control of my own life.

⭗⭘

The next morning, I got up bright and early, ready to attack the database with the requirements and even more prepared to be finished with that project and with Thomas. I had no clue what I would do after I completed the project, but I knew anything would be better than living with him.

I'd been home from London for ten days, and while the bruises were fading well, they were still too visible for me to go to the market. *Popcorn and vodka it will be tonight then.* Maybe I would finally lose those extra pounds.

I put my phone on silent and then focused on the work that needed to be done. I noticed Thomas called a few times, but I didn't stop to answer. Instead, I let him go to voice mail. It was late afternoon before I stopped working, having programmed a third of the database's requirements. At that rate, I should be done with that part of the project in about a week. Then I could start on the design phase and then testing, and then, if all went well, I would be free of Thomas and his web of abuse. It couldn't come soon enough.

It was getting close to happy hour. I picked up my phone and Kitty, went into the kitchen, and poured vodka and tonic into a glass filled with ice. It was another gorgeous island evening. The deck beckoned me to listen to the birds, breathe in some fresh air, and wait for another spectacular sunset. I set my glass down on the counter and picked up my phone to listen to Thomas's voice mails. By the third voice mail, his voice had the telltale signs of the beginnings of anger, and by the fifth, he definitely had turned to anger. Funny, I didn't feel paralyzed with fear. Was it because we weren't on the same continent? The reason didn't matter; I enjoyed the new feeling.

I smiled as I dialed his number. *Sticks and stones may break my bones, but words will never hurt me.*

"Where have you been?" he said in greeting.

Oh great. He definitely was in a mood. "I've been right here working on the requirements and database. Haven't you checked into the network to review the progress?" My voice was calm, sweetly so.

"Didn't you get my calls? I must've called ten times." He was agitated.

I said a silent prayer of thanks he was in London. "You called five times, and since I was focused on work, I let you go to voice mail. Surely you can understand why I didn't want to break my concentration on this critical part of our work."

He somewhat calmed down, and I briefed him on my progress, which he seemed pleased with. "Hey, love, I've been thinking of coming to the island. We can work together, and I can troubleshoot any database problems on the spot instead of eight hours later because of the time difference. I've been looking at flights, and I can be there in a few days. What do you think?"

My heart jumped into my throat and stopped. I hoped he hadn't heard my gasp at his suggestion. Oh God, that was all I needed. His coming there would ruin all my plans. My stomach turned, and bile burned my throat at the thought of being in the same house as him for more than a few hours.

"Well, I don't think that is necessary." I felt my newfound assertiveness dissolve. Why couldn't I just tell him no?

"It probably isn't necessary, but I'm lonesome for you, and I want to see the house again. I'll check on flights and let you know."

"Okay." How could I tell him to stay there? What excuse could I use?

"Look, love, I've got another call coming in. Chat later?"

"Sure," I said without conviction. How could I keep Thomas in London? I would never survive his rage if he found out I had lied to him about my divorce settlement. I had to think of a plan that would not raise his suspicions—and fast.

My thoughts switched to the phone call that had interrupted ours. Whom did he talk to so much? Last time I'd asked him, he'd told me it was "just a mate." He was on the phone with his mate more than a teenage girl was with her boyfriend. It bothered me more than I liked to admit. I wondered if he had another girlfriend. If he did, it might help me keep him in London until the project was over.

I watched the sky slowly turn to brilliant colors of orange, pink, and blue, which signaled the oncoming of sunset. While I watched the colors change their hues, I worked on a strategy to keep Thomas in London and off the island.

Chapter 45

Nothing is as deadly as the love of a powerful man.
—Nenia Campbell, *Cease and Desist*

If only I could find out who his supposed mate was, I could confront him over the phone about her. But what if I was wrong and it wasn't a girlfriend? What if it was his photographer friend? I settled back with my drink; I would need to think this through more carefully. It was a sensitive issue and would have to be handled just right.

I could be blunt and just come out and ask him again whom he talked to so much, which might be the best way rather than covertly, I thought. *He can't reach out to hurt me from three thousand miles and an ocean away.* But I thought the best way would be to wait to ask until the next time our phone call was interrupted. He couldn't avoid the question then, especially if I kept asking.

The month of May was always the best part of spring on Whidbey Island. The rhododendrons came into bloom and dotted the landscape with their gigantic flowers of red, pink, and purple. The breeze that came off the cove was not too chilly and signaled that winter was over.

The sunset faded into the blanket of night, yet I didn't want to go into the house just yet. I felt lonely to be with my friends, but it wasn't time to call them to let them know I had returned—not until my bruises and black eyes were completely healed. The last time I'd talked with Carol had been when we finalized the house purchase months ago. Thomas persuaded me away from the phone whenever I tried to call anyone—behavior typical of the cycle of abuse I'd learned about before my relationship with him. Courting came first, followed by isolation from friends and family, control of all aspects of life, and then physical and verbal abuse. Finally came the honeymoon period, when the situation was smoothed out before it happened all over again. Breaking free wasn't easy; staying was even harder.

Why did I stay with him? I supposed all victims of abuse had reasons, and mine were no different from others'. I loved him, and I saw a future with him, yet that future dimmed with each beating. He had changed me into a different person, from strong to weak, from a victim of my childhood to a victim of Thomas.

Darkness had fully extinguished the beautiful sunset, and the stars were dancing in the sky. The world seemed serene and simple, without the problems that life put on our path. Kitty meowed for her dinner, and my tummy grumbled for mine.

"Come on, Kitty. Let's go inside and rustle up some food for us."

I'd been home for twelve days. The days had turned into a boring routine. My only outlet for introspection and relaxation was the deck, which offered me the glorious gifts of nature and vibrant colors in the sky that lifted my mood. Work was going well; in fact, I was almost ready for Thomas to test the programming I had done. It wouldn't be long before the project was finished, along with my relationship with Thomas.

My black eyes and bruises were gone. I could finally join the rest of the world of the living. *Real food, chilled wine, more cat food and litter—this is what it must feel like to be sprung from prison.* Granted, my prison was of my own making, with help from Thomas, but now I was able to determine what my new normalcy would be.

First thing after my morning routine, I got into my car and drove to the post office to pick up my mail. Then I'd go to the market. Then I'd take a drive to Ebey's Landing to walk my favorite beach before going home. *Freedom at last.*

"You're back!" Jim exclaimed when I walked into the post office. I loved many things about living in a small town, and Jim, the postmaster, was one of them. He treated me like family and gave me a welcome like no other.

"Hi, Jim. It's good to see you again."

We chatted for a bit and caught up with each other, and then he disappeared in the back and came out with a tub full of my mail that had accumulated since I had been in London. I recognized a few people who waited in line for their turn to be served and gave them a smile and a hello before I carted the tub out to my car.

The next stop was Prairie Center, the town market where everyone shopped. I ran into people I hadn't seen for a while as I strolled the aisles and filled my cart. I was home—this time to stay.

Ebey's Landing, a pebbly beach west of town and the place where the first settlers of Whidbey Island had landed, was one of my favorite places on the island. I drove through Ebey's Prairie on my way, which led me down the winding, tree-lined road to the beach. I always marveled at the high bluffs and the trees gnarled into ghostly shapes by the wind that blew off Rosario Strait. As I walked among the pebbles, the waves sang a homecoming song to me. Yes, I was home. To stay.

On my way home, I decided to stop by the real estate office to say hello to Carol. I was on a high, back in familiar territory, doing ordinary everyday things, rediscovering my independence that I'd feared I had lost.

"Hi. Is Carol in?" I asked the receptionist.

"She just left to pick someone up at SeaTac's Whidbey shuttle stop to take them home. She should be back in just a few minutes, if you'd like to wait."

"No, that's okay. Would you please let her know Sara stopped in and ask her to give me a call when she has a chance?"

"Sure. She has your number?"

I confirmed she did and then left for home, eager to put the groceries away and sort through my mail. I drove down the long, winding, secluded driveway to the house and was surprised to see Carol's car parked in front of the garage. No one was in the car, and I didn't see her outside on the deck. *Strange.* She'd given us all the keys. She couldn't let herself into the house, could she?

Thinking she might be around back, I grabbed a sack of groceries and made my way to the front door with keys in hand. As I went to slip the key into the lock, I noticed the door was ajar. I hesitated and then pushed the door open and peeked inside. Not seeing anyone or noticing anything amiss, I stepped into the foyer quietly so as not to alert anyone if someone was there.

Thomas rounded the corner into the living room from the kitchen with Carol behind him.

"Oh shit." I gasped and dropped the bag of groceries.

Chapter 46

**Stepping into a tornado screams "This is the dumbest thing you will ever do."
—Shannon Messenger, *Let the Sky Fall***

My brain stuttered for a moment, and every part of me went on pause while I waited for my thoughts to catch up to the reality of Thomas standing in the living room.

"What are you doing here?"

"I live here, or had you forgotten?"

"You gave me a shock. Why didn't you tell me you were coming?" I gasped, trying to regain my composure.

"Don't be daft. I did. Don't you remember? I told you I would be flying over in the next couple of days—a couple of days ago."

I searched my memory, but I recalled only that he had been thinking about it.

Speechless and dumbfounded, I turned my focus to Carol for the first time. She looked from Thomas to me and back again with confusion on her face. I assumed Thomas was the person she'd picked up at the shuttle stop.

"Thank you for bringing him home," I managed to squeak out.

"I was happy to do it," she said as I bent to put the spilled groceries back in the bag, my entire body trembling.

"Why don't you stay and have a glass of wine with us to celebrate Thomas's homecoming?" I said. I wanted her to stay because I was afraid of what Thomas might do to me when she left. I knew Thomas had noticed my not-so-enthusiastic welcoming, and I didn't know if that would be enough to set him off. I silently prayed it wasn't.

"I'd love to, but clients are coming into the office in a few minutes. Rain check?" she asked. She looked as if she couldn't get out of the house fast enough.

"Of course." I was disappointed she wouldn't stay for a while, and my fear of being alone with Thomas overwhelmed me.

Carol gave Thomas a peck on the cheek and said a brief "Welcome home." I walked her to the door and thanked her again for fetching Thomas. I closed the door, took a deep breath, put a fake happy smile on my face, and then turned around to walk toward him.

"Wow, what a shock you gave me. I'm delighted to see you, Thomas; I had been missing you." I wrapped my arms around his neck, stood on tiptoe, and kissed him full on the lips. He didn't kiss me back.

Ripping my lips away from his, he held me at arm's length. "I don't think you are happy to see me, Sara. If you were, you would have come to kiss me and welcome me home long before this." He held me by the shoulders, away from him.

My brain raced and searched for the right answer, but the one I found was lame. "I was scared when I saw the door open; I knew I had locked it before I left. And then I was shocked to see you here." My words came fast and furious. I felt as if I were eleven again, trying to explain to Mom what her husband had done to me.

His eyes threw sparks into mine as he looked deeply into them. I felt naked and vulnerable, and with every minute that passed, my fear of him grew. It seemed as if hours passed between us before he lessened his grip on my shoulders. He pulled me close to him and kissed me with the passion a sailor might have given his girlfriend upon returning home from sea after six months.

"Welcome home," I said softly, my heart pounding. It wasn't the kiss that made my heart pound; it was fear.

"Now, that's better," he said with a grin. "How about fixing me a drink? Carol was kind enough to stop so I could get a bottle of Pernod on the way."

"Sure," I agreed. My heart was like an anchor around my chest, sinking with disappointment and fear. Earlier that afternoon, I had been on a high, enjoying my hometown and revisiting places I loved. My heart was crushed, aware that my brief feeling of independence had come to an end with Thomas's arrival.

I handed him his drink and sat in the chair opposite the sofa with a glass of wine. I remembered how he hated it when I didn't drink with him—another trigger point for his anger.

"How was your flight over here?" I tried to keep the conversation light.

"Yeah, it was boring. I hate that nine hours in the air—it feels like forever before we get here."

"Yeah, it is a forever-long flight," I said. "Did you watch any movies?"

"Naw, mostly slept and chatted with the chap in the seat next to me."

"Oh, he must've been interesting. What did y'all talk about?"

"Bollocks, Sara, let's drop this stupid conversation. Have you heard from your attorney about when your settlement comes in?"

His direct question took me by surprise, and my breath got caught in my throat. The money had been deposited in my account two days ago, but I wasn't about to tell him. He'd kill me if he ever found out.

"Um, well, I haven't heard from her about that. I've been busy getting things organized around here and catching up on the work on our project. It frankly slipped my mind," I lied.

He looked at his watch. "Too late to call tonight. Better give your attorney a call in the morning to see when we can expect it to be deposited."

I was relieved he didn't press any further, at least for that night. We drank some more and chatted for the rest of the evening. He drank three glasses of Pernod to my one glass of wine. How could a legitimate doctor have claimed he was not an alcoholic?

Our having a civilized chat seemed surreal. If others had looked at us, they wouldn't have guessed that the man on the couch was a monster and that I was his victim. Even I found it hard to believe I had not kicked him out as soon as I saw him in the house that day. *Why didn't you, Sara?* I had been strong when he wasn't there, but my strength dissolved when with him. Fear clutched at my heart while I tried to keep my outer demeanor calm.

I asked him whom he had contacted for work while in London, but all I heard was silence. I glanced over at him and saw his head lolled to one side. His empty drink glass rested on his knee and was about to fall to the floor. I reached over to take it before it dropped. I swung his legs onto the sofa, laid his head on a pillow, and covered him with the afghan I kept there to snuggle up on cold spring nights.

I watched him sleep. He looked peaceful and calm, with no hint of the rage that overtook him. Soft snores puffed from his mouth.

I looked down at his rugged facial features and marveled at how handsome he was. I'd had a vision of him as a monster for so long I had forgotten the attractive man I had fallen in love with.

I took our glasses into the kitchen and slipped them into the dishwasher, when it dawned on me: *I won't have to sleep with him tonight; we won't make love.* My relief was indescribable. *Miracles do happen.*

I tossed and turned throughout the night. No matter how confident I'd thought I was about hiding my settlement from Thomas, I trembled when I thought of what he might do if he found out. I knew I would not come out of his rage well. The thought added gasoline to the spark of fear. Above all else, I needed to keep secret the fact I had the money hidden from him.

The sun rising over the mountains in the distance signaled morning had arrived. My eyelids felt like sandpaper from my sleepless night. I looked down at the foot of the bed toward Kitty, who stretched her paws out with a yawn that could have fit two mice into her mouth. I didn't hear any noise, so I figured Thomas must still be asleep.

"Go back to sleep, Kitty, while I take my shower and get dressed." I gave her the chin rub she loved. I wanted to hurry to get into the office before Thomas woke up so I could change the password on my bank account. Idiot me had given him the password long before he started to beat me up. I shook my head. *You are naive, Sara.*

Showered and dressed, I wandered out to the kitchen for coffee. Kitty was at my heels, ready for her breakfast. I noticed Thomas wasn't on the sofa; the blanket I had thrown onto him had been neatly folded and placed on the back of the couch. The Mr. Coffee pot was half full of hot coffee, so I supposed he had been up for a while. I heard his voice faintly coming from the office. It appeared he had found his way around and made the office space his own. *Damn.*

I opened a can of cat food, spooned the food into Kitty's dish, and set it on the floor.

"Enjoy," I said to her. I grabbed a mug of coffee and made my way to the office.

I couldn't make out what Thomas was saying, but it didn't sound like a business conversation to me. This would be a good time to confront him about whom he talked to all the time, I decided.

"Morning," I said, speaking quietly so as not to interrupt his call. I sat down at my desk. We had two desks, mine and his, so we both could use the space to work when Thomas was there.

He looked up, mouthed a good morning, blew me a kiss, and left the room. I supposed he wanted privacy, as usual. It bugged me that he always was so private with his calls. I wondered what was so secretive that I couldn't be part of the conversation.

I let the thought go and settled in to open my bank account while Thomas was out of the room. My hands trembled on the keys, and my brain short-circuited, erasing my current password from my memory. I was frantic, and the more I tried, the more I couldn't recall it. *Calm down, Sara. Take deep breaths, relax, and clear your mind.* Finally, the numbers and letters that were my password came to me.

I was almost done typing the password in, when Thomas walked into the office with a glass filled with ice and Pernod. I wished he hadn't started drinking so early. I was afraid of what kind of mood he would be in if he continued to drink for the rest of the day.

"Wot's wrong? You look ill. You feeling okay?" he asked.

I quickly switched to a news website and prayed he hadn't seen my bank's website. "Oh, I was catching up on some news—not all of it good," I responded as calmly as I could.

I turned my attention to the tub of mail and started to sort through it. I opened the credit card statement with jaw clenched and a foreboding sensation deep in the pit of my stomach. How could the balance have gotten so high? It was now more than $35,000. It would take my entire divorce settlement to pay it off. I reviewed the new purchases made since the last statement; the Royal Chace amount was noted, along with Thomas's and my airplane tickets to Seattle. The rest were payments to the liquor store for his booze and a few charges to pubs. I dropped the statement onto the desk and stared out the window, not seeing the beautiful view ahead of me. What would I do? *I can't afford this bill, and Thomas will just put me off when I tell him how much his portion is.*

I had a strong urge to scream at him about the high balance and about his drinking so early in the morning, but I didn't say a word; I simply handed him the statement.

"Wot's this?" he asked, taking the statement from me.

"Just look at the balance owed, look at the new charges, and then tell me when you will pay the charges you put on the card. You need to pay this month's payment due. It is two hundred fifty dollars," I said with a half smile and a tone of voice that I hoped conveyed confidence.

He glanced at the statement and then threw it back at me. Icicles stabbed at my heart, and I feared what was about to come, but it didn't happen. Instead, he downed his drink in one gulp.

"We'll deal with this later," he said. "I'm getting another drink; then you can brief me on where you are with this project." He left the room.

I stared at his disappearing back, speechless and thankful. At least for now. We weren't fighting yet. But I knew it was only a matter of time.

Chapter 47

You fell in love with a storm. Did you really think you would get out unscathed?
—Nikita Gill

I set the bill aside and turned to my computer. He'd come back into the room at any moment. Suddenly, I felt the weight of all the stress I'd carried since he arrived, and I slumped into the chair. I was a dead woman if I couldn't succeed in putting him off about the money.

Thomas came back into the office and sat at his desk. "Okay, love, let's take a look at what you have gotten done."

I sat up in my chair and, with fear flowing through my heart, spent the next few hours going over the programming and design details of our project. He added his ideas, which enhanced the final product.

During a lull in our conversation, I turned my focus to the code on my screen. Thomas checked his phone for emails. Soon his soft voice interrupted the silence between us.

"When are you supposed to get that damned money from your divorce?" He was still looking at his phone.

His words bounced around the room and left me holding my breath and incapable of answering him. I kept focused on the screen ahead of me. My fingers pretended to make code while I tried to figure out the best way to tell him a lie he would believe.

"Did ya hear me?" he said with an edge to his voice.

"Yeah, I heard ya. Was just trying to finish this line of code." I turned to face him and put my best poker face on. "Shoot, I got so caught up in this project that I forgot all about it. I'll call my attorney tomorrow, but since I haven't heard anything, I'm guessing it hasn't come." Fingers crossed he bought into the lie.

"Bollocks, Sara. Why are you dragging your feet on this?"

"I said I will call tomorrow," I said with a forced laugh, and I turned back to the computer screen. It was apparent he wouldn't drop the issue of money. I bit my lower lip and tried to think of ways to keep putting him off. *The solution is obvious, Sara: you need to get away from him. Move out, and cut off all personal contact with him. It's the only way to safeguard your money—and your life.*

I knew enough about the danger victims faced when they left their abusers. I had to figure out a way to leave when he was not at home. The trouble with that scenario was that we had one car—mine—so if he was not in the house, he was somewhere in the car. *Don't let obstacles get in your way, Sara. Think this through, and get it right.*

When I turned to face Thomas, I was surprised to see he had left the room. I had been so deep in thought I hadn't noticed. The code on the computer screen sat idly, but I decided I didn't have the energy to deal with any more code. I saved my work and left the room for the kitchen to pour my first glass of wine of the evening.

Thomas stood in the adjoining dining room, gazing out the patio doors, talking on the phone, with a drink in hand. "It won't be long, love. She's calling her attorney tomorrow, and I'll know more then. Until then, just remember, I love you."

I froze, unable to move. His words echoed through my head. *Did I hear him right? Did he really say, "I love you," to someone other than me?*

"Sara, there you are, love. Knocking off work for the night? How about I pour you a nice glass of wine—you've earned it. You look pale. Are you feeling okay?" He acted nervous. Did he suspect I had heard his side of the conversation?

"I'm fine, I think. Who was that on the phone? Whom did you tell 'I love you' to, and why would they be interested in whether I called my attorney or not?" Shock had been replaced by curiosity and anger—a dangerous combination when throwing questions at Thomas.

"Jealous?" he responded with a laugh. "Don't be daft. I was chatting with my mum. She knows I have a few outstanding debts, one of them to her, and she wanted to know when I was going to pay her. I told her I'd pay her when you reimbursed me for the down payment on this house. That's all." He still looked at his phone, presumably to check emails that had come in while he was chatting with his mum.

I couldn't tell whether he was lying or not. I wanted to believe him, but something in my gut told me his story didn't ring true. However, I had no evidence he had lied. If I kept on questioning him, the evening would almost assuredly turn out bad for me, so I dropped it for now.

"How is your mum?" I asked, pouring myself a glass of wine. I stuffed my earlier alarm at his words.

"Same bitch as ever," he replied sarcastically.

"What a terrible thing to say about your mum!" I'd heard him say disparaging words about his mum many times. I always wondered what had happened to turn their relationship so sour. Yet just a few moments ago, he'd told her he loved her. Where did the truth lie?

"Let's talk about something else. Talking about my mum is depressing." He poured himself another glass of Pernod, walked into the living room, took up his perch on the sofa, and grabbed the remote to the television off the coffee table.

We settled into a movie and more drinking. I was not terribly interested in the film, and my mind drifted back to Thomas's phone conversation. Why hadn't I believed him when he'd said it was his mum on the phone? He hadn't looked me in the eye when he told me. Wouldn't he have if his story was really the truth? Was he talking to his mum all those times he spent outside on the phone? Maybe he would pass out on the couch that night, and I could sneak a peek at his phone to check numbers and messages, I thought.

"Earth to Sara," Thomas said, trying to get my attention. "Be a dear and fetch me another drink, will ya?"

I just stared at him, frustrated at being considered his personal flunky. *He's been drinking a lot today. Better to push my frustration down and do as he asked, or I might be sorry.*

"You drank all the Pernod," I told him once in the kitchen with his empty glass.

"Then make it brandy and Coke."

That sounded like trouble on the horizon. He wouldn't stop drinking until he drank all the booze in the house or passed out, whichever came first. I said a silent prayer he would pass out first.

"Cheers," he said as I handed him his brandy.

I tipped my freshly poured glass of wine in his direction and sat back in my chair. It probably was not a good idea for me to drink so much when he had been drinking so heavily, I thought. My brain was already fuzzy from the wine; I chuckled out loud, thinking his blows didn't hurt as bad if I was a little tipsy.

"What's so funny?" Thomas asked, turning to face me.

"Oh, nothing. I was just thinking about something funny Carol said." Still smiling, I hoped he bought into my lie.

"What did she say? Was it about me?"

"Naw, I can't remember it all, just bits and pieces, and it was a while ago. It was just a silly joke."

His eyes became more intense. His voice was thick and low, menacing. "Tell me."

"I told you I can't remember it all. I just remember it was funny."

"Tell me." He leaned closer to my chair—so close I could smell the alcohol on his breath.

I reached out and gently touched his knee as the cluster of spark plugs in my abdomen buzzed a warning. I tried to push the air from my lungs and softly spoke to him. "Please, Thomas, let's not go there. Not tonight."

Chapter 48

Broken people don't hide from their monsters.
Broken people let themselves be eaten.
—Francesca Zappia, *Eliza and Her Monsters*

Thomas's movement was sudden and sleek; he pounced like a cat. Before I understood what had happened, he flipped my chair over onto its back. He quickly jumped on me and pinned me to it. His weight knocked the wind out of me; his hands clutched my neck. His eyes were wild with rage; his lips curled cruelly. My hands tore at his as I tried to pull them away from my throat. My consciousness ebbed, and my grasp on his wrists became weaker. I fought against the darkness that tried to steal my wakefulness away, but the darkness was stronger than I was.

A cold splash on my face brought me back from the dark. Sputtering, I realized I was still on my back in the tipped-over chair.

Thomas stood over me with a brandy snifter in one hand and my empty wineglass, whose contents he'd thrown onto me, in the other.

"Get up, bitch," Thomas ordered. His voice sounded strange, like a sharp razor cutting through the fog the blackness had left in its wake.

I gently touched my neck and winced with pain. My throat felt like a ball of sandpaper when I tried to swallow. Every movement made pain stab at me.

"Come on, stupid cow. Get up," Thomas said, and he kicked me in the ribs.

"Oof, I'm trying, Thomas." Fear gripped my soul; that night would not end well. I struggled to stand so he wouldn't hurt me again.

"Not good enough, bitch." He scowled and kicked me again.

He left for the kitchen while I nursed my ribs. The pain was excruciating but did not deter me from finding a way to get away from him. I staggered toward the front door, but he came back into the room with drinks in hand. He quickly caught me just as I reached for the doorknob. He grabbed my arm and swung me around to face him. Without a word, he threw the full glass of wine he'd brought from the kitchen into my face.

I sputtered again, my eyes stinging from the alcohol. He raised his brandy glass over my head, tipped it, and let the brandy splash over me. It had been a mistake to stay in that house after he showed up, and now I was about to find out just how much of a mistake I'd made. *I've got to figure out a way to get the hell out of this house and away from him.*

"Make yourself useful, and go get us another drink. That's all you're good for anyway," he ordered, handing me both glasses.

I thought of breaking a glass, cutting him, and running out of there. *Crazy, stupid idea. That won't solve the problem, Sara. Think. Maybe if you just do what he says, he won't hurt you anymore.*

I didn't want another drink, but I figured he'd strike out at me if I walked into the living room without one. With hands that trembled, I handed him the brandy.

He sat back down on the couch, and I straightened the chair he had tipped over. I looked over at him and saw he had my phone. Fear clutched at my heart, and my lungs froze. I watched as he punched in my password and opened the messaging app. My secret and my lie would soon be found out.

"Sit down. We have something to talk about." He showed no emotion on his face, and his voice was as cold as steel in a Montana winter.

I took a seat in the booze-soaked chair. *If I come out of this alive, I will have to clean the upholstery on this chair*, I thought. *Jeez, Sara, quit thinking about the* if *and housekeeping and figure out how you will escape this madman.*

"So, Sara, I read something interesting in your texts on your phone. Wanna know what I found out?"

Oh God, please tell me he didn't find the messages from my attorney. "Thomas, my phone has a password and can't be unlocked without it." I sounded more confident than I felt.

"Sara, Sara, Sara, cracking passwords is my specialty."

"What did you find out?" I stammered.

"Well, some very interesting things. So you were going to break up with me, were you? When were you going to tell me?" His jaw was tight; his long legs were crossed. He took a sip of his brandy while he waited for my answer.

He'd found the texts between Carol and me. The texts in which I had expressed doubt about my relationship with him. I wrapped my arms around my middle and shuddered, powerless against him. "I wasn't sure I was going to break up with you, but I figured Carol could help me figure out how I was feeling and sort myself out." *Sara, you're babbling—stop!*

"So you weren't sure you were going to break up with me?"

"Thomas, I love you. I love the way you love me when you aren't hitting me."

He didn't say anything for a long time. The silence grew into a black hole between us, ready to suck me in. Why wasn't he saying anything? The longer he stayed silent with his eyes glued to my phone, the more my terror grew. I had to get away from him—and fast.

"Thomas, I have to go to the restroom."

He didn't say anything and didn't move. I got up from the chair with my arms still holding my sides and walked into the master bedroom. I closed and locked the door behind me. Would that lock be strong enough to keep him out?

I caught my reflection in the mirror and was sickened to see the bruises on my throat. Worse, the imprints of his fingers were visible on my neck; it appeared his hands were still strangling me. I pulled up my blouse and saw the evidence of his kicks to my ribs: ugly black, blue, and red marks up and down my rib cage. Horrified at what he had done to me, I slid down the door to the floor, hugged my knees, and sobbed quietly. *What have I done, letting this man back into my life?* How was I going to survive him?

A loud banging on the door made me scurry away from it. Trembling, with a panic attack about to tear into me, I called out in a shaky voice, "I'll be done in a minute."

Based on the noises coming through the door, he was tearing apart the bedroom; I feared he would tear me apart if I left. I cowered on the floor with my fingers curled into fists. My nails dug into my palms as if to create a pain that would wake me up from this nightmare.

"Sara, get your ass out here!" he roared, and he banged on the door so hard I thought it would burst.

Slowly, I rose with trembling legs and stared at the door, my eyes wide. *Don't do it, Sara. Don't open that door.*

As if in a trance, I reached for the lock on the door, turned it to the unlocked position, and slowly opened the door, coming face-to-face with Thomas. No words were exchanged before he grabbed me by my booze-soaked hair, dragged me into the room, and threw me onto the mattress he had thrown off our king-size bed. The linens were strewn about the place. As soon as I hit the mattress, Thomas rolled me up like a dead body in a carpet. The mattress was heavy and blocked the air from getting to my lungs. I felt him jump up and down on the mattress with me inside, forcing the little breath I had to gasp out of my lungs. My arms were pinned to my sides, as the mattress was wrapped so tightly around me; I couldn't move my legs. Black filled the edges of my vision, and I heard only my heartbeat and the ragged, shallow gasps of my labored breathing.

Just as I was about to succumb to the blackness that had engulfed me, he got off and unrolled the mattress. Sweet air once again filled my lungs. Thomas surprised me with a hard kick to my ribs. I doubled over in the fetal position, in instant pain, clutching my sides. Spasms from the abuse my ribs had taken that day rocked through my body.

"Get up, you stupid cow," he said. He grabbed me by the hair and pulled me out of the bedroom and down the hall into the office. "Sit," he ordered. He let go of my hair and pointed to my office chair. "Where's my money you promised me, fat bitch?"

Terror sucked the breath from me.

He knew.

I opened my mouth, but no words came out. He slapped me, knocking me off the chair. He leaned down, picked me up by my hair again, and set me back on the chair. *At this rate, I won't have any hair left. Funny how the mind works at times like this.*

"What did you do with my money?" he screamed, his face so close that the spittle from his angry words splashed against my face.

Still, no words came; terror held them deep inside my psyche. He waited a few seconds for my response, and then both his fists punched my face and knocked me onto the floor. Again, he dragged me back onto the chair by my hair. Blood oozed from my nose, and my tongue found a bloody loose front tooth. My head lolled to one side, and no matter how hard I tried, I couldn't hold it up to look him in the eye again. I had been beaten both physically and emotionally. All I could do was wait for the next blow.

Somehow, I found my voice, which was strained and low. "I haven't gotten the money yet" was all I could say. The room was spinning, and the now-familiar darkness had begun to creep into the edges of my vision.

"Liar!" he screamed into my face. "I read the texts between you and your attorney—you banked it the other day." Another punch came, this time in my stomach. In his rage, he picked up the paper shredder and threw it at me. Through one swollen eye, I saw it coming toward me. It hit the side of my head. I was dazed, unable to comprehend for a minute what had just happened.

I shrank into the chair with my head drooping and mouth slackened; blood was everywhere. I had reached the point where I wanted him to just get it over with, whatever his next move would be.

I raised the eye I could still see out of and saw the landline phone on my desk. A spark of hope emerged in my heart. Could I reach the phone before he stopped me? Shaking my head, I thought it would be a foolhardy attempt.

Thomas broke into my thoughts. "Guess what is going to happen now, stupid cow?"

I wanted to smack the smirk off his face and run far away from him. I slowly shook my head. Blood dripped from my nose and mouth.

"You are going to transfer that money into my account."

Unable to comprehend what he'd ordered me to do, I sat frozen in my chair.

"Now!" he yelled.

I jumped, with pain stabbing at my ribs and shoulders, and slowly moved my chair closer to my computer. He looked over my shoulder, his breath smelling of booze, and watched while I brought up my bank's transfer page.

"Get on it, bitch," he said, and then, surprising me, he left the office.

Why did he go? After catching me in my lies, he couldn't have trusted me. *Now's your chance—pick up the damn phone!*

I glanced at the door to the office to be sure he had left. White terror filled my soul—what if he came in before I could call? I looked at the phone within my reach and then back at the door. I strained to listen for footsteps, but all was quiet except for the sound of ice cubes plopped into a glass. *Do it now. Right now! Don't wait, Sara. Just do it.*

I grimaced at the pain in my ribs as I reached for the phone, picked up the handset, and dialed 911.

"Island County Sheriff's Office. What is your emergency?"

I kept my voice low so Thomas couldn't overhear me. "My business partner has been beating me and trying to steal—"

Before I could get it all out, I heard footsteps coming down the hall. I quickly hung up the phone, logged in to my bank account, and pulled up the account-transfer program.

He came into the room with a full glass of vodka. I supposed the brandy was long gone. He stood behind me and watched. I'd transferred monies to his account before and had his information saved in the program. All I needed to do was locate the information, tell the program how much I wanted to send to his account, and click

"Make transfer." What could I do to delay? *Think, Sara. Think!* Panic had nearly shut down my brain. *Hell, what would a delay buy me?*

The phone rang just then and startled both of us. I reached for it, but Thomas beat me to it. "Hullo?" he slurred into the phone. I couldn't hear what the caller said, but Thomas said, "No one here called 911," and he hung up.

He now knew I'd called 911. Oh God, what would he do to me? What more could he do but kill me? He wouldn't hurt me until I had the money transferred, but terror filled me enough to call up my fight-or-flight response. I pretended the computer was slow, to give myself just enough time to gather some of my strength and determination back.

The phone rang again, breaking into my thoughts and diverting them from my escape plan to the reality of his power against my broken body.

"Don't answer," he ordered.

I looked longingly at the phone and counted each ring until the answering machine took over. *Damn.* Hope deserted me.

As I clicked through the transfer program, lights shone into the office window as a car wound its way up the drive. My brain screamed what my mouth couldn't: *Help!* I didn't know who it could be, but I hoped it would be a rescuer.

The dark of the night didn't allow me to see if the car looked familiar. Footsteps—the kind that sounded as if they came from heavy boots—came closer to the front door. The steps stopped at the door, and the doorbell chimed its song of what I hoped was my freedom.

"Go clean yourself up. I'll take care of them," Thomas said.

The doorbell chimed again. As I slipped into the guest bathroom, I glanced back over my shoulder at the door he had opened and saw two uniformed deputy sheriffs framed by the doorjamb.

Chapter 49

I have faced death this night, and I have called his bluff.
—Lucien LaCroix

My fear hit a new level. What if the deputies left? *Help is here, Sara. Don't let them go away without helping you.* I knew I would tempt the rage monster if I left the bathroom without his permission. The sickening smell of my fear mixed with the fresh blood that dripped onto my clothes.

I heard Thomas greet the deputies as I quietly opened the door and peeked out. "How can I help you, Officers?" he said in a calm, confident voice with his back to me.

"We had a hang-up call from this address, and we're here to perform a safety check," one of the officers said. He looked past Thomas toward me and added, "Ma'am, are you okay?"

Thomas turned around and looked at me with fresh rage coloring his face. I looked at Thomas and then at the deputies, and then my eyes locked onto Thomas's stabbing eyes. "No, sir, I'm not okay."

Both officers stepped inside the door and closed it. "It looks like you two have had a pretty bad argument tonight," one of the deputies said.

Tears sprang fresh. They were going to help me! Maybe I wouldn't die that night.

He turned to Thomas and continued. "Deputy Parkinson is going to take you into another room to ask you a few questions while I speak with her."

Thomas's head swung from the deputy to me and then back to the deputy, his eyes wide and his mouth gaping open. I hoped he was afraid. I hoped his fear turned to terror, as mine had. Deputy Parkinson took Thomas by the arm and led him into the office for questioning.

The other deputy turned toward me and motioned for me to sit on the couch in the living room. He sat in the chair, but it was so booze-soaked he immediately stood and walked over to the love seat across from the sofa.

"My name is Deputy Reed. What's your name?" He sat on the edge of the couch and leaned forward, his voice gentle and kind.

"Sara," I answered in a meek voice, using the tissue he'd handed me to stem the blood dripping from my face.

"Want to tell me what happened?" he asked, and he took a pen and notebook out of his pocket.

I didn't know where to begin. My mind was jumbled, so I stumbled through the events of the evening. It was if I related someone else's nightmare. The more the story came out, the harder I trembled and shivered. To tame my body's jerkiness, I wrapped my arms around my waist and clenched my painful sides.

"How about we stop for a bit and give you some time to regroup? Can I get you some water?" Deputy Reed asked. I nodded, amazed at his kindness.

While he was in the kitchen getting my water, I overheard Thomas yelling about how I had scratched his face; the blood on his shirt was his blood, he said. My heart sank. What if they believed him? It would be my word against his. I knew from my experience as an advocate that one of us would be going to jail, and that person could be me.

Deputy Reed came into the living room and handed me the glass of water. The cold water felt like heaven on my parched throat, but the lump that threatened to turn to overwhelming sobs would not be swallowed away.

"I need you to fill out a statement form for me, writing down everything that happened tonight. Do you think you are up to it?" Deputy Reed asked.

I breathed deeply before looking up at him to say flatly, "Sure." The events of that night would be in writing, in detail, so Thomas could not shift the blame onto me and deny he had done those things—that was, if the legal system believed me and not him.

The deputy handed me the statement form, and I moved to sit on the stool at the kitchen counter to write. I felt outside of myself as I wrote every detail, every humiliating thing Thomas had done to me. I didn't stop writing until I came to the point in the story at which my finger had been on the key to transfer the money just as the deputies drove up. Relief washed over me like a surfer's wave. I hadn't clicked the button. I still had my money.

I wrote my statement antiseptically. I made no mention of the indescribable, paralyzing fear or the panic that had gripped me when I tried to find a way to escape. What I wrote painted a clear picture of the denial I had been in throughout our relationship.

Deputy Parkinson walked out of the office with Thomas in tow and led him to the door as I handed my statement to Deputy Reed. It took me a second to realize Thomas was in handcuffs.

"Where are you taking him?" I asked in a shocked voice.

"Thomas has been arrested for a domestic dispute. We'll take him to jail, and in the morning, he'll go before a judge," Deputy Parkinson said matter-of-factly. "You'll be notified regarding the court's decision."

Thomas looked at me with murder in his eyes as the deputy ushered him out the door and headed for the patrol car.

The monster had left the house.

"In domestic-dispute cases, we contact an advocate from the local domestic violence agency to talk with you before we leave. She'll listen, answer your questions, and offer support as you go through the legal process," Deputy Reed said as he dialed the number from my phone.

I knew the procedure from my advocate days. It never had dawned on me I would ever need the same support. Denial was alive and well in the depths of my soul.

It was two forty-five in the morning when they left with Thomas in the back of the patrol car.

"Hello?" I said into the phone to the advocate who waited on the other end of the line.

"Hi, Sara. My name is Amy, and I work with the local DV agency. I understand your partner abused you pretty badly tonight. How are you doing now?"

Another humiliation because of Thomas—I was speaking to an advocate about my abuse instead of listening to an abused person as the advocate. *If only I could close my eyes and open them again to a world in which I'd never met Thomas.*

"Are you still there, Sara?"

"Yes, I'm here. I—well, I don't know where to begin," I said, feeling bone-tired all of a sudden.

"Why don't I start? I'll give you some information about our agency, what an advocate can do for you, and the services we provide to support you as you try to make sense of this."

That was how I always had started; I'd done most of the talking at first to put the person at ease.

Amy went through her spiel in a soothing, friendly, nonjudgmental voice. I relaxed a little, and the sensations of panic slowly evaporated.

I already knew the information she gave me, but there was no way I would have told her I had been an advocate. I hadn't met her at the agency yet, so I hoped she had not recognized my first name. I wanted to be just another abused woman.

"Do you want to talk about what happened?"

I began to tell my story one more time, with the details openly spoken. Was it because Amy was a woman that I felt I could talk so freely? Or maybe it was because I had held the way Thomas treated me as a deep, dark secret, just like the secret of the way my stepfather had treated me. The dam burst, and all those secrets came rushing out.

When I hung up from my conversation with Amy, dawn slowly spread its fingers of light across the darkened sky. Amy had made sure I felt safe in my home and made me promise to call her when I found out what the ongoing legal issues would be with Thomas.

Kitty slowly crept out from under the sofa, where she had been hiding since that night's nightmare began.

"Come on, Kitty. Let's go to bed and rest. I'll clean up this boozy mess in the morning." Exhausted from the night's craziness, I felt strangely at peace, safe from Thomas and his rage, even if for just one night. He was locked up and couldn't reach out to me anymore. Not if I didn't let him.

I took a hot shower to wash the booze away and soothe the bruises, careful not to make my face and nose bleed any more. Kitty was already at the foot of my bed, sound asleep. She must have been exhausted too from all the turmoil that had happened that night.

I slept fitfully. Thomas's awful words filtered in and out of my sleep. Then he stood at the foot of my bed with a glass of ice and booze in his hand. He had the familiar look of rage about to explode. Icy fingers snaked up and down my spine. I sat up in bed and looked at him with wide eyes.

"Thomas, what are you doing here? Did they let you out of jail?" I squeaked out the words, hardly able to speak.

He didn't say a word and threw his glass of booze toward me.

Just as he moved to jump on me, I woke with a scream. Hot tears of fear ran down my cheeks. Kitty had moved beside me; she looked me in the eye and purred, as if to soothe me and reassure me it had only been a bad dream.

I reached out and held her close. My heart thumped in my chest; my breath came in huge gulps. The nightmare had felt real and tasted bitter on my tongue.

I didn't know how long I lay with Kitty in my arms and my eyes open and focused on the foot of the bed, ready to jump up if he came again. My rational mind repeated over and over again that he was locked up and couldn't be there; on the other hand, the irrational part of my brain kept the nightmare alive. It had felt so real I thought I could have reached out and touched him. *Please, Lord, don't let me make a ghost of Thomas, as I have with Mom.*

Kitty stirred in my arms and brought me back to the present reality of having had the worst nightmare I'd ever had. But it had been no ordinary nightmare; I had been living it.

Chapter 50

The sun always shines above the clouds.
—Paul F. Davis

I glanced at the clock on the nightstand: 7:30 a.m. I had no hope of falling back to sleep. I threw the bedcovers back and slowly and painfully crawled out of bed and made my way to the bathroom. I avoided my reflection in the mirror as I put on my robe and went to the kitchen to start the coffee. I grimaced at the boozy stickiness of the floor. Bits and pieces of paper from the shredder Thomas had thrown at me were stuck here and there. Kitty stayed where she was on the bed, apparently worn out from last night's hellacious events.

While I waited for the coffee to drip into the pot, I looked out the window and saw a doe and her spotted fawn grazing on the bushes. It was a sweet image, and my soul calmed as I watched the protective doe watch over her baby. Why couldn't my own mother have had that kind of protectiveness? Why couldn't she have kept me safe? I'd had a lifelong ache of sadness that my own mother hadn't loved me enough to protect me from my rapist, her husband. How would my life have been different if she had? How would I have been different? Would I have chosen to be with Thomas? To stay with him?

I supposed it was useless to have those thoughts. *What is, is.* Nothing would change unless I made a change myself. I'd lost my compass; I didn't know how to change a lifetime of feeling unworthy. Then there was Jackson, the one person who had been my anchor and kept me on course—but on course for what? I was a mess; my life was a disaster. How could Jackson ever be proud of his mom?

I looked away from the window, poured my coffee, and followed the shredded paper trail that led to the office. *What a frigging mess.* Piles of shredded paper covered the floor, and the shredder lay on its side under the desk, where Thomas had thrown it. Things had been pushed off the desks onto the floor, and I saw a dark spot on the carpet—blood.

My blood. Oh God, it wasn't just a nightmare. I hadn't dreamed it. It had happened. I doubled over with my hands on my knees and struggled to get my breathing back to normal. *How low you have fallen, Sara. People in your life have beaten you with sex, their words, and now their fists.*

I sobbed uncontrollably, grabbed fistfuls of shredded paper, and threw them at nothing in particular. My anger grew into a rage. *Oh, look at this: Thomas's favorite mug he hid his morning drink in.* I threw it against the wall, and it fell to the floor in pieces. It only fed my rage more. Totally out of control, I yelled obscenities, tore up his favorite magazine, and broke all the pencils on his desk in half. Laughing and cursing, I tossed his files onto the floor and stomped on the documents, mixing them up so it would be difficult to put them in order again.

My rage slowly evaporated. I looked around at the mess I had made on top of the mess Thomas had made. It looked as if a hurricane had blown through the office. I fell to my knees, laughing hysterically at the absurdity of my temper tantrum, but damn, I felt much better.

After a while, I pulled myself together and, laughing instead of crying, staggered out of the room to fetch the vacuum. The time had come to clean up the mess, clear my mind, and work on my plan to remove Thomas from my life.

⚭

It took the rest of the morning to put the office in order again. After hard scrubbing, my blood on the carpet turned to a light rust-colored stain. The kitchen floor was easier to clean, with lots of hot water and detergent. Bits of shredded paper were everywhere, so a thorough vacuuming of the entire house and the furniture was necessary.

I had taken a quick shower the night before, but that morning, I looked forward to a long, hot shower. I took a deep breath for courage before I looked at myself in the mirror. The woman who stared back at me was unrecognizable. Who was the woman behind the battered, bloody face and body? At that moment, I promised the demoralized woman in the mirror I would never allow that to happen to her again. Ever.

The hot water soothed the bruises and abrasions. My spirit was revived, and I adopted a new mantra to make it on my own. *I don't need Ray. I don't need Thomas. I will prove to both of them and the ghost of my mother that I can succeed and be happy without them. I can't go weak on myself and allow myself to go back to living for others.*

Change wouldn't be easy. I forced myself to look in the mirror again and let the bloody face and black eyes speak the truth of how easy life would be without a man.

I reentered the kitchen, dressed, refreshed, and ready to work on my plan. Just then, my phone rang. "Hello?" I answered.

"Hi, Sara. This is Amy, the advocate you spoke with this morning. I wanted to call to see how you are doing this morning and to see if you needed to talk some more."

I cringed. Humiliation crept back into my skin. "Oh, hi, Amy. So far this morning, I've had a meltdown about last night, but I'm doing okay right now. Today I want to start on a plan to get Thomas out of my life for good."

"Do you want some help with that? I know you were an advocate here, so you are familiar with the services we offer—we can get you into a shelter if you think you need the protection."

My humiliation was now complete—she knew who I was.

"Naw, I think I'll be okay. Have you heard anything about Thomas? Do you know when he might be released?" My heart pounded. I didn't know what time his hearing would be that morning.

"He has a hearing before the judge today, and it will be decided then if he gets bail to wait until his court case. Are you sure you want to be in the house if he gets released?"

I thought about Amy's question while a shiver trickled down my spine. There was no way I wanted to be in the same house, much less the same room. But other than to a shelter, where would I go? *I could go to Carol's, but then, well, she'd know. If Jackson found out …*

"Well, is there someone I could call to find out what is happening?" I asked.

"On the copy of your statement will be the deputy sheriff's number—give him a call. But be sure you are not to be found if Thomas does get released today," she said.

"I will. Thanks for your support and help, Amy." I understood the importance of the advocate's role even better now.

We said our goodbyes, and just as I hung up, my phone rang again. "Hello?"

"It's me."

My heart dropped, and the blood rushed through my veins like a tsunami. "Have you seen the judge yet?" I asked anxiously.

"I had my hearing this morning. This is my one phone call. Thought you would like to know that because you called the cops, I am being deported back to the UK."

Silence hung between us before I blurted out, "Thomas, you aren't being deported because I called the police. You are being deported because you beat me up." I surprised myself by being so direct with him and cringed while I waited for his angry reply.

"Actually, bitch, you know that visa waiver we go back and forth on? It clearly says to follow all laws of the country you are visiting. So I'll be deported not because you made me hit you but because I got arrested. No one cares about what happened to you."

Anger at his words spiked inside me, and I replied, "Obviously, you are incorrect. The deputies cared, as they carted you off to jail." I wouldn't back down from my promise to myself to be stronger.

There was one more thing I needed to know from him. I took a deep breath and asked, "Will you be allowed to come home before they send you to London?"

"No, you stupid cow, I'm in jail until they send me back to London. You need to send my clothes and laptop to the flat." With that, he hung up.

I looked at the phone, let my breath flow freely, and smiled. *Life just might be going my way for a change.*

Chapter 51

**If there's a single lesson that life teaches us,
it's that wishing doesn't make it so.**
—Lev Grossman, *The Magicians*

I set the phone down on the kitchen counter and felt as if my world had suddenly shed its blanket of darkness. Thomas couldn't come back to that house, to the United States, to me. I was free of fearing what he might do if he came home.

I'd helped many women plan for their escape from their abuser and knew the most dangerous time was when they left him. That was when the abuser felt his control diminish, which resulted in a desperate rage that served to escalate his abuse. Many women had been killed while the focus of abusers' anger. Relief flooded through me. I knew Thomas was safely tucked away in his jail cell. He'd eventually be moved to an immigration holding facility while he awaited his escorted trip back to the United Kingdom.

With a lighter heart, I fed Kitty her breakfast and went into my office. I had to think through the most immediate problem I faced: Where would I live? Thomas, as the house's legal owner, could have me evicted. With everything that had happened, I had forgotten to call the property management office to inquire if my old apartment was available.

A shudder shook my body. I didn't want to go back to that retro apartment. Just thinking about it, I could almost smell the odor from the bathroom wafting to my nose. With my divorce settlement secured in my bank account, I could afford something a little sweeter. Maybe an apartment with two bedrooms—one for Jackson.

Thomas's laptop on his desk caught my eye and my curiosity. Out of habit, I looked around the office to make sure no one would see me open it. *Why not?*

With sweaty palms, I picked up his laptop and moved it to my desk. I stared at it. Who knew what secrets I might find out? Would I be opening Pandora's box? Or would I just find work-related stuff I already knew about? Maybe I could crack his bank account to see if he had, in reality, received an advance from the modeling company for our latest project.

I slowly opened the lid, surprised he hadn't password-protected the laptop. *How strange.* I had access to all his files and his email. He had left his email account open when he last closed the computer. I leaned back in my chair and stared at his emails. To the left of his list of emails in the inbox, a folder named simply *A* caught my eye. I clicked on the folder and expanded it and then clicked on the latest email from a woman named Alice. Wasn't that the name of his ex-wife?

Hi, love,

After we talked yesterday, I was thrilled to hear it won't take much longer and that you will be home for good. I can't wait to have you in my arms and my bed again, and Melanie keeps asking where her daddy is. We went to the park yesterday, and she kept asking for Daddy to push her. Made my heart break. I hope this is all over soon.

I looked in on your mum the other day. She needed a few things from Tesco, so I took her shopping while Melanie was at preschool. She seems to be doing well after her hip replacement. Her pain has lessened considerably in the past few weeks.

Do you know when Sara will transfer the money into our account? Do you think she suspects? God, I hope not; we need that money. I'm barely keeping us alive over here.

I'll write more later—Melanie is waking up from her nap.

I love you and miss you,

Alice xoxo

I reread the email over and over. My mind was unwilling to take in the words on the page. Finally, through the numbness of my brain, the meaning behind Alice's words became apparent. Our entire relationship had been a setup. He hadn't loved me; he had used me. I had been his mark and nothing more. *How could I have been so naive? Stupid, stupid, stupid woman!*

He had stolen my heart, parts of my life, and almost my money. I wrapped my arms around my waist, clutched at my sides, and rocked back and forth while staring at the email. The pain of his deception was more excruciating than the agony of knowing he never had loved me. My love had not been sufficient for him. He had never loved me. I retreated into my prison of self-hatred and loathsomeness. A wail of torment erupted and broke the funeral silence of the office.

I didn't know how long I sat rocking and wailing. It had turned dusk outside when I calmed down enough to close Thomas's computer. After staring at it for a few moments longer, I got up, turned the lights off, and left the office for the night. I noticed for the first time Kitty had come in and parked herself at my feet.

I needed a glass of wine. I sat on the sofa with Kitty on my lap, my wine, the gas fire's soft glow, and my thoughts. Betrayal had been an enormous part of my life, first with my stepfather and mom, then with Ray, and now with Thomas. But just because I'd gone through it before didn't mean I was immune to the agony it caused. One would have thought I would have learned from my past life choices. When would I grow up anyway? I was naive—that was what my mom had always said about me. She'd relished telling others that I would be the first kid on the block to jump into a stranger's car if the person offered me candy. Every time she'd said it, people had laughed, and red with humiliation, I'd made myself as invisible as I could. Tears slipped down my cheeks. *The pity pot cometh.*

Just then, Mom, in her diva-like manner, appeared on the arm of the sofa. I didn't want her there that night. I wanted to be alone with my tormenting thoughts and pain without her inflicting more onto me.

"Go away!" I yelled, startling Kitty off my lap.

"Bad day, dahling?" she asked in her buttery, polished voice.

"You should know. Don't you know everything that happens in your pitiful daughter's life?"

"Sara, don't talk about yourself that way. Yes, I saw what happened. Honey, I'm so sorry. So he's married?" Her voice dripped with sarcasm.

"He's married and a thief. Mom, he planned on taking my money all along." It felt good to talk to someone—anyone—about what I had learned that day, even if it was Mom.

"I would have thought at your age you would learn."

I wasn't prepared for her answer; I felt she'd just thrust a pound of salt into the open wound of my heart. I looked at her as she took a long draw on her cigarette, and I replied, "I suppose I didn't have anyone to teach me not to be so naive." I hoped I'd hit the mark with my response, although I doubted it. "Look, Mom, I'm in no mood for you tonight. Please leave me alone."

"Well, if you don't need your mama, then I will leave you to feel sorry for yourself. Whistle if you want to talk." With that, she dissolved, leaving a wisp of cigarette smoke behind.

Was that all it took to get rid of her? I'd asked her to leave me alone a million times, and it had never worked before.

I thought about calling Jackson; I just wanted to hear his voice. I knew it was totally my need to call to call him, just to hear his voice. But I was so emotional after reading the email, I probably would blurt out things I didn't want him to know. Anyway, it was too late—he'd probably be studying. Just then, my phone rang.

"Hello?" I answered.

"Hullo. It's me."

Thomas. "They let you make phone calls this late?" Even though I knew he was not within striking distance of me, I cringed at the sound of his voice.

"They are taking me to the immigration holding place in Tacoma in the morning, and I need money. I'll give you my commissary account information so you can drop some money in it."

I took a sip for courage and then said, "I've got a better idea: call your wife, and tell her she can start paying your bills." I gave him a few seconds for that information to sink in. Then I hung up and poured more wine into my empty glass.

Chapter 52

Star light, star bright.
—Anonymous

I stayed on the couch, stroked Kitty's fur, and gazed into the fire. It was a fake fire, not a real wood fire, but it comforted nonetheless. I pushed the possibility of Thomas's evicting me to the back of my mind. I had time, at least until he got back to the United Kingdom.

So far, my life had been a series of contradictions.

"He raped you. No, he didn't."

"I love you. No, I don't."

"Let's make a life together. I don't love you anymore."

"I'm not married. I'm married."

Where in the fuck did reality fit in with all that? At fifty-two, my reality was I'd been living other people's realities: my mom's, my stepdad's, my husband's, and now Thomas's. What would it take to be strong enough to live authentically in my own reality? So far, the life decisions I'd made had been based on everyone else's expectations. I'd been told I always made the wrong decisions, and my choices made were based on what other people wanted for me and from me. Now, whining into my wine, I was damn mad.

On the coffee table, an empty bottle of wine sat next to the empty wineglass. I had two choices: I could crack open another bottle of wine or end this pity party and go to bed. Learning that Thomas would be deported and was married had drained and overwhelmed me. I looked at Kitty snuggled up beside me and wondered at how tightly by my side she was staying. She usually snuggled up by the fire, yet that night, it was as if she were attached to my thigh.

"Come on, Kitty. Let's end this day so nothing else can happen to shatter my reality, whatever that is." We both went into the bedroom after I turned the gas fire off, leaving the empty wineglass and bottles on the coffee table.

⬤⫤⟩⟨⫤⬤

Gasping for breath, I clawed at his hands, which squeezed my neck, cutting off my air supply. I bucked and kicked my legs, trying to knock him off me, but his grasp on my neck was too firm and held me in place. Fear gripped my heart; my bladder felt dangerously close to releasing its contents.

"Stop! Please stop!" I cried through my gasps, clawing vigorously at—nothing.

My own screams awakened me. I sat up in bed, terrified and dripping sweat droplets of fear. Kitty lay close beside me, purring loudly, and watched me with her beautiful golden eyes.

"A nightmare. Just another nightmare," I panted in a whispered breath.

I lay back down on sheets dampened with sweat, and a quick glance at the clock on the nightstand told me it was two in the morning. When I closed my eyes, the vision of Thomas's rage-edged face loomed above me. The sweet, sickening smell of his booze drifted into my nostrils and made my stomach churn its content of the wine. My eyes flew open, and tears of fear joined tears of anger—fear of him and anger at him for causing my fear.

I had fallen for his lies hook, line, and sinker, just hoping to have a little bit of love in my life. This was not where I'd thought life would take me. How would I pick up the pieces of my life? I didn't think I deserved to.

How had I not figured out there was another woman in his life—his wife? All those secret phone calls had been to her. The reality was, I had been taken for a fool. Again. Over and over again. The anger I felt toward Thomas was replaced by anger at myself for having fallen into his web of deceit. How could I have been so stupid? I knew the signs. I'd counseled women in those very shoes before. The abusers always found the most vulnerable, needy, hungry-for-love victims to prey on. Sure enough, there I had been in plain sight, ready for his grooming. Beating my fists against the bedclothes, I wailed at the stark reality that I had been had. Not only had I been had, but I had willingly played my part well. *Now, there's reality for you.*

I didn't know how long it took until I finally settled. I looked at Kitty, who still lay beside me, and stroked her fur, much as a child would have stroked a security blanket.

"Oh, Kitty, what a mess I have found myself in." I wondered if she understood my words. It was obvious she knew my moods and could sense my fear; I always found her close to me when I needed her gentleness and loyalty the most.

The nightmare had felt so real. I'd smelled the booze on his breath, and his eyes had looked dead, with nothing behind them but rage. The fear was real and slow to dissipate. I calmed myself by gazing out the bedroom window at the fir tree branches dancing in the wind and the stars twinkling down. I chose a star and whispered a little poem I used to say when I was a child, only that night's wish was different:

Star light,
star bright.
Wish I may,
wish I might
have the wish
I wish tonight.
I wish I were dead.

Chapter 53

Only the dead have seen the end of war.
—Plato

I woke the next morning to the drizzly gray skies the Pacific Northwest was well known for. Kitty was still snuggled up close to my chest. My new routine of an early morning nightmare came back to me in bits and pieces and brought feelings more than visions. Fear, anger, and despair mingled together in one hot mess. Sensing my mood, Kitty snuggled closer. My hand automatically went to stroke her fur, which calmed my jumbled mind instantly.

"Time to get up," I finally said to Kitty unconvincingly. I was tired. Even my soul was weary. My body hurt all over from the beating it had taken. I faced another day of trying to make sense of what had happened. I didn't want to get up; I had a strong urge to stay in bed all day and wallow in self-pity.

I hoped I'd feel better after my shower. *Funny word:* hope. *Why would I say that when I'm feeling hopeless?*

With a sigh, I threw back the covers, burying Kitty underneath them, which prompted a howl and a scornful look from her as she dug herself out from beneath them. "Sorry, Kitty," I said. She ignored me and strutted into the kitchen, supposedly looking for breakfast. "Breakfast after I shower!" I called after her.

The hot spears that came from the showerhead massaged my skin and threatened to uplift my mood, but the stubborn darkness remained. Lathering up, I wondered why Thomas and I had never showered together. I felt sick when I remembered he was married. We hadn't had much intimacy in our relationship; I guessed his marriage was why. It was easier to think that was the reason and not that my pudgy body was unattractive to him.

Tears of sadness and disappointment in what I'd thought was love ran down my cheeks as I slid down the shower wall, immersed in my despair. I sat sobbing, unable to make sense of my life, until the water lost its warmth. The sudden coolness jarred me out of my self-absorption.

I caught my reflection in the mirror as I reached for the towel. The bruises on my neck and elsewhere were stark and told the story of my relationship with Thomas. The outside of me did not begin to reveal the bruises and scars on the inside of me. With one look, everyone who knew me would understand the evil road to hell Thomas had taken me on. Yet if I could help it, no one would ever know how weak I had been to be duped.

Later that morning, I settled myself in my office to assess what I should do next. I felt compelled to work on the modeling company's project; I had given my word, and it wasn't their fault Thomas and

I had found ourselves in the personal mess we were in. It might be useful to immerse myself in work, I thought, but how would I know I would get paid for the work I did? Thomas was the point of contact, and as such, he would receive payment. I needed work that paid, not to give my time and talents away for free.

My phone rang as I mulled over whether to work or not. The number was unfamiliar, and I argued with myself whether I should answer. Curiosity won out, and I answered.

"Hello?" I said warily.

"You have a collect call from a detainee at the Tacoma Northwest Detention Center. Will you accept the charges?"

My throat went dry. It was Thomas. Married Thomas. Evil Thomas. A conflicted storm formed deep in my core. Why was I conflicted? Of course I should say no. I wanted him to know I did not want to hear from him ever again. But the curious side of me wanted to know why—why he'd scammed me and why he'd chosen me to scam. More importantly, in my heart, I wanted to know if he'd ever loved me.

"Yes, I'll accept the charges."

"Hullo, love," Thomas said as soon as we were connected.

Just hearing his voice again with that proper English accent made me shudder. "Do not call me *love*. Your love is in England, I presume." My voice was as cold as steel, but inside, I felt all marshmallowy.

"Don't be like that, mate." His voice was that of the gentle, loving Thomas, not the married Thomas, the monster.

"I'm not your mate either. Why did you call?"

"I was worried about you."

"You tried to kill me!"

"Look, you know I would never hurt you."

"But you did—over and over again." The heat of anger burned

my cheeks. "Don't you realize what you—you and your wife—have done to me?"

"It takes two, baby, and you know just what to do to push my buttons."

I removed the phone from my ear and stared at it with disbelief. I heard his voice coming from the receiver, the voice that once had enamored me but now sent chills down my spine. I clicked the off button and silenced that voice.

The quiet of the office posed a stark contrast to the turmoil that grew inside me. The awareness that he had almost killed me several times struck me. How could I have stayed with him after even one attempt? *Oh, Sara, what a fool you are. A lifelong fuckup.*

"I've got to quit thinking, Kitty." There was no way to know if she understood, but she looked at me with her big golden eyes as if she did.

A drive to the post office to get the mail would help, I thought. Fresh air in my bruised lungs would set the refresh button. I knew my bruises were visible, but I needed to get out of the house. If someone asked, a lie about having been in an accident would put to rest anyone's curiosity.

It still drizzled as I pulled up in front of the post office. It was a small building, just big enough to service the residents, who numbered almost a thousand. The mail was deposited in our boxes by noon, and it was not uncommon to bump into people I knew and spend at least an hour catching up on the town gossip. That day, I was not disappointed: my ex-husband, Ray, entered the post office as I came out with my mail. Oh God, would he believe my accident story? I was desperate to turn around and walk the other way before he saw me, but he had already seen me.

"Hi, Ray," I said with hesitation and head down.

"Hi, Sara. How's it going?" Shock registered on his face when, not thinking, I looked up at him. "God, Sara, are you okay?"

"Yeah, sure. I was in an accident last week, and lucky me, I got the worst of it."

"You got the worst of it all right. I did some work for that Amy who works at the domestic violence center, and she told me differently. She told me what Thomas did to you, and by the looks of you, he beat you pretty bad."

My mouth dropped open, and I felt the blood drain from my face. "That's supposed to be confidential," I stammered. "Amy wasn't supposed to tell you or anyone." Humiliation had struck yet another blow below the belt. Now that Ray knew, he would spread the news island-wide. My stomach twisted when I realized he would surely tell Jackson.

"She recognized my last name and put two and two together. So why did he beat you up?" he asked with a hint of a smirk crossing his face. The tone of his voice told me he had no empathy or concern, only curiosity.

Anger percolated in my stomach—anger at him for his laid-back attitude and at Amy for telling him. "Please don't tell Jackson. I'll tell him when I'm ready."

"Okay. Well, gotta go. I'm picking up a package for an out-of-town client. Take care of yourself. See ya." With that, he walked into the post office.

Was that all the compassion I would get from him—a simple "Take care of yourself"? I clenched my fists and stared at him as he walked into the post office. Anger overtook my humiliation, and I wanted to swing out at something—anything. I was angry at Amy and the agency she worked for. My story was supposed to be confidential, and now, of all people, my ex-husband knew. Anger seethed through my pores as I realized he would relish spreading such a juicy bit of gossip. I got in my car and vowed to call the agency as soon as I got home. I could sue. But if I did, how many people would be left without the necessary services when something like this happened to them?

I pulled out of the post office parking lot with tires squealing and figured it didn't matter about anybody else. Maybe the time had come for me to think of myself first for a change.

Chapter 54

One of the greatest regrets in life is being what others would want you to be, rather than being yourself.
—Shannon L. Alder

By the time I returned home and parked the car in the garage, my anger had evolved into full-blown fury. Hot tears of rage burned my cheeks while I banged my fists on the wheel. How dare Amy violate the confidentiality of her job as my advocate? How dare Ray smirk at me when he told me he knew?

"Haven't I suffered enough?" I yelled to the universe. "When will it stop? When? My life is in the sewer, and you give me one more punch in the gut! How much more can I take?"

My voice became hoarse. My throat felt like sandpaper from the combination of yelling and crying. I didn't know how long I threw my tantrum. It all seemed futile anyway; bad things happened to me whether I was looking for them or not. Maybe I had done something terrible in a previous life, and this life was my punishment for those misdeeds. *Or perhaps I'm too naive and stupid, like my mom always told me I was, and an open invitation for others to abuse me.*

I had been beaten by my relationship with Thomas and by mom's and Ray's betrayals, battered by life. I had no hope left.

After slumping out of the car, I shuffled into the house, set the mail and keys on the foyer table, and let my raincoat fall into a heap on the floor. I didn't care what time it was; it was time for wine.

It took two glasses to think through whether I should sue or work with the agency to prevent something like this from happening to someone else. My soul was too beaten up to go through the legal process, I decided. I would undoubtedly be made the villain in the scenario, accused of financially harming a much-needed service. No, I wasn't strong enough to face that kind of criticism. Besides, then everyone would know, which would bring more humiliation. The other option was less painful to face: I'd keep the situation between the director and me. I took a deep breath of conviction I had made the right decision. I didn't have the energy to invite more angst into my life by suing. The thought made me nauseous.

I picked up the phone; dialed the agency's number the deputy had given me; and, once connected, asked for the director.

The call went surprisingly well. The director listened to my story, asked a few questions, and then told me she would circle back with me once she'd had a chance to look into it. I was surprised. I was so conditioned to being accused of lying that I assumed she would come back to me with some see-through explanation of punishing Amy, making her shadow a senior advocate, and putting a note in her personnel file. Yet she had listened and asked questions. Maybe

I could hope for a better outcome. I knew Amy was in the office, and I wondered if I would hear back that day.

A few hours later, my phone rang. I recognized the agency's number on the caller ID and picked up on the first ring.

"Hi, Sara. This is Debbie." Debbie related that she had talked with Amy, who'd confirmed my story. Amy had admitted what she had done. *Hallelujah!*

Debbie apologized for Amy's unprofessional behavior and told me she had scheduled a staff meeting to discuss system and policy changes to prevent anything like that from happening again. My chest puffed out when she asked me what solutions I might suggest, and I gave her a few that, as an advocate and victim, I thought were important. As the call ended, she promised to keep me updated on their progress with the changes. I felt validated for the first time in a long time.

"Come on, Kitty. Time to celebrate." I coaxed her into the kitchen for another glass of wine.

The phone rang just as I got into the kitchen, and without looking at the caller ID, I answered it. My heart dropped when the familiar recording from the detention center where Thomas was held came across the line. I stood and stared at the phone; my stomach churned with anxiety. If I didn't answer, I wouldn't know when he would be returned to the United Kingdom. If I did answer, I was opening myself up to more of his bullying.

I needed to know when he left. Once I knew he was out of the country and unable to return, I would feel much safer. I accepted the charges.

"Hullo, love. How are you doin' today? This place sucks. Wankers are constantly yelling, food is horrid, and I'm in the same area as murderers and drug runners."

"Have you told your wife about your conditions?" Sarcasm dripped from my voice.

He ignored my comment. "They refuse to move me somewhere else. They called me a criminal. Bollocks, can you believe that?" He still refused to acknowledge he was married.

"Well, you are a criminal. You broke the law."

"But I didn't kill anyone, for Christ's sake!"

"You almost killed me." I surprised myself with my bold answer.

"Quit imagining things. You aren't dead, are you?"

Every muscle in my body tensed; once again, I had been called a liar. I didn't answer. I couldn't answer.

"Look, I've got information about an immigration lawyer who's pretty good. I want you to talk to her about my case and see if she can get the deportation lifted."

I sucked my breath in. My mind questioned if he'd said what I thought he'd said. "Lifted?"

"Yes, lifted. I was told she charges a hundred and fifty dollars an hour, and if you present the case right, it should take only an hour."

Oh my God, what is wrong with him? Why in the hell would he ever think I would dish out money to save his ass? "I won't be contacting her."

"Stupid cow, you're the reason I am in here. I expect you to get me out of this hellhole. I am sitting next to killers. Get me out!" he yelled.

I pulled the phone away from my ear and hung up. A snicker bubbled up from deep inside. *No way, Thomas. There is no way I would pay for an immigration attorney after what you did to me.* I felt empowered, confident I had made the right decision.

"Hello, darling child of mine. Looks like you've had a good day."

Her words stabbed my heart. I whirled around and saw Mom's apparition sitting precariously on the arm of the sofa. Her flowing white negligee parted at the thigh to show off her long legs and ruby-red high heels. Her ever-present cigarette dangled from her long fingers as she blew smoke rings into the air. It had been so long since she had shown up. I had hoped she was gone forever.

"What? Cat got your tongue, sweetie? You don't have anything to say to your loving mother?"

"Why are you here?" I turned to face her.

"Well, it seems you are celebrating. Why don't you tell me what happened today to give you such confidence?"

"If you were any good at being a spirit, you would already know."

"Don't be like that, dahlin'. I want to support you, but don't you think you should help Thomas with the immigration attorney?"

"Let his wife pay for him to fight the deportation."

She inhaled her cigarette smoke deeply and puffed it out in more smoke rings. I admired her ability to do that; I never could blow smoke rings when I smoked.

"What's a measly hundred dollars or so? Look, you need to do the right thing by Thomas. He has been good to you. Look around you. Where do you think you would be if it weren't for him? Living in that shabby, stinking apartment you called home—that's where."

Anger at her unwillingness to see my side of the story heated my veins. I grabbed a fresh bottle of wine from the fridge, opened it, and poured a full glass into my empty one.

"Look, my sweet, you are the reason he is where he is. If you had just listened to him and quit pushing his buttons and making him angry, he would be here with you instead of in a cell with degenerates, where he does not belong. You owe him."

I shook my head, not believing what I had heard. A flash of white light blinded me, and I threw my full glass of wine in her direction. She was gone by the time my sight returned to normal.

For the second time that day, I had heard I was the reason he would be deported. Grabbing a towel to clean up the wine mess on the sofa, I vowed I would not allow Mom or anyone else to take away my newfound sense of empowerment. I hoped I could live up to my vow.

Chapter 55

When others cannot find something to hold onto ...
we can reach out and be their anchor in that moment.
—Aaron Woodall

I was shaken by my mom's appearance and her words. My newfound empowerment threatened to dissolve into a deep, dark well of depression. The *blame* word kept whirring through my brain. First Thomas and then my mom had told me I was to blame. *Maybe I brought all this on myself. Indeed, I made the choices that got me here. I knew about the red flags to look for in an abusive personality and ignored them. But I don't think I consciously ignored them.* Thomas had been at once charming and manipulative. Almost immediately, he'd seized my desire to be loved and cherished, blinding me to his faults until it was too late. He had locked in my heart and my finances, I'd depended on him, and it had been impossible to break free.

But why had it been impossible? Had I been so needy that I'd stayed because when he did show me he cared, I pretended it was like the ending of the fairy tales I had read as a child? I had been fooling myself. Why hadn't I seen it earlier? It had been easy to explain it away to myself: *He is under pressure; it was the booze that made him do it. Otherwise, he wouldn't have hurt me.* Even though I had always been weak inside, others saw me as a strong woman. It was a facade. Having to explain to others that I had been in an abusive relationship and had stayed scared me almost as much as Thomas did.

I hadn't really left him, though, had I? Would I still have been with him if the deputies had not arrested him that night? I knew the answer to that question, and it sickened me. I would have stayed.

Abuse wasn't supposed to happen to women like me. I'd been a middle-aged woman successfully building a business who had a network of friends and supporters in the community when I met Thomas.

Now I thought there was nowhere I could go for support. How could an advocate for abused women allow herself to be abused?

I'd thought I could fix the relationship—fix him—so he wouldn't abuse me anymore. I'd begun to believe what Thomas had told me all along: that I was to blame. I had been sucked into his web of abuse. I'd become accustomed to a lie.

He never had physically abused me in public, so who would have believed me?

Then I'd found out he was married. I couldn't fit that fact into my brain. I never had seen that coming. What a fool I had been to think he actually cared for me and loved me even. He'd beaten me, said foul things to me, and made me do things I didn't want to do, yet the only thing that had woken me up to the reality of our relationship had been finding out he was married.

An empty wine bottle sat on the coffee table, and an empty wineglass sat beside it. I didn't remember drinking the bottle empty. I slogged into the kitchen, retrieved another bottle of wine, and felt blessed it was a screw-cap bottle. I didn't think I could handle anything more complicated than twisting the cap off.

After slogging back to the sofa, I turned the fire on and sat back down. The quietness of the house surrounded me. Outside, an owl hooted. I remembered from a book my mom had read that supposedly, if one heard an owl call his or her name, then death would follow. I strained to listen carefully and hoped I would hear the owl call, "Sara."

Hours slipped by. Several more bottles of wine were emptied. I lost track of whether the owl called my name or not. I put my favorite CD on the player, one filled with mournful, self-pitying music by my favorite artist, Sarah McLachlan. Just what the doctor ordered to throw me entirely into the well of despair. My thoughts rambled. Nothing seemed real to me. It was as if I had been playing a part in someone else's life. This couldn't have happened to me, yet it had. I'd been beaten, scammed, and thrown away.

I replayed the same haunting song repeatedly and continued to drink while the words spoke what I couldn't. I felt I didn't belong in the world anymore, and those soothing words convinced me I would be better off not there. Why should I reside in a world that treated me with contempt at every turn?

A burst of energy flowed through me. I tucked Kitty under my arm, grabbed the bottle of wine, jerked the CD out of the player, picked up my car keys, and headed for the garage. If the owl wasn't going to call my name, I'd take matters into my own hands.

Kitty sat comfortably on the passenger seat, where I had placed her. Her trusting eyes watched me while I turned the key in the ignition and put the CD in the player.

"It's okay, Kitty. We'll soon be together in a much nicer place with none of this pain for us to go through together again."

She blinked and then laid her head on her paws and closed her eyes.

I turned the volume up so that each word of the lyrics, each syllable in the song, reverberated in my soul. It was the song I wanted to be played at my funeral. It would be a beautiful, low-key funeral without all the people who'd betrayed me in attendance. I leaned my head on the headrest and thoughtfully planned out what I wanted my interment to be like. The song played over and over again while the car idled and poured its poisonous gas into the closed garage. I'd opened all the car windows to quicken the deadly result.

Sleepiness and nausea began to take over my body, letting me know the end was on its way. I glanced at Kitty on the seat beside me; her eyes were closed as if she were sleeping. I relaxed and settled back to let the gas take me away from the world that had been like hell to me. Closing my eyes, I gave in to the darkness and thought, *It won't be long now.*

Jackson's voice broke into my fog as if he were begging me to open my eyes and get the heck out of there. I hadn't given a thought to how my suicide would affect him. His heart would be broken. Would he hate me for taking his mother away from him? I couldn't do that to him. I wouldn't do that to him.

My eyes flew open, and I frantically turned the car off, grabbed Kitty, opened the garage door, and ran out into the fresh air. I fell to the ground on my hands and knees, coughing and gasping as the clean air made its way into my poisoned lungs. I glanced over at Kitty lying next to me. Her still body looked lifeless in the garage's light.

"No, Kitty. No," I gasped through my burning throat, and I

frantically turned her over to give her CPR. The gravity of what I had done sobered me and froze my heart with fear.

Tears blurred my vision, but when she started coughing as the clean air worked to push out the carbon monoxide, a deep sigh of gratitude left my own lungs. I picked her up and held her close, even while she still coughed, thankful for each clean breath she took.

"I'm so sorry, Kitty," I sobbed.

Chapter 56

Your memory feels like home to me. So whenever my mind wanders, it always finds its way back to you.
—Ranata Suzuki

Jackson, my son, the anchor of my life, had saved us both.

My lungs burned as I gently carried Kitty into the house. I laid her in her favorite chair by the fireplace. She looked up at me with a furious look and curled up to rest, still coughing every few minutes. I had been at the lowest of lows and had scared myself more than Thomas ever had scared me. What had I been I thinking? No matter how depressed I'd gotten in life before, killing myself had never entered my mind. And what right had I thought I had to take Kitty with me?

It had turned late, and the evening's failed suicide attempt drained me of every last bit of energy. I wanted to go to bed, close my eyes, and shut out the world. But at the same time, I feared another two o'clock nightmare visit from Thomas.

I decided the last thing I needed was another glass of wine but opened the refrigerator door and took out the bottle. As I poured the wine into a glass, I thought maybe if I got drunk enough and passed out, there would be no opportunity for a nightmare to occur—so I finished off the bottle. Each glass downed eased little by little the pain that stabbed at my soul, until the numbness began to release the pain into unconsciousness.

Somewhere in the distance, I heard a phone ringing. Deep within my drunken slumber, I realized it was my phone and reached out to answer it without a thought of who it might be. The now-familiar message from the detention center greeted me. Against my better judgment, I accepted the call, hoping to learn when Thomas would be sent back to the United Kingdom.

"Hullo, love," Thomas said once we were connected.

"Hello." My mouth felt like the Sahara Desert in the dead of summer. "Any news on when you are going back to the UK?"

"Why? Eager to get me out of the States?"

A groan escaped before I could check myself. He was good at exploiting my feelings. With the drunken stupor I was still in, I was even more susceptible to his manipulations. *Tread lightly, Sara.* "No, I just thought that's why you called."

"I'm leaving the day after tomorrow. I will be escorted back in handcuffs to the UK by two ICE officers. It's like they think I am some sort of criminal." His voice had an edge to it. Was that fear I heard?

"I see." I didn't know what else to say. I wanted to say he deserved that and more.

"Have you contacted the immigration attorney yet?"

I paused before answering, mulling over whether I should lie and tell him yes or tell him the truth that I had not contacted her yet.

"No." It was a simple word, one that would cause his anger to rise. I hung up the phone before his rage could be unleashed toward me.

He would be in London tomorrow afternoon and unable to come back to hurt me. How long could I stay in that house before Thomas realized I was not paying him the down payment and kick me out?

I didn't know how long I stayed on the sofa, still in the clothes I'd wore last night, staring off into space when I wasn't napping. It was late afternoon when I decided to get up; feed poor Kitty, who must have been starving; and change into my pajamas. Who cared if it was midafternoon? It felt good to have the freedom to do what I wanted when I wanted. In fact, that night's dinner would be popcorn and wine. I grimaced at the thought of more wine. I didn't know if the hangover I had was due to the carbon monoxide or the massive amounts of wine I'd drunk last night.

I felt restless, as if I should be doing something. I could work on the modeling company's project but had no energy to stare at code. I glanced over at my knitting basket in the corner of the room, which I'd neglected for so long. The abandoned project, a pink baby blanket, looked forlorn, with knitting needles stuck into the yarn like spears. After taking it out of the basket, I moved to the sofa, refamiliarized myself with the pattern, and tenderly stroked the soft yarn. Whose baby was I knitting it for? Knowing how long it had been since I had worked on it, I figured the baby had to have been a toddler by then.

Soon the needles were in my hands and followed the pattern as if I had just put it down yesterday. The rhythm of working the needles with the yarn was soothing. Focusing on the pattern kept my mind organized and forced out the clutter left over from my earlier call with Thomas. It was a basket-weave pattern—knit five, purl five, knit five, purl five. The routine was hypnotic. Knit five—thoughts turned to Ray. Purl five—I thought about Thomas. I was still in love with both, and that saddened and angered me.

Had I given myself enough time to grieve over the loss of Ray and the life I'd had with him before entering into a relationship with Thomas? When I'd lost Ray, I'd lost the only life I had known for twenty years. Up until the last few years, we had done everything together and always with Jackson. But in the last five years of our marriage, I had gone my own way and worked toward my lifelong dream to build my own business and travel. Ray always had known about my goals and even supported them throughout the years. Until the time to actually put my business plan in action had arrived. Building my business had dramatically changed the journey our lives had been on. I naively had plowed ahead without consideration of the changes I forced onto Ray. I'd cheated on him, not with another man but with my passion spent on my business rather than on him. Was it any wonder he'd looked elsewhere for tenderness, understanding, and normalcy?

Knit five, purl five, knit five, purl five.

All the knitting and thinking made me thirsty. It was time to have a nice cold glass of pinot grigio, check on Kitty's food to see if it needed to be freshened, and make a potty run. I felt strangely calm. I knew the owner of the house—on title only—had been kicked out of the States, which gave me more time to figure out my housing. It would be just me and Kitty from now on—and my anchor in life, Jackson.

Shoot, I needed to call Jackson and tell him about Thomas before Ray told him. With my bladder relieved, Kitty fed, and a full wineglass in hand, I picked up the phone and called.

Chapter 57

Life's under no obligation to give us what we expect.
—Margaret Mitchell

"Hi, Jackson," I said when he answered. "How're things going for ya?"

"Hi, Mom. Things are good. I raised my grade in calculus. It was a tough class, especially because I took physics at the same time."

"That's awesome. I knew you had it in ya!"

We made small talk for a time; it took me time to build enough courage to tell him what I needed to. He had only met Thomas a few times, and their relationship had been contentious. What I had to say to him held the possibility of coming between him and me in ways that would be irreparable. At the very least, the way my son thought about me would forever change.

"Look, there is something I have to tell you about Thomas."

"Dad already told me."

My heart sank. I had known Ray wouldn't be able to keep the news to himself. I wondered how many others he had told. "Oh, honey, I'm so sorry. I wanted it to come from me." I swallowed the lump in my throat.

"You know how Dad is—he can't keep anything to himself. Is Thomas with you now?"

Evidently, the only part of the story Ray had felt was necessary to tell Jackson was that Thomas had beaten me. I told him the full story, including that Thomas would be deported back to the United Kingdom tomorrow.

"So how are you now, Mom?" Jackson asked with concern in his voice.

"I'm doing okay. Still in the house, trying to get my head on straight so I can figure out my next steps." I didn't mention my deep depression or my suicide attempt. There were some things he didn't need to worry about. Nor did I say I could be homeless if Thomas evicted me before I had those next steps figured out.

"You aren't going back to London, right?"

"Right. I'm not going back to London. Thomas won't be able to come here, and I have no reason to go there."

"What if he flies to Canada and crosses the border at Blaine? He could easily slip into the States, and Whidbey is only a two-hour drive from the border."

"I hadn't thought of that," I said. "Who would I contact about that—Homeland Security?" Fear gripped me once again. I quickly looked toward the front door, imagining Thomas walking through it. My fear turned to terror. I'd left a hole in my safety plan, the plan that immigration had taken care of for me by deporting him.

Jackson thought for a moment and then agreed that Homeland Security would be an excellent place to start. We chatted for a bit longer until he had to leave to study for an important exam in the morning.

"Good night, Jackson. Thank you for being you. I love you."

"G'night, Mom. I love you too."

I smiled with the knowledge my confession had not jaded Jackson's view of me.

First thing the next morning, I went into my office to google Homeland Security. I found the number, but just as I was about to dial it, the phone rang. I looked at the caller ID; it was the detention center. Without hesitation, I pressed the decline button and then calmly dialed Homeland Security. I was surprised to be connected to an agent on the first ring. I explained to her the purpose of my call: my business partner had just been deported for a domestic violence charge, and I had a restraining order against him.

"I would like to know the process of marking his passport so he cannot cross any border into the United States. I live just two hours away from the Canadian border. Conceivably, he could fly into Vancouver and drive into the States, crossing the border at Blaine."

"I'm sorry, but we have to follow the Privacy Act—we cannot red-flag his passport, because he has protections under that act."

Her response lit the spark plugs in my stomach and fired up my anger. *Thomas has rights, and I do not?* "Ma'am, he has tried to kill me three different times. Are you telling me, as an agent of the US government whose salary my tax dollars help pay for, that the man who tried to murder me has more rights than the person he tried to kill?" I worked to keep my voice even and low without yelling.

"Yes, ma'am, that is what I am telling you. Is there something else I can help you with?" Her voice was cold, with no empathy or compassion.

Unbelievable. Everywhere I'd looked for justice for myself, I had run into a stone wall. Amy at the domestic violence center had betrayed my confidence. A judge had deported him not on the grounds he'd beaten me but because he'd broken the visa-waiver agreement by getting arrested.

I knew it wasn't the agent's fault for the law being what it was. I turned my attention back to the phone. "No, thank you."

I threw my phone onto my desk and stomped out of the office, fuming at the audacity of the United States to put an alien's rights over and above the protection of the rights of a citizen. I paced through the living room, kitchen, and bedroom and finally went out onto the deck. I hoped the fresh fall air would cool me down. The more I thought about the possibility of Thomas sneaking across the northern border and driving there while my hands were tied to stop him, the angrier I became. What was I supposed to do—be there like a sitting duck, waiting for him to come? Even if I moved, he'd find me.

"No!" I screamed to no one, banging my fist on the deck's rail. I stomped back into the house, determined to find help somewhere. I'd contact my congressman, and if that didn't work, I'd call the *Seattle Times* newspaper with my story. "Woman Beaten by Boyfriend from the UK Has Fewer Rights to Protection Than He Does"—a long headline, but it would get the point across.

I googled my congressman's contact information, pulled up a blank email, and detailed my problem. As I saw it, the solution would be to red-flag Thomas's passport for every border crossing into the States. I read through what I had written, and when I was confident it all made sense, I clicked the Send button.

I sat and stared at my email program on the computer screen for a long time, confident, with hope for the first time in a long time. *Now would be an excellent time to celebrate.* I left the office to fetch a glass of the lovely pinot grigio and then settled in for the rest of the afternoon with my knitting. Knitting and wine—the perfect combination.

Knit five, think. Purl five, think. Knit five, think. Purl five. Whether it was the wine or the routine of knitting, I soon became sleepy.

"I can't keep my eyes open any longer," I said to Kitty, who was sound asleep next to the fire. I put my knitting back in the basket and took my empty glass into the kitchen to rinse out. "Come on, Kitty. Time for bed." She didn't need much coaxing and followed me into the bedroom.

I changed into my pajamas, left my clothes in a heap on the floor, crawled into bed, and snuggled under the covers. I wished I could open the windows to let the fall air spread its freshness into the room, but I didn't dare. I still didn't know for sure if Thomas had left for the United Kingdom, where he'd be three thousand miles away.

I struggled against him—he had poured the dirt from my poinsettia plant into my mouth, gagging and choking me. I couldn't breathe. Every breath forced the dense soil down my throat. I tried to make him stop, but my blows weren't strong enough to push him off me. Words that begged him to stop came out garbled by the dirt. Consciousness faded as the soil was packed into my mouth. I fell deeper and deeper into the blackness.

I sat up screaming, jolting myself out of the nightmare. *Oh God, it was so real.* I spit out the musty taste of dirt—the same taste I'd had when Thomas forced the dirt into my mouth last Christmas. Tears ran down my hot cheeks, and my heart beat so loudly I was sure the neighbors could hear the drumming. Kitty was there beside me and purred as she watched me, as if to tell me it was okay. I was okay. Reliving the horrible things Thomas had done to me had become a regular occurrence at two in the morning.

I must have cried myself to sleep after calming down, for when I woke again, daylight lit up the room. Kitty, with her caretaker's role over for now, was sound asleep at the foot of my bed again. I felt as if I had a hangover, even though I'd had only two glasses of wine last night. My eyelids scraped against my eyeballs, and I had a headache that hammered nails into my teeth.

Life seemed bearable after a shower, eye drops, and some aspirin. Eager to get into my office to check if my congressman had responded to my email, I skipped my coffee routine. I knew I had written only last night, but miracles could happen.

Hope once again leaked slowly into my battered soul. Hope that my inbox held a solution.

SIX

Healing, Homeless,
and Hopeful

Chapter 58

> Your life is on the line, and we all know that deep down, beneath your bravado, you're nothing but a coward
> —Kayla Krantz, Reanimate at Dawn

What if my congressman hadn't responded? Congresspersons were probably inundated with emails every day. I steeled myself against disappointment. I shook my mouse to wake my computer and navigated to my email program. I placed the cursor over the program icon, closed my eyes, and clicked. When I opened my eyes again, I saw the congressman's response in my inbox. It wasn't from the congressman directly but had come from his office, which was enough for me.

Dear Ms. Matthews,

Thank you for your correspondence concerning your situation. I too had a similar situation and know of actions we can take to protect you.

By return email, please send a scanned copy of your statement to the police, the police report, the arrest warrant, and all court proceedings, including the deportation order. Once we have that, we will review the documentation and contact you regarding what action we can legally take toward resolving this issue.

In the meantime, please do not hesitate to call or email your questions and concerns.

Sincerely,
Denise Jacobsen
Administrative Assistant, Congressman
Rick Larsen's Office

I must have read through the email twenty times before it sank in that someone was actually going to help me. I felt light-headed, lighthearted, and giddy with a feeling I had not experienced in a long time: happiness. I picked up Kitty, who had followed me into the office and watched me with suspicious eyes, and danced with her around the room, spinning, giggling, and feeling almost free of Thomas. I set her back down on her chair and got busy gathering and scanning the documents Denise Jacobsen had requested. Thank goodness the prosecuting attorney and deputies had made sure I had copies of everything; it made the chore a breeze. Soon I had all the documents scanned in and attached to the return email.

Dear Ms. Jacobsen,

I want to thank you so much for your quick response. I don't know what I expected, but it wasn't an overnight reply—thank you.

You will find all the documents requested attached to this email. Please let me know if you need anything further.

I anxiously await your answer regarding my situation.

Sincerely,

Sara Matthews

I read through it once more and then clicked Send. Off the message went into cyberspace, ready to land in Denise Jacobsen's inbox. I hoped her next reply would be as quick as her first one.

I was on a high. Self-confidence felt pretty darn good. I realized I had not heard from Debbie at the domestic violence agency in a while and decided that morning would be a good time to call. However, the call could wait until after I made my morning coffee and stoked myself with some much-needed caffeine.

While the coffee dripped from Mr. Coffee, I watched the doe and her fawn graze on the weeds outside the kitchen window and remembered how unloved and uncared for I'd felt the last time I had watched them. I didn't feel that way now. That day, I had started to love and care for myself.

Back in the office, I placed my mug on the desk, picked up the phone, and dialed Debbie's direct line.

"Hi, Debbie. This is Sara Mathews. How are you doing?" I said after she picked up the call.

"Hey, I'm fine, Sara. Thanks for asking. I'm glad you called. I want to update you on our progress in changing policies and procedures for working with our clients."

"Great. That's why I'm calling, along with an idea I have. Please fill me in."

Debbie went on to explain the new procedures to ensure a client's anonymity in great detail. I was thrilled with the progress they had made and was convinced their new processes would never again put a client at risk.

"Wow, that all sounds perfect, Debbie. Thank you for your efforts to protect your clients, and please thank your staff too. Is Amy still there?" I hesitated to ask, but my curiosity got the best of me.

"No, she moved to Florida. I did get a call for a reference for her at an agency there. I couldn't give a good one, based on what happened to you."

That was good news. Amy would never have the opportunity to wreck someone else's life, as she had mine. I silently said a prayer of thanks.

"Well, now for my idea. I know that once a month, all convicted abusers are ordered to attend a victims' panel before they start court-ordered treatment. I understand professionals from various services talk to them about what they can expect during treatment. Law enforcement is there to speak to them, as well as the prosecuting attorney. I also am aware there is usually a victim who comes to talk to them about her experience with her abuser. I know it hasn't been so long ago for me, but what do you think of me as the next panel's victim?"

"Wow, you surprise me. Are you sure? Your emotional wounds must still be raw. But really, that makes me think this is a good opportunity for you. Expressing your raw emotions will provide a good opportunity for the abusers to see the impact of their own violence against another."

"I think so too. I believe my story would come across as authentic. I admit it is a scary thought for me to stand up in front of strangers to talk about the pain and my humiliation. But as the saying goes, it also might help one person to think before he abuses again."

"I'm proud of you, Sara. When most would be taking care of their own emotional needs, you are willing to help others. How do you feel about next Tuesday? That's the next panel."

I hadn't thought it would be so soon, but I had committed to doing this. "Okay. Yes, Tuesday will be fine." I knew I had work to do to prepare myself.

"Perfect. Let me know if you have any questions and if I can help you in any way," Debbie responded.

We said our goodbyes, and I leaned back in my chair and watched the mussel rafts below from the office window. *What have I done?* Was I ready to tell a bunch of strangers my story? I hadn't even told my friends what had happened, although I was sure they all knew via Ray's island-gossip grapevine. What if when I got up to talk, no words came out or, worse, I babbled like a friggin' idiot? *Or, Sara, what if you allow your emotions to show the reality of what happened to you?* If I was going to do this, I wanted it to be worthwhile—for them and for me.

Kitty and I went into the living room. I picked up my knitting and spent the rest of the afternoon thinking about whether I could do what I'd promised. The more I thought about it, the more I was convinced it wasn't a question of being ready to talk about my story. It was a question of whether I could deliver my account authentically.

Kitty meowed, letting me know she was ready for dinner, and I felt a little hungry too. Darkness had hidden the daylight for another day. After setting my knitting in the basket, I sauntered into the kitchen and fed Kitty before I poured a glass of pinot grigio and took the popcorn down from the pantry.

"It looks like a wine-and-popcorn gourmet dinner tonight for me,

Kitty." I winked and smiled at her while she ignored me, eating her own gourmet dinner of Friskies salmon.

I marveled at how nice the evening had turned out to be. That day, I'd had two successes: the reply from Denise Jacobsen and the progress made at the domestic violence agency. I felt better than I had in months and almost could see the light at the top of the deep, dark, dank well the horrid depression had thrown me into.

The ringing of the phone disturbed the peace I was feeling. *Thomas.* I wrestled with whether to answer it or not, but my need to confirm he was no longer in the States won out.

"Hello. You must be back at the flat. How was your trip?"

"Hullo, love. Yeah, it was a nightmare being handcuffed to those two wankers. They made a good show of taking them off at immigration at Heathrow. Bollocks, Sara, this didn't have to happen if you hadn't called the coppers."

"What about our current project?" I diverted the conversation to prevent him from playing his blaming game.

"Have you done any work on the project?"

"No, I haven't had time or energy to give it. I'll send you a status report tomorrow. But I'm here to tell you I won't be working on it if I do not get paid."

"Sara, where are you living rent free?" he asked sarcastically.

"That isn't the point, Thomas, and you know it. You haven't paid me for our last project or your charges on the business credit card. Let's just call it even and call the outstanding balance your rent."

"Or what, Sara? What ya gonna do if I don't?"

"You won't know what I'll do until I do it. Just sort this out."

"Look, I'm to the point of having you evicted," he said.

My hands clenched the phone. My jaw tensed as if to chew through the line and attack him. How many empty threats had he made to me? I prayed this was yet another one. I needed time to get myself together and get out of that house.

"I guess you don't know yet." His voice was as sweet as honey.

"Know what?" Something was up, and it wouldn't be a threat.

"All charges have been dropped. Guess the wankers figured that since I couldn't return to the States, they didn't want to go to the time and expense of going through a trial, when they knew they would lose."

Chapter 59

So let's raise our glass to the accident season,
To the river beneath us where we sink our souls,
To the bruises and secrets, to the ghosts in the ceiling,
One more drink for the watery road.
—Moïra Fowley-Doyle

They'd dropped all charges? How in the hell could they do that? I would not get the satisfaction of watching his face when they pronounced him guilty. My stomach had just received another swift gut punch.

The judge had deported him not because he had tried to kill me but because he had gotten arrested. It didn't matter why he'd been arrested; being arrested had been enough to deport him.

I hung up without saying goodbye and reached for my glass of wine. The popcorn was long forgotten. This was the newest betrayal in the long line of betrayals of my life.

⚬⊰⊱⚬

The phone woke me the next morning. *Thomas.* My head was not in the right space to talk to him. The regularly scheduled nightmare had shown up at two in the morning, and sleep had evaded me for the rest of the night. I let the call go to voice mail and slowly got out of bed to get my day started. The news that the prosecuting attorney had dropped all charges against Thomas threw me back down my well of depression. After my morning routine, I reluctantly went into my office with Kitty close behind and reviewed the status of my current project.

It was difficult to concentrate on the details of the project. My mind drifted to what Thomas had told me last night. How could they have dropped the charges without telling me? Maybe he had lied—he was good at that. It seemed a prudent idea to call the prosecuting attorney's office to check out his story. The receptionist answered my call on the first ring. After I told her who I was and gave her my case number, she connected me to the prosecuting attorney.

"Hello, Ms. Matthews. I was just about to call you regarding the status of the case against Mr. Hunter. Because it will be impossible to prosecute him due to his deportation back to the UK, we have decided to drop the case against him without prejudice. This means the charges against him are not dropped, and if he should ever return to the States, he could be tried in the courts."

"So that's it?"

"Unless he comes back to the States," he replied. "Do you have any questions?"

"Um, well, no, not now. Thank you for the information."

"I'll follow this phone call up with a letter for your files to explain everything we just talked about."

"Thank you," I said in a slow, quiet voice, and I hung up, unwilling and unable to continue the conversation.

So that was what being a victim felt like. I'd been victimized by Thomas and now victimized by the law. There was no justice. The only punishment Thomas would get for lying, stealing, and attempted murder was deportation to his mother country.

I couldn't concentrate on the project. Instead, I went into the living room and lay on the sofa with Kitty on my tummy. She purred so loudly the vibrations felt like a massage. The conversation with the prosecuting attorney played through my mind. The bottom line was that I had been deserted by everyone, including the law.

The doorbell woke me from a troubled nap, and while I didn't feel like company, I got up to answer the door anyway. I peeked out the window on my way to the door and saw it was Carol. My body tensed. *Why is she here?*

I put on a smile and pulled the door open. "Hi, Carol. What a surprise. Come on in. I just woke up from a quick nap."

Carol was dressed elegantly in clothes that spoke of success; on the other hand, I had on oversized sweats and no makeup, and my hair was uncombed. Next to her, I felt frumpy.

"Hi, Sara. You look like shit," she said.

My bruises and cuts were still visible, and I still had a slight limp. "Thanks, Carol. Just what I love to hear. Have a seat. Can I get you something to drink? Maybe a glass of wine?" It was just barely wine time, but after the news I had heard that day, I needed more than one glass.

I walked into the kitchen and poured our wine while Carol sat on the sofa. Once back in the living room, I handed her a glass of wine and sat in the chair next to the couch. "What's new with you?"

"I didn't come here to talk about me," she responded. "Did Thomas beat you? Is that where you got those bruises and cuts?"

"Whoa, nothing like cutting to the chase. Ray's gossip must have reached you."

"Yep, so answer, please." Carol was her usual blunt self.

Slowly, I related my story to Carol through embarrassment and tears. She listened without interrupting as I sobbed through the entire tale of Thomas and me. The silence between us when I was done was heavy, as if we both were internalizing what I had just told her, to make sense of it all. Finally, Carol, in a soft, nonjudgmental voice, broke the silence.

"You never mentioned the why of wanting to break up with him when we messaged. I could have helped you then."

"Carol, I just couldn't. I was humiliated about what he had done to me. Everyone thinks I am this strong person and knows I worked with abused women—how could I let anyone know I was deep into Thomas's abuse?" I said through sniffles and gulps for air between sobs.

She didn't say another word; instead, she came to sit on the arm of the chair and held me while I wept. The last time she had held me, we had been in my apartment. It seemed so long ago.

"Sara, please don't ever feel you are alone. I'm always here for you, and I will always have your back. I may tell you things you don't want to hear, but that feedback is based on what I see and hear you say. I love you and would never think less of you, no matter what choices you made."

Her words brought more tears. No one, even those who had professed their love for me, had ever said such powerful words to me before. I didn't know how to respond; I had no skills to let her know how much her words meant to me, so I just cried and hugged her tighter.

My tears finally stopped. We spent the next few hours talking and drinking wine. I began to feel more comfortable with letting Carol in on the secret of my childhood and what my stepfather and mother had done to me. It became clear to me that Carol did not take our friendship for granted and saw me as a person who deserved to have love and to fulfill her hopes and dreams. She didn't see me as Thomas's victim. The realization sparked something in me, though it wasn't clear what yet—perhaps a determination to take baby steps to make my life work and shed the title of victim in favor of the title of survivor.

After Carol left, I poured another glass of wine and retrieved my phone from the office. Sighing and with a heavy heart, I noticed more than twenty calls and voice mails from Thomas. I didn't want to talk to him. He was the last person I wanted to call. I felt upbeat, with a new sense of inner strength, and calls with him always brought me down and forever took the wind out of my sails. If I called him, I knew it would be the same.

Just then, my phone, still in my hand, vibrated with an incoming call. *Speak of the devil*, I thought, and then I giggled at how appropriate my thought was. *I might as well answer and show him my newfound strength.*

"Hello, Thomas. Reunited with your wife?" I snapped, encouraged by the wine and, through my conversation with Carol, the inner strength to call him on his bullshit lies.

"We aren't together, you stupid cow. We are separated. Why would I have been with you if I was still with her?"

"Oh, Thomas, the lies you tell. You told me you were still married, remember?"

"Look, let's not do this now. I need to know where you are with our current project."

Short, sweet, and to the point, he effectively had deflected us off his married status.

"I didn't get around to reviewing the status today; some things came up. But while we are on the subject, if you want me to continue to work with you on this and future projects, I will need an international business contract, signed by you and me. It must specify timelines, expectations, and especially how soon after the client signs off I get paid."

"We don't need a contract, love. Why would we need one? We've done okay with verbal agreements, haven't we?"

Ah, he had left the door open for me to blast him. "At my last count, you owe me one hundred thousand US dollars for our previous project, including expenses, and seventy-five thousand US dollars for your half of the business credit card, with most of the expenses not deductible as business expenses, like your booze. If I continue with the current project, you will owe me another one hundred thousand US dollars. That makes the total you owe me two hundred seventy-five thousand US dollars. That is why I insist on a contract."

"You are overthinking all this. But okay, look, to make you happy, I'll get an international business attorney to draw one up and send it to you to sign. In the meantime, would you please send me an update on the project and move forward with it?"

"I want it notarized, so don't send it to me without your notarized signature. I'll give you an update tomorrow."

With that, I hung up, in control of myself and my future for the first time in—well, I couldn't remember when. *I won't have to see Thomas again. I don't have to talk to him if I don't want to.* Still in the office, I heard the ding of an incoming email. My eyes lit up when I saw it was from my congressman's office.

Dear Ms. Matthews,

I'm pleased to give you some good news! We worked with the State Department and have red-flagged Mr. Hunter's passport at all ports of entry into the United States. This includes Canadian and Mexican borders, as well as all ports of departure from the United Kingdom leaving for the United States. This means Mr. Hunter will be unable to enter the United States altogether.

Please let me know if you have any further questions or need our assistance in any way. Be safe, and take care of yourself.

Sincerely,
Denise Jacobsen
Administrative Assistant, Congressman
Rick Larsen's Office

As with her first email, I read the message over and over. I hadn't believed what I read. After the news from the prosecuting attorney's office that afternoon, the email was a message from heaven. No more lying awake at night while fearful he would find a way to come to the island and hurt me again. It was all I could do to contain the relief and joy her email had brought me. *Oh, hell with it—why hold it in?*

"Come on, Kitty. We have some celebrating to do."

Chapter 60

The truth of the story lies in the details.
—Paul Auster, *The Brooklyn Follies*

I made progress on the project but didn't publish my work on the network. I would not give Thomas access to my work until my demands had been met, and I was still waiting.

Before I knew it, V-Day arrived: the day of the victims' panel.

With doubts surfacing, I rose from bed and went through my morning routine. I dressed in blue jeans and a red sweater before I had a cup of coffee. I cuddled with Kitty while visions of what Thomas had done to me throughout our relationship haunted me. The images were real, the pain was real, and the humiliation was real—as authentic as when I'd lived through it. I crawled back into bed and lay in the fetal position. The movie of terrifying memories of Thomas played through my mind. The visions had a direct impact on my emotions. It had to be a good thing, didn't it, to take those real, gut-wrenching emotions with me to talk to a roomful of abusers about the impact my abuser had had on me?

The time came to leave. The panic began as a cluster of yellow jackets in my abdomen. I opened my eyes to the misty gray afternoon, which mirrored my mood. I cleaned myself up and applied some concealer, hoping it would hide the redness and puffiness around my eyes, not to mention the still-visible black eyes. I gave Kitty a pat on the head and then headed out the door with a few yellow jackets still humming around my stomach.

The panel was held in a small courtroom. I was seated in the jury box, along with a policeman, a probation officer, and several representatives from local treatment centers. The convicted abusers were sitting in the gallery, guarded by a few deputies strategically placed around the room. Some of the abusers had their partners—their victims—with them. I sort of had expected the abusers to be dressed in orange jumpsuits with *Prisoner* stamped on the back and was relieved they were dressed in their regular everyday clothes.

While the other presenters took their turns speaking to the group, I tried to pretend I was an actress preparing to play the role of a lifetime, one filled with love for her abuser at first and then disbelief, humiliation, and hopelessness every time he directed his anger at me. But I hadn't been in a role. It all had been real; it had really happened. This was not the time to playact.

My turn to present finally came. As I stood to walk to the center of the courtroom, my hand went automatically to my abdomen to still the yellow jackets. I had an eerie sense that Thomas and I could have been in the gallery, waiting to hear a victim tell us her story. I looked each person in the eye and tried to determine if he or she would just blow me off. It was up to me to tell my story so they would never be able to ignore it or forget it.

"Hello. My name is Sara, and I'm here to tell you my story. It starts out okay, not unlike many other stories women have to tell. But the ending comes right out of your favorite horror story." The yellow jackets hummed a little louder and threatened to throw me into a full-blown panic attack.

I paced back and forth in front of my captive audience and continued. "As I tell you what happened, you will hear me laugh, cry, yell, and sometimes use words that may be offensive to you. I don't apologize, for this is what happened to me, not what I did to someone else to make them violent toward me." My hands curled into fists. I didn't know if I could go through with it. *Just do it, Sara; it's essential. But essential for whom?* I wondered.

"Not long ago, I was a happily married, successful woman with a wonderful son. I thought I had it all, and the world was mine. Until my life started to crumble. First, my marriage was gone. My son left for the university, and my business was limping along."

I paused again. *You can do this, Sara. Look them in the eye.* "I had a business partner who lived in London. We worked together for five years, designing and developing systems for clients. After I separated from my husband, my partner and I became closer, until we became romantically involved."

I looked at the audience and saw a few yawns; a few looked down at their hands, suddenly interested in their fingernails. I would have to get to the hard part. I took a deep breath, closed my eyes to focus on what I would say next, and continued.

"To make a long story short, we fell in love with each other. At least I thought it was love. It wasn't too long before we moved in together and even bought a home on the island. And then it started."

Another pause came with more pacing. With fists still clenched,

I continued. I explained how he had lured me into his web of manipulation and deceit by playing on my vulnerabilities. I detailed all the violent episodes from my perspective. I shouted about how it had felt to be rolled up in a mattress, how each of his punches had hurt me, and how powerless I'd been against his rages. I explained how I'd hidden from others when my eyes were blackened and my lips were cut by his fists. I told of the humiliation I'd endured when I walked into a hotel, looking as if I'd just stepped in from a war and smelling like a distillery, and no one had tried to help me.

My voice softened as I looked into the victims' eyes in the audience and related how he had kept me from my friends and family and isolated me from everyone who cared about me. I displayed my raw emotions, and after I finished, I quit pacing and stood in front of them as rivers of tears wet the floor.

When I finished, the silence in the room hung over us all. I looked up toward the gallery, and through my tears, I saw that all eyes were riveted on me; some had tears of their own.

"Thank you for listening," I said in a hoarse voice, and I turned back to the jury box. The room exploded with applause, not just from the gallery but also from the other presenters. I was shocked. Goose bumps pricked and tickled my skin.

"Thank you. Please remember my story if you ever feel like striking out against another again."

After the panel ended, many in the gallery lined up to shake my hand. They thanked me for sharing my story, some still with tears in their eyes. A few of the men told me my story had changed their attitude toward beating up their partners. They had never looked at the situation from their victims' eyes before. I hoped my account would stay with them for a long time. It was the single proudest moment of my life, and to think I had Thomas to thank for it.

I walked out of the courthouse with a mix of emotions. I felt washed out from speaking with such intensity, yet there was a lightness in my heart. The guilt and shame I carried around as an integral part of who I was didn't seem to weigh as heavily as before. The light had broken through the top of my self-imposed deep, dark well.

To think I had almost not gone that day. I'd nearly allowed my fear and shame to continue to hold me as their prisoner. I had broken the grip they had on me, an essential first step in my healing process. I still had a million miles to heal, but that step was a huge one and started me on a positive path toward being emotionally and physically healthy.

I presented to the victims' panel one more time. Presenting took a toll on me. To be authentic, I had to relive Thomas's rage each time. Presenting kept me stuck in the nightmare, and while I was proud that what I shared probably changed at least one person's life, the time had come to turn the focus onto my own well-being.

Chapter 61

My life is a perfect graveyard of buried hopes.
—L. M. Montgomery, *Anne of Green Gables*

Thomas followed through with his agreement to arrange for a signed international contract between us. Would he actually honor the contract? That was a huge concern of mine since he had not paid me yet for anything.

The ringing of my phone brought me back to the present. Since I was on a short break from work, I decided to answer it.

"Hi, Thomas," I said tersely with my thoughts still on the past hurts.

"Hullo, love."

I cringed at the word *love*. I certainly was not his love anymore.

"Just wanted to know where the project is at and if you think we are still on track to meet our deadline."

I spent the next few minutes updating him again; evidently, he had not read the email I'd sent to update him that morning.

"Great. Good to hear. I want you to come to London for the launch. They are planning a soiree in the crypt at Saint Paul's Cathedral and have invited all the movers and shakers in London. I want you there with me."

"I'm not coming to London, Thomas. I've got an idea: take your wife," I responded calmly. "I don't relish the thought of walking on top of dead people while sipping champagne and listening to jazz and hobnobbing with the London elite. And I don't relish the idea of seeing you again."

"You will be there," he ordered.

"No, Thomas, I won't. I never want to see you again. Our current project will be our last project together. I thought I made that clear a while ago."

"You did not make it clear, and if you refuse to come, you will be sorry."

I clicked the phone off at Thomas's threat. I didn't need to hear any more of his orders and ultimatums. He didn't own me. We were partners in one last project together, and I wouldn't have him marginalize me ever again.

The phone rang again almost as soon as I had hung up.

"Hello?" I answered in a happy, singsong voice.

"Hullo, love. You hung up on me before I was through talking to you." His voice sounded strange, deep, and more authoritative than usual.

"We don't have anything more to talk about," I responded, still using my singsong voice.

"Oh, we do have one more thing. I am contacting Carol and

putting the house on the market. If I can't be there to enjoy it, I may as well not have it. I want you out as soon as possible."

I was speechless. Surely he was joking. I hadn't expected that, but maybe I should have. He hadn't paid me. I hadn't inquired about alternative places to live. Where was I supposed to go? What would I do with all the furniture? Who would help me move? How was I supposed to pay for a move? With each question, the panic grew in my chest, ready to take over.

"I expect you out by the time the house sells."

"Thom—"

He had already hung up. Sucker punch number two.

Disbelief and panic scrambled my thoughts. I had to call Thomas back. Surely he had been joking. After dialing his number with shaky hands, I took a big gulp of wine and waited for him to answer.

"Hullo, love. What do you need?" he said.

"I need to know you were joking about selling the house. You were kidding, right? Just to wind me up?"

"I'm not kidding, Sara. I don't want a house that I cannot be in and that you live in rent free. I need to sell it and move on."

"I'm not living here rent free! You owe me money for the credit card and for our last project as well as the current one. You must be crazy to think I am living here rent free!" I shouted over the phone.

"You know, I can easily call the sheriff and have you evicted, or better yet, I know people over there who could convince you it would be in your best interest to leave the house."

"What do you mean?" I asked in a shaky voice.

"Don't be a stupid cow, Sara. If you can't figure it out, use your imagination. I hope your medical insurance is paid up." With that, he hung up.

I had a fortune to pay in bills, nowhere to live, and no hope left. I had been thrown back down my familiar well of despair. Its darkness clung to me like slime.

Ray's words echoed in the stillness of the house: "You will never make it without me."

Right now, I had to agree with him.

Chapter 62

Death ends a life, not a relationship.
—Mitch Albom, *Tuesdays with Morrie*

Only moments ago, the tiny flicker of hope for a better life had become an extinguished wick of despair. I sank to my knees on the carpet. My brain refused to comprehend that Thomas had essentially evicted me from my home. Even though he owed me a tremendous amount of money, I had no recourse. His name was the only one on the deed. I stared into nothingness, unaware of how much time passed. Kitty sauntered up to me, rubbed against my thigh, and purred her love song, which finally broke my zombie-like state.

"Oh, Kitty, this is bad. Very, very bad," I whispered to her as I picked myself up from the floor and headed to the kitchen for more wine, even though the thought of moving again threatened to paralyze me. Everything that had seemed to come together just an hour ago had unraveled at warp speed and left a million questions and no resources to figure out the answers.

Did I believe he had friends who could convince me to move? I didn't know if I did or not, but I leaned toward the side that he did, considering the scam he had pulled on me, a lonely, vulnerable woman who had fallen for his act like a fish taking bait.

Finishing my wine, I decided to go to bed. There was nothing I could do about my predicament that night. I shivered and knew the nightmares would probably visit. I wondered why Mom hadn't shown up lately. Maybe her haunting license had expired.

I slept fitfully and found it challenging to go back to sleep after the usual two o'clock nightmare. I had no idea what I would do or where I would go. Without Thomas's expert database knowledge, the web design work I did would provide minimal income. I was a college dropout and had no degree, and I feared my skills on a résumé would not be marketable. I had more questions than answers and felt the well of despair close in on me. I looked out the bedroom window at the darkened sky and a million twinkling stars.

"Lord," I said, "I don't know what to do. I don't want to be homeless. But if that is where you think I need to be, on the streets, then I promise I will work to discover what your purpose for me is."

My prayer surprised me; I was more spiritual than religious. I hadn't prayed since my bedtime prayers as a young child. But while my prayer was a surprise, after I whispered it into the darkness, I fell into a deep sleep uninterrupted by nightmares.

The next morning, I woke somewhat rested and committed to find a job. I didn't care what or where, just one that paid and had excellent benefits. My only job now would be to find a job, but because I desperately needed the money, I would have to finish up the modeling company's project. First things first, I had to update my résumé and highlight the skills I thought would be marketable.

I sat down at the computer and opened up Microsoft Word to begin a list of my skills and abilities. I stared at the blank page and tried to think of what I should type. While I didn't have a college degree, I'd had lots of learning experiences, including graduate-level college courses. All I had to do was translate my personal education so the reviewers understood I had a lot of skills and knowledge.

I leaned back in my chair with a huge sigh. Was I kidding myself? I wasn't twenty anymore. I was a divorced, jobless, homeless middle-aged woman who was not where I'd thought I would be at that age. I was starting over as if I were twenty. What was I thinking? Where did the homeless go on the island anyway?

Stop it, Sara. Quit feeling sorry for yourself, dammit. You know what you must do: get yourself in gear, and get that résumé done.

For the rest of the morning and afternoon, I researched what made a sound, well-formatted résumé and then compiled mine with my new knowledge. Hours later, I was confident the finished product spoke truthfully to my skills and abilities. I believed I had a good chance of having the door opened for an interview.

"Time for a break," I said to Kitty, stretching to get the kinks out of my neck and shoulders. I looked out the window at the darkened sky. "Where did the time go? I bet you're hungry for your dinner."

In the kitchen, I frowned when I realized Kitty hadn't eaten her solid food from breakfast. That was strange; she usually gobbled it up as soon as I put it into her dish. Stranger still, she did not follow me into the kitchen. I went back to the office and found her again curled up on her chair.

"What's the matter, Kitty?" I asked, kneeling down to stroke her.

She responded with a growl, jumped off the chair, and ran toward the living room. That was weird; she'd never growled at me before. I followed her into the living room and saw her on her chair by the unlit fireplace. She kept a steady eye on me, ready to run if I came near her. Her behavior was out of the ballpark for her. I struggled in deciding whether to call the vet or not—it would be another expense to my already stretched budget. The bills I had were well over the amount of money in my bank account, even with my divorce settlement. But in the end, it was a no-brainer. Kitty had been loyal to me and taken care of me when I needed tenderness and to know someone cared for me.

The next morning, I called the vet and made an appointment. Luck was on our side: an appointment was available within the next hour. Kitty would not let me put her in the cat carrier; she growled if I came near her. I put the fire on and hoped she would hop onto her chair, curl up, and fall sound asleep. Sure enough, she did. I took my opportunity and gently picked her up off her chair and swiftly placed her in the carrier. She howled and spat at me when she realized I'd tricked her. She didn't like the car ride any better and growled a low growl all the way to the vet's office.

Soon we were called into the examination room. It always surprised me that while the vet took care of hundreds or maybe even thousands of animals, he remembered Kitty's name. Perhaps it wasn't surprising after all—a kitty named Kitty.

He gave her a proper examination and finally made his way to her mouth. He gasped when he gently opened her mouth and turned Kitty toward me to see what he had seen. It was my turn to gasp. Her swollen left jaw looked raw and bloody.

"Good Lord, what is wrong with her?" My heart twisted, and I feared the worst.

"Bone cancer. Looking at it, it appears to be pretty advanced."

"Don't you need to run some tests or something to confirm?"

Hope sparked in my voice. "How come she never showed symptoms until now?"

"I'm not sure why she didn't let you know something was wrong before now. At the stage her cancer is in, she should have been eating less and sticking to herself. She is at the stage where tests would only confirm what I can see with my eyes. She has advanced bone cancer in her jaw."

I paused and let his words sink in—*bone cancer.* Any kind of cancer sounded ominous to me. I couldn't lose her. I just couldn't. Why hadn't I seen any symptoms before? Had I been so involved with my troubles that I hadn't noticed until that day? Guilt joined my fear and sadness.

"What can we do to help her get better?" I asked him hopefully.

"Sara, we could do chemo and radiation, but at this stage in her disease, I don't think it will eradicate cancer. It is also costly. It's totally up to you, but I recommend you take her home and spend the next few days loving her. She will let you know when she is ready."

"Ready for what?" My heart knew what he meant.

"To be blunt, to put her down. Her pain will only increase, and I would guess she has less than a week."

Tears jabbed at my eyes. *This on top of everything else life has dumped on me.* I looked through blurry eyes at the vet, slid Kitty back into her carrier, and thanked him.

"Call when Kitty is ready, and we will take good care of her and you as she crosses over." His voice was gentle and filled with empathy. I wondered if it would be as hard for him as for me.

I didn't say anything. I couldn't. My precious Kitty would not be with me much longer. She was my protector when I had nightmares but would no longer be there to comfort me. Kitty, my sounding board, always seemed interested in everything I told her, and now she would be leaving me. Leaving the world. Forever.

I cried all the way home as the reality of losing my best friend dug into my soul. Once in the house, Kitty popped out of the carrier and immediately ran for her place by the fireplace. It wasn't that chilly, but I didn't care; I flipped on the gas, and the comforting flames surrounded the fake logs. She loved sitting by the fire, and if needed, it would stay on until she was, as the doctor had put it, ready. I knelt down next to her, not touching her but letting her know I was there. My heart was broken; my eyes wept.

"Kitty, I don't know what I am going to do without you. Who will protect me when you're gone? Who will soothe me when the nightmares come?" We sat next to each other and watched the fire. We felt each other's pain, hers in her bones and mine in my heart.

The next day, Kitty showed me she was ready. She didn't eat or drink her water, and she ran from me, growled, and spat when I tried to hold her. How could I not have seen the signs? How could I not have known she was suffering? Had I been so into my own suffering that I had ignored the warnings?

My heart was heavy with sadness and guilt when I phoned the vet. The receptionist told me to bring Kitty right into the office. I didn't know if I could go through with it, but I couldn't allow her to suffer in her pain.

It took a while to get her into her carrier, but she was weak and tired quickly. The vet took us right in and, once in the exam room, slid Kitty from the carrier onto a soft towel on the table. I snuggled her, put my arms around her, and locked my eyes onto hers. The vet shaved her paw in preparation for the needle. Kitty took care of me again, thanking me with her eyes for releasing her from her pain. I didn't see the needle go in, but I knew the instant she left our world.

Chapter 63

**A friend is someone who walks into a room
when everyone else is walking out.**
—Gary Moore

"What would you like to do with Kitty's body?" asked the vet softly. I hadn't moved; my arms still held Kitty, and my tears fell onto her beautiful, soft fur. She was really gone, and now I had to decide how to honor her life in her death.

"I think I'd like to have her cremated and keep her ashes." I didn't move from Kitty's body. My eyes remained locked on her lifeless ones.

He nodded and then explained the process and timeline. "We'll call you when Kitty is ready to be picked up."

He came around the table to where I still held her in my arms, pulled me away, and hugged me. I took it as my cue to leave, so I picked up the empty carrier and my purse, gave Kitty one last kiss, thanked the vet, and left.

I sat in my parked car beside the vet's office and let the tears fall unchecked. My heart was broken. Each time I looked over at the empty carrier on the passenger seat, my sobs became uncontrollable.

Come on, Sara. You can't sit in the parking lot forever. I swallowed my sobs, started the car, and began the lonely drive home. Kitty wouldn't be there to greet me.

Once home, I hesitated to go into the house. The feeling of loss was immense. It was time to begin my life without Kitty, but that didn't mean she wouldn't be in my heart forever. Once in the house, I saw her food and water dishes and her litter box, and the pain grew larger. I cleaned them all and then took them and the carrier to the garage, out of sight.

But her empty chair waiting for her by the still-lit fire broke me. I rested my head on her chair, smelled her scent, and sobbed until I had no more tears to give.

I decided I needed a distraction for the rest of the afternoon, or I would wallow in grief. The perfect solution seemed to be to browse online job sites. I realized the jobs available on the island would not pay enough for me to pay my bills, live, and have benefits too. I would need to search off the island also.

It was arduous and tedious work. I found openings for training and communication consultants, both of which I had experience in. For each job application, I tweaked my résumé to ensure I met the requirements, which took longer than I imagined. Hours passed, but I submitted applications to at least fifty job openings. *Good job, Sara. You deserve a glass of wine.*

I turned to Kitty's office chair to say, "Let's get out of here." For a moment, I was confused when I didn't see her there, and then I remembered. Fresh tears wet my cheeks. I left the office and shuffled to the kitchen. The effects of losing Kitty and a new threat from Thomas had wiped my hunger away. I opened another bottle of pinto grigio and sat on the sofa, where I spent the night drinking. I thought about Kitty and worried about what lengths Thomas would go to in order to get me out of our house.

The next morning, I woke in my bed with no memory of a nightmare for the first time in a long time. I stretched my sleepiness away and then looked down at the foot of the bed for Kitty. The hole in my heart got bigger. *God, I miss you, Kitty.* I got out of bed.

With my morning routine over with, dressed in my well-worn sweats and no makeup, I looked forward to brewing coffee and taking that first sip. I shuffled into the kitchen and grabbed the coffee basket to put the filter in it, when I spotted the doe and her fawn. I smiled at the peaceful scene and felt a bit of happiness mixed with my sadness at the loss of Kitty.

I headed to the office with a full coffee mug, eager to check my email for any responses to my résumé. I was astonished that three responses had come in overnight. As I read through them, I figured I had three good chances to secure a position. All three had requested a phone interview, so I spent the next few minutes responding with an enthusiastic "Yes. When?" As Grandma had always said, I wasn't willing to count my chickens before they hatched, so after I sent the emails, I checked the job sites for any new job listings. There were a few, so I went back to tweaking my résumé and submitting it.

What do I do now? I can't sit here and watch my inbox for new responses to come in. I decided to work on the modeling company's project for the rest of the day. My work was close to being completed, and I wanted it done before I had to move out—or became homeless.

I heard the dings that indicated I had new emails in my inbox. I set the project aside and, with butterflies in my stomach, checked my email. *Woohoo!* I had received formal meeting invitations for phone interviews with all three companies. Two of them were video game companies that wanted a trainer to work with their salespeople, and the other was a corporation that requested a training and communication consultant. They were located in the Midwest, in the South, and on the East Coast.

I accepted all three phone interviews and felt lucky I had enough time to research the companies, prepare, and formulate my questions. The interviews were spaced just far enough apart so that one would not bump into another.

I reviewed the companies again and noticed they all required a move to their location. I hadn't seen that before. One was located in Gainesville, Florida; one was in Washington, DC; and one was in Bloomington-Normal in central Illinois. If I took one of the jobs, I would have to move far away from Jackson. Did I have a choice if I didn't want to be homeless?

I figured Florida would be hot and humid, as would DC. I couldn't see myself going from a small island to a busy metro area like Washington, DC. Central Illinois, rich in farmland and rural but close to Chicago and St. Louis, sounded like the best place for me to relocate to. But I needed to get an offer first. *No eggs before the chickens.*

The phone calls went surprisingly well. Florida and DC wanted to fly me out for on-site interviews, and Illinois wanted one more phone call. State Farm Insurance, the company in Illinois, had been in business since 1922 and had been stable throughout the years. I was concerned about the video game companies' longevity—they'd be around at the whim of the gamer population. I put my answers to them on hold until my second call with State Farm.

A few days later, the second call with State Farm went like a dream; it felt as if the interviewer and I were old friends and not potential boss and employee. Not long after that, I received a proposal: a salary more than I ever could have made on the island and full benefits. They would pay for movers to pack me up and move me there; I wouldn't have to lift a finger. There would also be a rental car for me at the airport when I landed and a corporate apartment to use until I found other living arrangements. I was gobsmacked. I'd received a job proposal that offered everything I needed to make the transition. I looked upward and whispered a grateful thank-you.

They sent the proposal immediately by email. I reviewed it carefully, and with no questions or concerns, I signed it electronically. I called the other two companies to thank them for their interest and tell them I had accepted another offer.

I leaned back in my office chair with my hands interlaced behind my head. I had never felt so blessed. Someone thought I had value and talent, and they wanted me. *I am not worthless after all.* I thought my heart would burst. I was on a high after last night's low.

I would need to call Jackson to give him the good news. It was mid-December, and my start date was January 6, so I wanted to firm up our plans to celebrate Christmas together. It was his last year at the University, and since he was in the Air Force's ROTC program, he would join the Air Force upon graduation, with his first duty station in Hawaii. We had no idea if we would be able to celebrate Christmas together next year.

But that night was meant for a mix of celebration and mourning, and for once, I would allow myself to do what I wanted to do without fear of reprisal.

⊷⊰⊱⊶

My phone woke me the next morning. I got out of bed slowly and muttered, "Uffda," at my wine-induced headache. I hadn't thought I celebrated that much, but the evidence was in the hammering inside my head.

"Hello?" I said through buckets of sand in my dry mouth.

"Hullo, love. I just wanted to call to see if you heard footsteps on the deck last night."

My brain moved slowly and became confused with his question. What had he meant? What footsteps?

"Hullo? Are you still there? Didn't you hear me?"

"I heard you; I'm just confused. What did you mean?"

"Are you that thick? I sent someone to the house to see if you were still in it. He had my full agreement that he could remove you with as much force as it took if he decided to. Obviously, you're still at the house."

I took deep breaths to settle the yellow jackets in my abdomen. I steadied my voice and said, "I will be moving by Christmas, and I can move that up if your buyer wants to close early. Do you have a buyer? Actually, I haven't seen Carol. There is no lockbox on the door and no For Sale sign."

"We just got the listing papers finalized electronically, and the sign will go up today. I'm sure Carol will get the lockbox on the door as well. So where are you moving to?"

I would never tell him where I was moving. He had threatened me again just now. How did I know he wouldn't send his thugs to hurt me in Illinois?

"In town," I lied.

"Well, you be careful. I'm not sure if my friend will return tonight or not," he said, and he hung up.

I was petrified. Part of me didn't believe Thomas, but what if he had told the truth? Just then, the doorbell rang. I threw on a bathrobe, quickly ran a brush through my hair to tame it, and left the bedroom to answer the door.

"Morning, Carol," I said as I opened the door. "Come in, and have some coffee."

"I'm not happy about this whole thing with Thomas." That was Carol—to the point.

"Well, look at it this way: this is your livelihood, and I'd rather have to deal with you through this than anyone else. But you need to know that Thomas is dishonest and has stolen money from me—money I earned. Be careful, and make sure you get your commission before he gets his money. Come in, and sit down. I'll put the coffee on."

"I just came to put the lockbox on the door and to let you know Ray will be out sometime today to place the sign."

Crap, that's right. My ex-husband placed the For Sale signs for all the real estate offices. I wondered if he would come to the door to rub in what a loser I was. But I wasn't a loser anymore; I had a job.

"I have some news to tell you," I said to Carol while the coffee was brewing. "The good news is, I have a job. The bad news is, I will be moving to Illinois at the first of the year. My job starts January 6. The even worse news is that you cannot tell anyone where I am. Thomas has been threatening me. He says he has friends here who would hurt me if he asked them to. I don't want him to have access to me when I move."

Carol was ecstatic for me. She was not happy I would be moving away but understood. I knew she would guard my secret; I'd never trusted anyone more than Jackson and Carol. She wanted to know about my plans, so over mugs of coffee, I told her from beginning to end how I would get to Illinois.

"I am so happy for you, Sara. You deserve a break more than anyone I know." She prepared to leave and gave me a huge hug at the door. "I'll keep you updated on the progress with the house."

I watched her walk to her car as tears trailed down my cheeks. She had always been a good friend. I loved her and wondered if I would find another friend like her in Illinois.

Chapter 64

Christmas is doing a little something extra for someone.
—Charles M. Schulz

As I watched Carol's car wind down the drive, the reality of what I was about to embark on landed on me like a two-ton black cloud. What was I thinking? I'd be leaving Jackson, lifelong friends, and the island I loved—all that was familiar—to go to a place where I had no friends, no familiarity, and a job I wasn't sure I could deliver on. The totality of the change that faced me was overwhelming. Would I have the strength to face all that alone? Wouldn't it be easier to stay on the island and develop small websites to supplement a welfare check? I was too proud to accept a handout, I reasoned; my shame would have been unbearable.

I closed the door, turned around to a lonely house, and felt the silence that surrounded me. The sensation of total aloneness was crushing and enveloped me like a silent fog; my perception of myself seemed surreal. I hadn't even moved to a new town yet, but as I stood among everything familiar, I felt like a stranger in a strange land.

I pulled myself out of my quiet reverie and knew I had to call Jackson with my news before Ray had the chance to. Finding the right words to break the news to Jackson plagued me. Ray and I had split up, breaking an unspoken vow to Jackson and tearing his safe, loving world apart. Now I would be doing it again.

I picked up the phone and dialed Jackson's number.

"Hi, Jackson. How's it going?" I began with my usual greeting, hoping he couldn't hear the stress in my voice.

"Hey, Mom. What's up?"

"Got some news to share with you." I decided to get right to it, cutting out the chitchat crap. "I got a pretty good-paying job with great benefits. I start on January 6."

"Wow, that's awesome! What kind of job?" He always had been my biggest cheerleader.

"The position is for a communication and training consultant with State Farm." I paused, taking a deep breath, and then, with eyes closed, continued. "In Bloomington, Illinois."

He didn't hesitate with his response. "Wow! Are you okay with leaving the island?" He knew what was important to me, which brought tears that blurred my vision.

"I have to be, Jackson. There is nothing on the island that would match the salary I'll be making, and I need something with benefits. The only thing that gives me second thoughts is moving so far away from you." I didn't want to load any guilt onto him, but I needed to be honest.

"Mom, don't worry about me; we can always go back and forth

to visit. I'll be in Hawaii anyway, so we wouldn't be close even if you stayed on the island." He paused and then continued. "Mom, you've been through a lot with the divorce and Thomas. I think you need to think about yourself for a change and go after what will make you happy."

Tears streamed down my cheeks. He didn't know, and would never know, that somewhere along my journey in life, I'd lost the knowledge of what made me happy. All I'd known was what I needed to do to survive.

"Thank you, Jackson. You will never understand what you just did for me. You allowed me to give myself permission not to carry with me to Bloomington guilt about leaving you and this island."

It hadn't been as hard as I'd thought to tell him I was leaving the island to live thousands of miles away. Our conversation changed to stories of his college life that had tears rolling down my cheeks from laughter instead of sadness.

As our conversation started to wind down, I turned it toward Christmas. "I'll still be in the house on Christmas. I would love for us to spend it together. What are your plans?"

"I planned to spend the day with you. I'll be on winter break, so I thought I'd spend Christmas Eve with Dad and then spend Christmas Day and a couple of days after with you. I could help you pack."

"I love the idea! The packers will be coming on December 27 and the movers on December 29, so we'll have plenty of time to celebrate before we box up the decorations and get organized for the packers."

The rest of our call was spent firming up our plans, and by the time we hung up, my heart was much lighter, and reality found a firm footing in my mind. I wandered into the living room. I would miss that view when landlocked in central Illinois—the sun glinting off the water, the boats bobbing as the tide rose.

Movement at the bottom of the drive caught my attention; Ray was installing the For Sale sign. He glanced up and waved at me. I half-heartedly waved back. Did he think I had been turned out on the street, homeless and jobless? Had Carol told him I would be moving across the country to take a new job that paid three times what I had been making when we were still married? My heart gave a tug and hinted at the residual feelings I had for him. Was it possible to be married to someone for twenty years and just shut off all feelings for the person? I missed him. I missed the familiarity of him. While we hadn't had a great intimacy of minds, our romantic intimacy had been special. I missed his touch, which was gone from me forever, given to another.

I had better things to do than feel sorry for myself with those melancholy thoughts. They were nothing but memories now, and that was where they would remain. Christmas was just a few weeks away, and I had lots to do to plan for the holiday and organize the move, which left no time for negative thoughts to take up residence in my mind.

I counted on house sales remaining slow in the winter. With less than a month to go before I moved, I didn't think I needed to worry, unless Thomas evicted me. I decided not to think along those lines and pulled out the holiday decorations.

After all that had happened, I still believed in the magic of Christmas. It wasn't all about religion for me, although I believed Jesus was the Messiah. It was the aura: the warmth of the hearth, the smells of sweet treats wafting throughout the house, twinkling Christmas lights, holiday music everywhere I went, and, most importantly, the surprise on the faces of loved ones when I found just the right gift.

My heart took up residence in my stomach when I realized my finances severely restricted the quality and number of presents I'd be able to purchase that year. There would be no lavish Christmas dinner with turkey and all the trimmings. I'd be lucky to afford to make a nice meatloaf. Yet none of that mattered. Jackson and I would be together, making new memories and new traditions.

I ramped up to high gear. I knew I would not be able to spend all my time on Christmas preparations; I had to prepare for the movers. Still, I baked Jackson's favorite cookies, bought a few inexpensive gifts for him, and purchased a small roast for dinner. The closer Christmas Day came, the more excited I became, like a little girl in anticipation of Santa's arrival.

Except when Thomas called. I didn't bother to answer anymore, but that didn't stop him from leaving threatening voice mails. His threats remained the same: he said he had friends who would visit and force me to leave the house. The real threat made in every voice mail was on my life.

That day's voice mails were no different. I knew I shouldn't listen to them, but I did. Every single one. If his goal was to make me afraid, it was working. I left all the lights on at night and lay awake, listening for footsteps on the deck. *They can't get in*, I reasoned. All the doors and windows were locked and dead-bolted.

Then I remembered Thomas still had keys.

Chapter 65

Sometimes you have to lose all you have
to find out who you truly are.
—Roy T. Bennett, *The Light in the Heart*

The minute I remembered Thomas still had keys to the house, I
googled a local locksmith and called. I hoped they could change out
the locks that day. I couldn't take the chance he'd send the house
keys to his so-called friends, who then would let themselves in and
do his bidding, whatever that might be. Luck was on my side: the
locksmith would be there within an hour.

Within a few hours, I had new locks on the doors and new keys.
I had to get the new keys to Carol for the lockbox so she could show
the house to potential buyers.

What a relief. I felt empowered to take steps for my own safety, not to mention my peace of mind. But while I felt safer in the house until I left, the reality was that Thomas could follow me everywhere with his threats of hurting me, even if I was thousands of miles away from there. I had to make one more phone call that day, without delay, to figure out how to be safe figured out.

"Hello. May I speak to Debbie? This is Sara Matthews." I figured if anyone would know what I should do, the director of the local abuse center would.

Debbie's calm but cheery voice came over the phone line. "Hi, Sara. How are things with you today?"

I explained my situation and asked for her advice about how to rid myself of Thomas's threatening phone calls and keep my location a secret to all but Carol.

"First, I'm surprised you haven't changed your phone number; you should do that immediately. Next, we can help set you up with a blind post office box here that you can use for mail. We will forward your mail to your new address in Illinois; you and our agency will be the only ones to know. How does that sound to you?"

"Wow, you make it sound so easy. I didn't know how easy it would be to become anonymous," I said with a laugh.

"I understand the next step may be difficult for you, but you need to stay off social media. That means Facebook, Instagram, Twitter—all social media. You may get by with a made-up account; it depends on how frequently you saw Thomas use social media. You should also report Thomas's threats to the sheriff. We know they won't do anything toward Thomas due to his deportation. Still, perhaps they can patrol your area more frequently until you leave."

I promised her I would do as she recommended. We made a date for me to come to the office after the holidays to set up the blind post office box. I hung up and felt more in control of my situation than ever—I had new locks and would have anonymity when I left. I felt less like a victim of Thomas and more like a survivor of him.

I decided to change my cell number once I got settled in Illinois. I called the sheriff, explained my situation, and asked for frequent patrols in my neighborhood. He promised they would patrol more, which lowered my stress level a notch or two.

Christmas Eve arrived. Jackson called to let me know he was on the island, at his Dad's house. We chatted for a few minutes and then hung up so he could join in the festivities of new traditions with Ray and his new family. A twinge of homesickness went through me. I was homesick for the old days, when I'd made fudge and dozens of cookies and prepared a huge dinner with all the family in attendance; Ray had stocked up the wood bin for our holiday fires; and Jackson had secretly searched the house for gifts, trying to pinch back the wrapping paper to see what was underneath. The warm glow of favorite memories surrounded me, and I felt a tingle of excitement to make new memories in a new life.

A new life. Wow, that sounds like a curse and a gift. I would be starting over. I imagined myself crawling out of the deep, dark well of despair I had been in when things were terrible with Thomas and standing on the edge of a mountain. I could fall to the depths of the well, or I could soar, free from past shame and guilt. It was my choice; it always had been.

The only lights on in the house were the tree lights, which gave the room a soft glow. Everything felt perfect in my life. Presents had been placed under the tree, and the wrapping reflected the tree lights. All that was missing was a fire and Kitty. She used to lie on my lap while watching *It's a Wonderful Life* every Christmas Eve, and I missed her. I walked over, flipped on the fire, and placed her chair near it, where she used to love to sit. I got the box that held her ashes, which the vet had delivered, and put her on the chair. I whispered a "Merry

Christmas Eve" to her and stroked the box as if I were stroking her fur. We would be together in spirit.

I turned on the television and settled on the couch with a glass of wine and *It's a Wonderful Life*. That night surely felt like a wonderful life on Whidbey Island.

Then Thomas called. *Nope, no way.* I would not allow him to ruin my lovely evening. I reached for the phone and, with a determination and conviction I had not experienced in a long time, turned it off.

⚬⟨⟩⚬

"Merry Christmas, Mom," Jackson said when I opened the door the next morning, and he gave me a big hug.

"Merry Christmas, sweetie," I said as I hugged him with tears of happiness flowing down my face.

"Hey, what are the tears for?" he asked as we broke apart.

"Oh, you know, the holiday, and I am so happy you are spending the day with me," I blubbered.

In the living room, I took his coat and beanie and hung them up while he fished a couple of presents out of the bag he carried and placed them under the tree.

"Are you hungry?" I asked, making my way to the kitchen. I loved cooking for him and hoped he had saved his appetite for his mom's traditional Christmas breakfast of pancakes, bacon, and eggs.

"You bet! I left Dad's house before breakfast was ready because I didn't want to miss your pannycakes."

I laughed. He had called pancakes pannycakes since he was old enough to talk.

"Mind if I go get a shower while you fix breakfast?" he asked.

"Not at all. Food should be ready when you get out."

Humming "Waltz of the Flowers" from the *Nutcracker Suite*, I set about making breakfast for the two of us. I set the table with my favorite china, which had a Christmas pattern. It was a special day, and I wanted every detail to reflect how much Jackson's being there meant to me. Dancing as if I were in the ballet, I placed the dishes gently on the table, flipped the bacon in the pan, and mixed up the pancake batter, ready to provide just-off-the-grill pannycakes for Jackson when he got out of the shower.

"Ah, there you are," I said, spotting Jackson as he walked into the kitchen just as I ceremoniously floated my way to the stove.

"What the heck—am I getting my own *Nutcracker* ballet?" Jackson laughed.

"Not quite." I chuckled and placed the bacon on a paper towel to sop up the grease and then put it on a dish to serve.

We spent the rest of the morning talking, laughing, and reminiscing over our breakfast. Jackson helped clean up when we were done. After the kitchen had been cleaned up, we adjourned to the living room to share the gifts we'd gotten.

"I didn't want to get you anything big because you would just have to pack it up and move it," Jackson said as I oohed and aahed over the warm boots and beautiful purple scarf he'd gotten me. "I hope they keep you warm in those Illinois winters."

"Very practical, Jackson. I love them. Thank you."

In turn, he was happy with the gift cards and new wallet I'd gotten him. Ever since he had been a teenager, he had forbidden me from picking out his clothes, so gift cards were the ticket. I also had gotten him a gift card to Dick's Drive-In, *the* place in Seattle to go for a burger and fries. All in all, the magic that the season brought to me every year seemed to be multiplied tenfold.

"Hey, Mom, what's that box on Kitty's chair? And by the way, where is she?"

I swallowed the lump in my throat and explained what had

happened and why Kitty was not with us. "The box holds her ashes, and last night, I set it on her chair by the fire just to feel her close."

Jackson came over and gave me a hug, whispering in my ear, "I'm sorry." What a loving young man his dad and I had raised.

For the rest of the day, Jackson watched football while I read a book I had wanted to read. We were comfortable just hanging out together, secure in the knowledge we were in the same room.

Time seemed to slow down for us that day. The football game must not have been that exciting, as Jackson fell asleep. A nap on Christmas Day was a luxury to take advantage of. Just as I entered a dream filled with wonderment, I heard my phone buzz. I rolled my eyes when I saw it was Thomas. I clicked the phone off just as I heard the crunch of gravel in the driveway as a car drove up.

I peeked out the window and saw the sheriff's car. Fear clutched my heart, almost stopped the blood flow, and made my ears hiss. Was the sheriff coming to kick me out of the house as a vagrant on Christmas Day?

With Jackson here? Please, God, don't let this happen. Not with Jackson here to witness how far I've fallen. Not on Christmas.

I opened the door before the deputy could ring the bell, so it wouldn't wake Jackson. I closed the door behind me and walked a few steps onto the deck.

"Hello, Deputy. How can I help you?" I asked in a voice that sounded vaguely like Minnie Mouse's.

"Hello. Are you Sara Matthews?" he asked with authority.

"Yes," I stammered. *Here we go. I'm homeless. And Jackson is here to witness what a failure his mother has become.*

"We got a call from you about threatening phone calls and a request for patrols in the area. I wanted to check to see if you were okay."

All I could do was stare at him. Had I heard him right? *I'm not getting kicked out?* I let my breath out in one big whoosh and said, "I'm fine. Thank you, Deputy."

"Well, let us know if anything strange happens. We will be patrolling the area more frequently to make sure you are okay. Merry Christmas, Sara."

"Thank you, and merry Christmas to you." Relief washed away my fears of becoming homeless and having to figure out how to move everything on Christmas Day. I waved as he walked to his car, and then I went back into the house and closed the door, shivering. I hadn't noticed how cold it was outside. I walked over to the fireplace and turned it on.

"Who was that, Mom?" Jackson asked sleepily from the couch.

"It was the sheriff. They are patrolling the area and wanted to know all was well here."

He didn't ask me anything more.

⊶⊰⊱⊷

The days after Christmas were happy yet melancholy. Jackson helped me pack up the things I didn't want the packers to touch and then spent some time with friends with whom he had graduated high school. We spent long evenings together just talking, as we always did. I felt close to him again. It was as if the divorce and all the angst that had come with it had been erased.

One night, Jackson told me he had something important to say to me. I thought it might have something to do with his girlfriend, although I hadn't thought they were serious about each other.

"Okay, I'm listening," I said, eager to know what he had to say.

"Mom, you have gone through so much. First the divorce and then Thomas, and now, well, look at you. You are on the edge of reinventing yourself. You made things happen when most would have fallen apart and not moved forward. I respect you so much. You are my hero." He finished with tears in his eyes.

I almost crumpled into the puddle that my tears made on the chair. Had I heard him right? I was his hero. He had reminded me I was a survivor and would never be someone's victim again. His loving words and that moment would be locked in my heart forever. I was speechless and felt honored; my heart felt as if it would burst. I went to him and hugged him tightly as our tears mingled together.

⊶⊷

Life would never be the same again, but that was not a bad thing. *Life*, I realized, *is growth. Without growth, we become stagnant and fall into situations that are not good for us. Sometimes being stagnant can be downright dangerous because we are afraid of the change growth brings to us.* It had taken all my fifty-five years to come to terms with that truth. For the rest of my life, I would never forget it, for the sake and safety of my life.

At SeaTac, while waiting for my flight to Chicago, I gazed out the window and watched the baggage handlers load the plane. It was January 2, the second day of my new year and the first day of my new life. Thoughts of Thomas crept into my brain, along with the lessons he had taught me. The most important lesson had been how to spot a man who was manipulative and controlling. I recognized what was still in my heart: my affection for him, not hate, as many might have thought. He would likely never know happiness, know the power of a soft touch instead of a punch, or feel unconditional love from someone. How could I have hated him? No, I felt pity for him. His was an angry, unfulfilled life.

When the bags were loaded, along with the passengers, the door to the plane closed. I buckled my seat belt while the jet's engines ramped up. The plane jerked backward, and in anticipation of our takeoff, I hugged the bag that held the box Kitty was in. I had questioned reality before, and now I was sure of mine. I was leaving the past behind, where it belonged. I'd been given a chance to soar until peace was finally mine.

I had a plan. Success would be my revenge to all who had taken so much from me.

Acknowledgments

The cover of *Success Is the Best Revenge* lists my name as author. However, I did not write this story alone; I had a few helpers I want to give my thanks to.

Sheila Athens worked with me as my book development coach. She has an intuitive sense of how a story should go and how to bring characters alive on the page and was instrumental in keeping my tenses consistent.

Marty Thomson, Carmen McFadyen, and Annee Brizo were the best beta readers ever. All three bravely gave what some might consider hard-to-hear feedback and were instrumental in pointing out inconsistencies, typos, run-on sentences, and so much more.

While many gave their encouragement and motivation for me to continue writing, even in the darkest days of putting trauma on paper, the Women's Fiction Writers Association never failed to nurture me through the hardest parts.

The book *Intuitive Editing* by Tiffany Yates Martin gave me confidence and insight not only with editing but also with elements of good writing.

Most importantly, I give a world of thanks to you, the reader, for reading Sara's story.